Logan and Christian have been best friends since kindergarten. After spending their entire childhoods together, it makes sense they would go to the same college: the first step toward making their futures intertwine forever as blood brothers.

But being away from home means discovering freedom Logan and Christian have never had before, and their journey of finding who they really want to be—and how they want to fit into each other's lives—is a messy one.

When a double date with their girlfriends turns into a new, erotic experience, both Logan and Christian are shaken by it. Suddenly, they can't continue to see each other in a platonic light. Exploring their curiosity feels dangerous even when their girlfriends aren't an issue, but ignoring their changing feelings is impossible.

PLAYING AROUND

Rough Play, Book One

Suzanne Clay

A NineStar Press Publication

Published by NineStar Press
P.O. Box 91792,
Albuquerque, New Mexico, 87199 USA.
www.ninestarpress.com

Playing Around

Printed in the USA
First Edition
April, 2019

Print ISBN: 978-1-950412-60-0

Also available in eBook, ISBN: 978-1-950412-46-4

Warning: This book contains sexually explicit content, which may only be suitable for mature readers.

For Disa—my earliest fan and dear friend

Chapter One

LOGAN

For years, Logan resented how his parents had made him into a workhorse. Whether the boxes of supplies were for the funeral home or the drug store, they were heavy and unwieldy, and no matter how much he protested, his parents never tucked an extra dollar into his pocket for his trouble. There was no choice—just required labor without a word of gratitude.

Moving his belongings into his college dorm was the first time he welcomed the labor. No parents telling him how to set things up. No last-minute delivery showing up right as he finished. No demands or expectations. Just welcome quiet.

He set the last of the boxes on the floor with a grunt and rubbed his arms as he studied the small room. The tight quarters weren't much—barely the size of his bedroom at home and stuffed with twice as much furniture to accommodate two men—but he wasn't going to complain. Not even about the bunk bed. He'd heard from his RA, Aavai, they could be broken down into two beds, and he'd get Christian to help him do so later.

"Lazy ass."

Speak of the devil. Logan glanced over his shoulder with a smirk as Christian came in with both hands full of bags, as many as seven hanging from each hand.

"At least I know how to pack a box," Logan said. "I can't believe your parents let you bring all your shit in grocery bags."

"Not all of it," Christian fired back. He set the bags down on top of their mountain of stuff in the corner. "Shut up. You're still lazy. You're standing there, not even starting to unpack..."

"Why the hell am I gonna unpack when we need to work through logistics?" Logan gestured around the room. "Look at this. Two beds. Two desks. Two dressers. C'mon, we've gotta do some rearranging. This place looks like shit."

"I don't give a damn how it looks." Christian leaned forward and launched himself face-first on the bed. Unsurprisingly, his feet hung off the edge. "Perfect." The word was muffled, but he already sounded half-asleep.

Logan walked over. "Now, who's the lazy ass?" He spanked him and darted away with a laugh when Christian turned on him like a wounded animal. "Get up, man! Want you to help me break this bed down."

Christian scoffed. "Weren't you the one who just said we've got too much shit in here? And now you wanna move the bed? No way."

"If you like the bunks so much, you can sleep on top."

Christian shot him a frown. "Me? On the top bunk? Are you kidding me?"

"You're over six feet tall. How are you afraid of heights?"

Christian shrugged and rolled onto his side, the wall protecting his ass from another slap.

Logan rolled his eyes. "All right. Are you gonna make me spell it out for you?"

"Yeah, go ahead, spell it out."

Of course. "If you think I'm gonna meet some girls who're chill with crawling up a ladder to get some alone time, you've got another thing coming."

The grin Christian shot him spoke multitudes. "Your ugly ass couldn't get a girl in the first place."

"I'll be stealing *your* girl first."

"I'd like to see you try!"

Logan laughed as he turned away. He took in the placement of the furniture and tried to visualize the best place for everything—once he moved things, he was unlikely to do it again. "Listen, just help me break apart the bed, and we can put it by the wall."

The mattress creaked when Christian sat up. That was definitely going to put a damper on trying to be quiet when they had company over. "Nah. I wanna get a couch and put it there."

Logan glanced over his shoulder. "We've got a couch in the living room. The whole point of a suite is to have another room to put our shit in instead of clogging up the bedroom."

Christian shrugged. "So? The couch can only fit three of us anyway. What if I wanna sit down somewhere and you and our suitemates are taking up all the cushions?"

"Then you sit your ass on the floor."

Christian stood, his eyes sparking with a familiar competitiveness. A fire lit up in Logan's chest as Christian faced him. Logan squared his shoulders, head tipped back to look him in the eye. Christian didn't seem the least bit intimidated when he replied, "I'm getting a couch. And I'm putting it there."

Logan crossed his arms over his chest. "And I'm taking apart the bed and putting it there instead."

Christian took two dangerous steps forward. Already, his hands dangled by his side, open and ready for grabbing. Logan planted his feet and held his gaze. "Winner chooses?" Christian asked.

Logan bit his bottom lip through his smile. "Bring it on, motherfucker."

Christian barreled toward him like a bull, grabbed hold of Logan, and they began their dance.

Like any two guys who had known each other since kindergarten, they'd always done their fair share of horsing around. They'd thrown each other in the dirt on the playground when they were seven, much to the panic of their teachers, and Logan's mom had blunted the end of a broom with the number of times she'd banged it against the ceiling when they wrestled too loudly.

They knew each other's moves by heart at this point. Though Christian had the stronger body from years of soccer, Logan played dirty.

Christian's hand wrapped around the back of Logan's neck, and Logan batted his arm away before going for Christian's waist. An early takedown might not be the best strategy, but the more unpredictable he could be, the best chance he had.

Unpredictable didn't work. Christian spun with his tackle, and all the breath knocked out of Logan when he landed on his back on the cold tile floor, Christian's weight on top of him.

"Couch," Christian said with a certain smugness.

Logan lay limp for only a second to catch his breath before he exploded with energy, lashing out legs and grabbing at Christian's shirt to get some leverage. "No deal! I didn't give yet!"

"You're gonna!" Christian was never out of breath this early. He sounded as calm as he'd been a few seconds ago. He caught Logan's wrists, then pinned them to the floor over his head, his bright white teeth shining against his dark skin. "We're getting a fucking couch."

"No way!" Logan squeezed his thighs around Christian's hips and twisted, trying to roll him over, but Christian pressed a hand against his stomach and held him there, as if it was easy. The full weight of Christian—most of it bearing down on his wrists, the rest coming down on his hips—was too much to shake off.

Maybe if I just tire him out... Logan didn't stop thrashing around, his teeth gritting with the effort, and Christian laughed, the only sign of his exertion the slight tremor of his tone.

Christian bore down on him, one of his muscular legs tangling up with Logan's to pin it down too. Their bedroom door opened just then, and they both whipped their heads to see the mortified man backing away with wide eyes.

"Oh, fuck, sorry!" And then the door slammed shut.

Silence. Christian stared at him for a few seconds.

They both started to snicker.

Christian sat on his knees, letting Logan pull away and rub his back. "Oh my God, you don't think he—"

"I absolutely think he thought that," Logan said through his laugh. "Holy shit. Should we go tell him?"

"Nah." Christian's eyes gleamed as he stood and offered Logan a hand to tug him to his feet. "He'll figure it out when he sees all my girlfriends I'm bringing back."

"Right." Logan rolled his eyes, elbowing him as he walked past. "C'mon, we might as well go introduce ourselves or whatever."

Christian got to the door first—*competitive to the end*—and opened it for him. "And then we go couch shopping."

"Fuck you."

"I won," Christian said with a smirk.

"That wasn't a win!" Logan led him into the living area of their dorm's suite. "We got interrupted! That wasn't even *close* to a win!"

"We don't have technicalities in the rulebook."

"I'll put it in tonight." Logan rolled his eyes. "If we're getting a couch, you're fucking paying my medical bills after I go to the hospital for my broken back."

"Weenie."

"Shut up."

After a moment of searching the empty living room and their kitchen nook, they peered in the second bedroom and found the man who'd walked in on them.

"Hey." Logan knocked gently on the half-open door. "Sorry, you, uh, caught us at a bad time."

The guy threw his hands up as if he'd been stopped by police. "I'm so sorry—"

"Dude, you don't have anything to be sorry about." Christian leaned against the doorframe as if his head wasn't almost brushing the top. "Just taking care of some unfinished business."

"Shut up," Logan threw over his shoulder and held out a hand. "I'm Logan. This is Christian. Guess we're gonna be your suitemates?"

"Yeah, guess so!" The guy smiled as he shook Logan's hand, though his eyes still flitted between them as if he were watching a tennis match. "My name's Daiki. It's nice to meet you both."

"Daiki?" Christian asked.

"Daiki." He nodded, but didn't say anything more. "Have you guys met my roommate yet?"

"Nah. We just got here, but Aavai said we were the first ones in." Logan shrugged. "We left last night, got a hotel room, got some breakfast this morning...guess we were ready to get here."

Ready was an understatement. After twelve years of being in the same tiny town and barely able to remember where he'd first lived, the change of scenery was what Logan had been desperate for. It didn't matter that Fulton State University was in the same state—tuition was cheaper for his parents, and the view outside Daiki's window showed him something different.

A city, for example, that wasn't too far away, barely visible over the roofs of their college buildings. He didn't know what was down there besides a Waffle House, a hotel, and a gas station that carried an incredible array of candy for late-night snacking, but he looked forward to learning the lay of the land.

"I guess he'll be here later." Daiki rubbed the back of his neck. "Do you guys think I can go ahead and claim a bunk and start unpacking, or..."

"Tell your roommate to go fuck himself if he doesn't like the bunk you picked." Christian was succinct as always.

Logan laughed and shoved Christian out of the doorway. "Don't pay him any attention. He doesn't think much. Sports scholarship, you see."

"At least I got a full ride." Christian lifted his chin and smirked. "Don't see my parents having to rob a bank just to pay for the damn place."

"Mm-hmm. Yep, and you're gonna be a big soccer star, and we're all gonna say we knew you when. Uh-huh." Logan rolled his eyes.

"I, uh, I guess you guys know each other...pretty well?" Daiki asked. "Have you been...together long?"

"I've known this idiot since he was trying to eat crayons, if that's what you mean," Logan drawled. "But that's about it."

Daiki's eyebrows shot into his hairline. "Really? You're not dating? But I thought—"

"We're straight. Sorry to disappoint." Christian turned on his heel and headed into the living room. "Logan, I'm hungry! Buy me a burger!"

"Buy your own burger!" Logan called and glanced at Daiki. The expression on Daiki's face made Logan hesitate. "Hey. Sorry if you're..." *How do I phrase this?* He'd heard it put a number of ways back home, and all of them had made his mom's lips thin. He'd learned what the wrong words were only after she washed his mouth out with soap. "...he doesn't mean anything bad. Promise."

Daiki stared at him hard. "I hope he doesn't, or he's going to have an awful time at this school."

Logan chuckled. They'd already walked past several couples holding hands around the busy campus as they found their way to the parking lot—most of them a guy and a girl, but a couple of girls and a couple of guys together too. The open display of affection would take some getting used to. "It's fine. Seriously, no problem. It's just not something we saw very often at home."

Daiki leaned against his desk and glanced down at his feet, and Logan took the opportunity to size him up. The gay couples weren't the only thing he'd have to get used to. Though Daiki didn't appear mixed like Logan was, he still wasn't *white*. As he'd carried his boxes in, Logan had seen more people of color than in his entire life just in the lobby. Their floor RA was Indian and Sikh. The girl checking them in downstairs was white, but she was being helped out by someone with dark brown skin.

FSU was a different world, one appearing as though the campus had come out of some movie that was really making a point out of being diverse. As though it had been intentionally done. As though some guy was gonna point the diversity out in his review as being unrealistic.

But here he was, standing in a room with someone who wasn't white and who wasn't like his best friend Christian either.

Logan spent the past twelve years thinking the white, heterosexual climate of Greenbarrow was normal. But the other students didn't seem as surprised by their surroundings as Logan—and he wasn't sure what he thought of that yet.

Going home after this was going to feel fucking weird.

"I guess you guys are both from down here, then," Daiki finally said.

"Around Georgia? Yeah." Logan shrugged. "Greenbarrow's a couple hours south of here. Why, is my accent that bad?"

Daiki chuckled. "It's pretty thick, but that's not *bad*, I mean—"

"I got you." Logan grinned. "You always apologize this much? What, are you Canadian?"

"No! No, I just..." He trailed off. "I guess I don't want my roommates to hate me immediately. Especially if you two are some united front that could make my life pretty terrible."

Daiki wasn't a tiny guy, but he carried himself with the air of someone who was ready to be pushed around right now. Logan wasn't a bully, and with the school's star jock as his best friend, he'd been pretty immune to targeted violence by his classmates. But he'd never exactly stepped in and stopped anyone from being an asshole either. *This is a sign. I've got some penance to do here.* Logan was pretty sure his social calendar was going to be filled with nothing but Christian for the next four years, but he could try to do better.

"I'll only make your life terrible if you eat whatever food I put in the fridge," Logan said dryly, and Daiki laughed. "I'd better go catch up with Christian, or I'm not gonna get any lunch, but it was nice meeting you. Maybe we can hang out before classes start."

Daiki stood tall, as though he'd been waiting his entire life for this moment. "Yeah! I-I mean, that'd probably be cool or whatever."

"Cool." Logan backed out of the room, putting his hands in his pockets. "And, uh, hey, listen, if your roommate's an asshole, let me know. I'll make sure he doesn't mess with you."

Daiki gaped at him. "Y-yeah, I'll do that. I'm sure things'll be fine, but..."

Penance. Logan shrugged. "Just saying. I'll see you later."

When he popped into his bedroom, Christian was shoving clothes haphazardly in the drawers of one of the chests. "You're an idiot," Logan said, huffing. "I wanted to move stuff around before we started unpacking."

"And I wanted to get these bags out of our fucking way." Christian scowled at him. "What? Your noodly-ass arms can't move furniture when it's full of boxers?"

"Fuck you." Logan grabbed Christian's sleeve and started walking backward, dragging him along. "Let's go get burgers. I'll pay if you drive my car."

"*Finally.*"

Chapter Two

CHRISTIAN

College mixers were one of those things Christian didn't really understand the point of. He was going to meet new people in his classes. They'd lucked into a coed dorm, and the floors above and below them were full of girls. He didn't need to be herded into a massive room of scared freshmen in order to actually meet people.

Are these even the kind of people I wanna meet? He skimmed the room. He could pinpoint three guys who were throwing themselves at the first people to lock eyes with them.

They were all needy fuckers, and Christian already had his main man. The only reason he'd need some of these other guys would be for homework help, since he and Logan didn't share every class.

The girls, though, he could work with them. He didn't mind their desperate eyes quite as much.

"So." He elbowed Logan and nodded toward a little copse of girls gathering in the corner, all in high heels, minidresses, and flawless winged eyeliner. "What do you think—sorority girls?"

"Duh." Logan grinned. "Aiming high, aren't you?"

"I mean, I'm a jock." Christian puffed out his chest. It was an old habit from when he was still short and surrounded by older kids finding some reason to push the black kid around. He'd hadn't broken the need to seem more imposing, even though his towering height had kept bullies at bay for years now. "It's not that high, is it? It's not as if I'm going after the college president's daughter. They've got a little money, that's all."

"A little money and a lot of expectations." Logan shook his head and glanced elsewhere, and Christian followed his gaze. "No, man, listen. If you're *already* looking for a girl, then you've gotta find somebody who's gonna be *fun*. Besides..." He nodded toward a trio of girls smoking outside, practically bathing in the sunshine like lazy cats. "...why not try something new, huh?"

Christian wandered toward the window, frowning. They certainly seemed different enough. No camouflage jackets to be seen. No four wheelers. No boots for function rather than for show. He was used to a very specific aesthetic of girl who'd populated their high school, along with a few stereotypes hanging around the edges—the dramatic theater girl in heavy makeup, the metal girl with piercings lining her ears from top to bottom, and the jock girls with their sports bras and challenging eyes.

"What do you think about the artsy type, huh?" Logan asked as he brushed up beside him and sipped his punch. "Nice change of pace, right?"

There was one girl in particular with red curls and skin as darkly colored as his who caught his eye. Her clothes didn't quite match, as far as his inexperienced eye could tell—conflicting patterns—but the color of her eye shadow seemed intentional, since it brought out the dominant color scheme. The freckles were what caught him; thick clusters over her cheeks, the same color as her hazel eyes.

One of her friends nodded at Christian, and the girl followed her stare, quirking a brow. And then she held his gaze with the same directness that had always made him sweat a little more, like a girl challenging him one-on-one on the soccer field.

He liked it.

"Maybe," Christian murmured before he offered her a nod.

She blinked a few times and took a long drag off her cigarette. She tapped the ashes from the smoldering end and tilted her head to the side as she pulled a fresh cigarette out and held it toward him.

Logan whistled softly, then elbowed him. "Go on, man, this is a better invitation than you're ever gonna get."

"I hate smoking," Christian mumbled.

"Fake it. *Fake it*. Take two or three puffs and you'll get yourself a date."

When Logan egged him on, it was impossible to turn him down. He glanced at Logan, looked through the window, and sighed. "Fuck it."

"That's my boy!" Logan called after him as Christian headed for the front door.

As he walked, he thought about exactly how big a load of shit this entire experience was. He'd spent eighteen years figuring out who the fuck he was as a person—liking most of his discoveries and discarding the rest. He'd gotten entrenched in the legend of Christian-and-Logan, all one word, always in that order, and their friendship gave sense to his galaxy. If all of the people he'd ever met were planets, then he and Logan were the twin stars they were orbiting.

Even now, only going to talk to some girl who might not end up meaning anything, he glanced over his shoulder and made one last moment of eye contact with Logan before slipping outside.

Logan stared back. He grinned widely.

I believe in you. You've fucking got this. Don't get intimidated by some girl just because she's pretty. And don't be a fucking idiot either. The words rang in his head in Logan's voice, clear as day, and he took a deep breath, sucking in new confidence that he held close to his chest.

Tension eased. He put on a small, natural smile and came around the corner, where the three girls were waiting for him.

Nice of them, really. He wouldn't have been surprised if they'd disappeared around the corner the second he started walking.

"Hey." He gave a little wave.

"Hey there," one of the girls said. At about a foot and a half shorter than him, she was a tiny little thing with the build of a flier. "What's up?"

"Not much." Christian shrugged and shoved his hands in his pocket, trying to seem as relaxed as he possibly could. He leaned against the wall. *Smooth.* "What about y'all?"

"Same. Just getting some fresh air," the closest girl said. She was chubby, and the glamorous pinup makeup she wore, paired with the pretty crop top and cut off shorts, told him she had more confidence in her little finger than he had in his entire body. He liked it. "I'm Natsumi. What's your name?"

"Christian." He glanced at the petite girl next.

"Kavya." She grinned and waved enthusiastically. "It's nice to meet you."

"You too." Though every cell in his body trembled with nerves, he gulped and studied the redhead last, quirking his brow. "And you are?"

She turned her head and sent a puff of smoke away from them before she extended her free hand. "Charlotte. Christian, you said?"

"Yeah." He shook her hand and was impressed with her firm grip. "So, where're y'all from?"

"Y'all," Kavya teased, giggling. "I'm from New York. What about you? Are you from around here? You sound pretty Southern."

One tour of the campus had prepared him for how strange it would be to see people who were different like him. Kavya, for example, had brown skin, Natsumi was Japanese, and Charlotte had his same sepia skin tone. But he hadn't anticipated the oddness of being one of the few people with a discernible accent. "Yeah, I'm, uh, from a few hours south of here, still in Georgia."

"Oh yeah?" Charlotte asked as she offered the cigarette she'd gestured at him with. He hesitated for a few seconds before plucking it away. "I've got folks in Georgia. Said the college came highly recommended. It isn't too bad, I guess."

As Natsumi offered him her lighter, he forced himself to push down his distaste and took a long drag, just like he'd seen his dad do the few times they'd been together. Thank God he didn't cough as if he'd never had a smoke or anything. "Y'all know each other from somewhere?"

"Nah." Charlotte chuckled. "We all drew the short straws. We're in Wayfield Dorm."

"What's that?"

"The dorm where they decided to shove three freshmen girls in a tiny room." Natsumi rolled her eyes. "I get it, everybody wants to come here, you admitted too many people, you're overcrowded. But geez, there's barely any room to walk in our dorm now. That's what we get for being the cheapskates, though."

"It's not bad!" Kavya crossed her arms. "You're gonna make me think you don't even *like* me, Nat."

Natsumi's cheeks flushed as she chuckled. "All right, fine, I guess you're not that bad. I could've been stuck with worse."

Are they flirting? Christian met Charlotte's gaze, and she smirked with a little roll of her eyes. She noticed the teasing and curiosity too, then.

Kavya took the cigarette out of Natsumi's hand and shoved it in an ashtray, then started pulling her away. "C'mon, we're gonna go get a drink. You want anything, Charlotte?"

"Nah, I'm good." She shifted her weight and cocked a hip, lifting an eyebrow. "Anyway, Christian here'll get me anything I need, won't he?"

Oh, so she's one of those *girls.* He chuckled. "Well, I don't know about that."

She grinned and put her cigarette out as well, then started wandering away, her hands tucked behind her.

Was he allowed to follow her? What was the protocol here? He peered through the window, and Logan was still there, scanning the room and bobbing his head lightly with the music playing. Christian tapped on the glass, and Logan jumped, spinning around and immediately flicking him off when he saw him. When Christian thumbed over his shoulder toward Charlotte, Logan blinked a few times before he shrugged and gave him a thumbs-up.

That was all the encouragement Christian needed. He gave him a wink, flicked the cigarette onto the large ashtray, and turned on his heel to follow her.

"Is it okay if I walk with you?" he asked when he was still a couple of feet away.

"You'd better." She peered over her shoulder. "I just gave you that cigarette. Did you already put it out?"

"Oh, I, uh…" He cleared his throat. "…I-I don't actually smoke much. I sort of—"

"You made me waste my cigarette rather than owning up to it right away?" She kissed her teeth and shook her head. "My God, man."

"Sorry. You've got a point." When he caught up to her, he settled for walking side by side, attention caught by the luxurious texture of her hair. "Can I ask you something?"

"I can't stop you." But there was teasing in her tone that he enjoyed, as if she was testing him somehow, and, so far, he hadn't let her down. Interest flashed in her glance, her eyelashes thickly curled, and her eyes glistened with the low light of the setting sun. "Go on, then."

"Your hair color…?"

"It's natural, yeah." She scoffed and bumped her arm against him. "I should've known you'd be predictable. Yes, I'm black. Yes, I have red hair. Yes, I have freckles. You'd think I was an endangered species."

"Hey, listen, I didn't—"

"I know; you didn't mean anything bad." Charlotte came around a bench not too far from the student union and sat before stretching her legs out in front of her. "Guess I should be used to it."

Christian hesitated before he sat beside her. "I like your hair, though. I think it's gorgeous."

She narrowed her eyes. He got the sense she was analyzing him as though those pretty eyes were wired up to some kind of computer, and she was feeding herself results from the little things she saw. She smiled. "Well, thanks."

He shrugged. "No problem."

"You're not too bad either. I like your hair too."

He resisted the urge to touch his head. He'd gotten his hair trimmed right before leaving home, and the pattern buzzed into the sides had been a new experiment. "I mean, it's no head of fire, but..."

"But it's nice." She reached up and then paused an inch away. "Can I?"

Why not? He leaned over, and her fingers brushed over the bare skin between the edges. Tingles buzzed down his spine like a lightning strike, and he licked his lips and stared at the ground, embarrassed by the sharp reaction. *She's just a girl, dude. You just met her. Don't be getting all heart eyes now.*

But she was beautiful, and she was interesting, and she was touching him already, and that was something he couldn't ignore.

"Awesome." She beamed. "My dad's white, so I never really got to see someone do cool edges before."

"You've got a white dad?" Christian grinned. "My, uh, my mom's white, actually. And my stepdad."

"So you've got that syndrome too, huh?" Charlotte turned on the bench to face him and pulled her legs to her chest. She wrapped her arms around her shins. "Like, you look around your house sometimes, and everybody's just...they're different from you."

"Man, talk about my entire life." After his mom and dad divorced when he was young, Christian barely saw him anymore—Christian's own decision. Logan was his only other black friend. A definite lack of color. "Logan and I, we live in Greenbarrow, and I swear to God, he and I are the only black kids in our whole town."

"Really?" She crinkled her nose, one of the cutest things he'd ever seen in his whole life. "I've never heard of anything like that around here. That's gotta be one tiny-ass town."

"It is. We've got three stoplights. Everything else is farmland and some quiet, little family-owned joints, and that's about it." After living there his whole life, the isolation never seemed too strange. But coming somewhere like Fulton—it was a different beast. "There were about four really big families everybody was related to, and then five of us smaller families that ended up there for some reason. Like, my best friend Logan—he came to Fulton State with me too—the whole reason his family ended up down there was because his grandparents died. So they either had to sell the funeral parlor or come down and work. His mom took over the funeral parlor, his dad took over the pharmacist position at the drug store from the guy that should've retired ten years before, and there he was."

"That's trippy."

"Man, you have no idea." Christian trailed off when his phone buzzed in his pocket, and he pulled it out to check the text message.

Did you get laid yet?

From Logan, of course. Christian snorted and shook his head, putting his phone away.

Charlotte was staring at him when he met her gaze again. "Everything okay?"

"What? Yeah, that was Logan. He's back at the mixer. Probably lost as hell now that I'm not chained to his hip."

Charlotte smiled. She had a gap between her two front teeth that she didn't seem the least bit embarrassed about. "So you guys are close?"

Close didn't begin to describe their relationship. He let out a deep breath and scratched the back of his neck.

"Yeah, he's been like my brother since the day I met him in kindergarten, I guess. We were always inseparable in high school. And, uh, now we're here, I guess." He shrugged. "I got a scholarship for soccer, and he just sort of came right along."

"Is he a jock too?"

"Him? No, he's a writing nerd. Writes scripts for plays and movies and shit." *Good ones.* He had a number of incredible memories surrounding them. Whole DVDs full of his amateur acting were stuffed somewhere in his basement, surrounded by a million other things his family wouldn't throw away. "He's got a great mind for writing, though. He's gonna be an English teacher once we're done here, and I'm gonna be some kind of accountant, and we'll have a hell of a time wherever we end up..." As he trailed off, he saw how she was watching him with amusement.

Right. People don't start making life plans with their best friend.

Christian cleared his throat and shrugged. "Anyway—I don't know—he's probably just bored at the mixer, fuck him."

Charlotte burst out laughing, her eyes sparkling. "Oh my God, some best friend," she teased, nudging his thigh with the tip of her shoe. "Remind me never to try and be one of your best friends."

As if she could try. And what was up with having more than one best friend. Didn't that sort of break down the whole *best* part of the idea? He chuckled, though, and shrugged. "Hey, if you roll with me, you've gotta be tough; you know what I mean?"

"I think I do." Charlotte checked her phone and got to her feet. "Hey, listen, I'm gonna head back, I think. Gotta grab dinner with my family in town. But there's this thing tonight..."

"Thing?" Christian stood as well.

"A party, I guess. I don't know. An old high school friend of mine who started here last year invited me. Anyway, it's gonna be fun, and you should totally be there." She opened her phone and gestured. "C'mon, gimme your number. I'm gonna text you the address later. Don't get there any later than, like, nine o'clock. Only losers get there after that."

"I sure wouldn't wanna be a loser," he drawled.

"You're right." She pushed her hair away from her forehead and peered up at him against the setting sun. The light played off her skin, bringing out beautiful warm tones, and he caught himself staring a second too late. "So, are you in?"

He was pretty sure he'd never once made evening plans without Logan's input. But things were different now, weren't they? This was college. This was a whole new world. A galaxy rather than the tiny planet their hometown had been. And maybe that meant taking a chance on something new, even if it meant Logan might not be there with him.

So he shrugged. "Yeah. I'm in."

THE WALK TO the party was a silent one. Tension lurked in Logan's chest as he tugged at the hem of his shirt, his eyes flitting toward Christian and away again every few seconds.

I'm not mad, he wanted to say. *This is just...weird.*

He hadn't imagined their first college party would be a gathering he had to be coerced into. Something like this should've been an experience to brag about. And yet here he was, putting one foot in front of the other, hoping the party would be over soon? He was an embarrassment to college freshmen everywhere.

But he wouldn't know anybody there, except for Christian. And Christian had made it perfectly clear he wasn't going for Logan.

Charlotte. It was a name Logan steeled himself to hearing a lot.

"So, you think she's actually gonna be there?" Logan hated the grit he heard in his tone, but Christian didn't seem to notice.

"C'mon, man, she'll be there. Why wouldn't she? What, she's gonna invite me to play a prank?" Christian snorted. "You've been watching too many movies."

"I mean, I might not be wrong. Could be she was looking for a reason to get rid of you. She was the one that walked away, right? And you're the one that followed her?"

That got him a glare. Christian frowned. "I asked."

"Maybe she didn't feel like she could say no."

Christian scoffed and rolled his eyes. "Will you quit? What the fuck, dude?"

"I'm just saying, you don't know her! She could be a bitch!"

"And I'm not gonna know until I hang out with her. What the hell's wrong with you?" Christian nudged him, bumping their arms together, and Logan pulled away and shoved his hands in his pockets. "Just 'cuz I won the bet. Just 'cuz I'm pulling a girl before you can."

"You're not gonna pull her," Logan muttered.

"Yeah?" Christian winked. "Watch me, brother."

He hated tonight already.

As they turned the corner down another side road, cars filled the street and people milled around on the front lawn of a house. *And these are college kids?* Logan studied the other houses they passed. Pretty damn impressive specimens. Getting his parents to help him pay for a place like this might be easier if he was able to prove renting houses was normal for college kids here. Could be cheaper than their dorm, if they swung it the right way.

You think Christian's gonna be able to afford living with you if his scholarship won't cut it, man?

The truth hurt. He nudged the dream aside and took a deep breath as they started walking up the front path.

Logan was as out of his element as he was at the mixer. Christian drew eyes with how he loomed above everyone like a giant. Logan was used to falling off to the wayside next to him. It didn't matter that Christian didn't have the timing to tell a good joke or that he was all bark and no bite—he would always get attention first.

And Logan would follow him, until he invariably got left behind.

Christian pushed the front door open and ducked under the frame. "All right, keep your eyes open for some pretty red hair."

Logan rolled his eyes. "Oh, don't you worry."

The house was a little different from what he was used to, but maybe that was the new normal—everything being a little more peculiar, as if he'd walked into a maze. Parties back home had been held in rickety old houses, or barns that weren't used anymore when families moved away from their old roots. More often than not, there'd be people around a bonfire in the middle of a huge field, shooting up a new and expensive drug that didn't have a name yet.

Not this. This seemed like a movie. Low lighting, people clogging up the halls, music playing, dancing in a room where all the furniture had been shoved against the walls. Walking in was as surreal as stepping onto a Hollywood set.

Logan didn't realize he'd stopped, but his eyes followed Christian's head bobbing above them all, and he hurried after him, swallowing hard.

A drink was the most important thing to get his hands on right now, and he grabbed the first can of beer he saw. The brand was shit, but that was okay. He wasn't after alcohol for the taste.

"Oh, fuck, there she is."

Logan followed Christian's line of sight, and sure enough, there was the goddess of the evening, sitting on a couch and chatting with some meticulously groomed guy with thick glasses and jeans rolled up around his skinny calves. Logan wrinkled his brow. He didn't know much about fashion, but—

"I'm gonna go for it." Christian called his attention back as he grabbed two cans of the beer. "I've got this, right?"

Logan shrugged. "I mean, you've got *something*."

"I'm serious."

He huffed. He touched Christian's back and leaned up on his tiptoes, closing the distance between those four and a half inches separating them. "You're Christian Fucking Daniels. You beat out a hundred other guys for your scholarship even though you've got shitty grades. You could take that hipster's head and juggle it on your knees for hours. How the hell wouldn't she be impressed by that?"

Christian stared down at him, brow wrinkled. "You're gruesome as fuck."

"And you're incredible." Logan slapped him on the arm. "Go on, go show off. Give me the signal if you need me to come save you later."

Christian chuckled. "You've always got my back," he tossed over his shoulder as he walked away.

Yeah. Yeah, I do. Logan started squeezing his can, and then backed off before he spilled beer over his hand. *Got you covered, brother.*

Of course, Christian walked right up and didn't say a word before Charlotte was grinning up at him and scooting over and making just enough room that he had to squeeze in beside her with their legs touching and whatever. He didn't have to try. Charlotte turned completely away from the other guy and faced Christian, wearing the biggest smile Logan had ever seen.

No matter what Christian might think, he didn't need Logan's help anymore.

Logan took a shallow breath and scanned the room for a familiar face. He'd met a couple of people at the mixer—no one of any real consequence—but he'd take anybody who seemed alone right now, anyone who might want some pathetic hanger-on like Logan Brown.

And then he saw him.

Daiki.

His suitemate was watching a game of beer pong with his head tilted to the side, as if he was analyzing it. Logan drifted toward him. Hanging out with him was the least he could do, especially since Daiki didn't seem to be speaking to anybody else. *Maybe we could both use the company. And hell, I'm doing him a favor, right?*

"Hey, dude."

Daiki looked up as Logan came closer. He blinked and brightened. "Hey. Didn't know I'd see you here."

"I'm pretty sure the entire student body is here," Logan drawled as he leaned against the wall. "What's up?"

"Nothing. Trying to figure out how..." Daiki gestured toward the table covered in glasses of beer.

"Oh, that? Easy stuff." He and Christian had been old hat at beer pong before they were sixteen years old—not exactly information he ever planned on telling his parents. "I mean, it's just trying to get this ball in one of those cups, and if you do, the other person has to drink the whole thing. It's normally beer, but it can be pretty much anything."

Daiki frowned. "Isn't...like... That ball is absolutely covered in germs."

"Oh, for sure," Logan teased, parroting his tone. "When you play beer pong, you take your chances with life and death—or mono and strep."

"Disgusting." But Daiki tilted his head a little further, his dark eyes focusing intently. "Have you played before?"

"I would, unfortunately, kick your ass halfway to Sunday if I played." Logan chuckled. "Christian can't throw shit. That's why he never did basketball, right? So, I'm pretty much the reigning beer pong champion of my class."

"Well, I mean, losing doesn't sound so bad, right?" Daiki smirked, more mischievous than Logan expected. "You get drunk. Wow, big whoop."

"Unless the beer sucks." He lifted the can. "Which it does."

Daiki took the beer out of Logan's hand. "If you hate it so much, *I'll* drink it."

Logan's eyebrows lifted. "You're just gonna take a dude's beer, Daiki?"

All his bravado drained away in a second, much to Logan's amusement. "I-I mean, that's, no, I only thought—"

"'Cuz if you're gonna take a dude's beer, you've gotta chug the whole thing." Logan crossed his arms, his lips quirking at the edges. Daiki was almost as tall as he was, but his thinness didn't speak well for an ability to hold his booze. At the very least, the aftermath would be funny. "So, go on, then."

Daiki stared at him. His eyes gleamed with the same mirth bubbling up inside Logan. "Oh yeah?"

"Yep."

"Is that a challenge?"

"You bet your ass it's a challenge."

Daiki looked at the can, looked at Logan, and then threw his head back and started chugging.

"Yeah, dude!" Logan immediately clapped his hands, and the other eyes drawn to them followed with instinctive cheers. There was a power in being watched, Logan had learned a long time ago, that made him feel as though he could do anything. As long as the focus was on him, he could practically sprout wings and fly.

Daiki seemed to fill up with similar energy, and he made a valiant effort, as shitty as it was. Though some beer dribbled down his chin, by the time he pulled off to take his first breath, he'd nearly drained the whole goddamn thing.

More cheers rose up around them, as though they were in a pantheon of warriors rather than some rich kid's house, and Logan laughed as he tossed an arm around Daiki's shoulders. "My man! You kicked that beer's ass!"

Daiki wiped his face clean. "You're right. It was shit."

He snorted, took the can away, and drained the rest of the dregs without thinking. Then he crushed it in his hand and chucked it in the nearby recycling bin. "We don't drink for the taste, buddy; we drink for the buzz."

Daiki tilted his head toward the table, which was being cleaned of the red plastic cups. "So let's get buzzed."

Logan stared at him for a few seconds before he flicked his eyes across the room. His heart stopped cold in his chest.

Christian had his hands buried in Charlotte's curls, kissing her. She was halfway in his lap, her hands sliding down his sides. As if he felt the attention, Christian opened his eyes, and their gazes locked before he winked at Logan.

I kicked your ass, he might as well have been saying. *You're over there playing the Good Samaritan with some kid you barely know, and I'm getting some action.*

It might have been fairer to pit Daiki and Christian against each other. Christian might've been a little more in the kid's skill range. But now, Logan wanted nothing more than to kick someone's ever-loving ass.

"Yeah. Let's do it."

Daiki whooped and clapped his hands together just the once, then grabbed someone's sleeve. "Hey, can you help me get this set up again?"

"Sure, man!"

Logan pulled himself out of the fog and turned to help them both. His thoughts wouldn't slow, try as he might.

Christian was going to leave him behind. He always knew the split would happen one day. Twelve years of friendship were nothing compared to the pull some girl would have on him. Christian would be the one who broke off first, too—Logan would always drag behind. It seemed appropriate that Logan had been adopted into money and opportunities while Christian lagged behind with his long legs and cleats and nothing else to his name. Logan would end up alone while Christian found somebody who actually gave a shit about him.

He just hadn't known it would happen so fast.

After the table was set up, he made sure to keep his back to the couch and his eyes on Daiki. But he had to risk one last peek over his shoulder.

Christian and Charlotte were stirring, coming off the couch. She led him toward the hallway with a secret smile. Christian wrapped his arms around her shoulders from behind, charming a laugh out of her before they disappeared behind a door.

"You ready to get your ass kicked?" Daiki asked brightly.

Logan turned away, facing the table. "Yeah, sure, man."

For the first time in his entire life, someone creamed him in beer pong.

There was something pleasant about the soft haze from the shitty beer in his system, though. As all the other people who'd been ignoring Daiki now surrounded him, declaring him a beer pong prodigy, Logan snagged a water bottle and drained the lukewarm liquid halfway.

This was what he did. He found people who didn't quite belong, and he lifted them to a level way above his own head—to a level he couldn't reach, no matter what opportunities were handed to him.

He'd accepted that a long time ago.

He disappeared to the bathroom and took a leak, then spent an inordinate amount of time washing his hands of every drop of sticky beer and sweat. As he left the bathroom, he hesitated in the hallway.

Under the thudding music, he caught a sharp moan through the door they'd disappeared through, followed by a bright laugh. Christian couldn't tell a joke to save his life, but apparently, she liked him anyway.

Logan was a wallflower for the rest of the night, seeing life as a series of impressions that didn't seem real. Maybe he talked to some people. Maybe he didn't. Maybe he watched Daiki start dancing, fueled by his beer. Maybe Logan forced a smile when Daiki ran over to him and grabbed his hands and pulled him onto the floor. Maybe he finished out the song with him before he returned to his post on the wall.

Either way, when Christian reappeared, his hand loosely captured by Charlotte and his eyes sparkling, Logan didn't make his way over. He'd leave them to their happiness, and he'd wait.

Charlotte was pulled away by a group of girls Logan didn't recognize, and Christian finally floated back to him with a sigh. "Man..."

Logan grunted. He sipped his water again. He didn't reply.

"She's something else. She's..."

Logan stared as Charlotte left the house, her purse in hand. "She gone for the night?"

"Yeah. Gotta get ready for classes on Monday." Christian leaned against the wall with him, tipping his head back, caught up in his wonderland, and Logan didn't try to pull him away. Thirty seconds later—the longest thirty seconds of his life—Christian bumped their shoulders together. "Hey, wanna head to the dorm? Kind of late."

So we came here for her, and now we're leaving because of her. Logan crumpled up the water bottle and tossed it away. "Yeah, I'm beat."

"Did you kick Daiki's ass in beer pong?"

"Nah." Logan walked toward the door, leaving Christian to catch up with him. "Guess I lost my touch."

"What?!" Christian laughed and opened the door for Logan, then held it for him to go through first. "What the fuck! Did you get trashed before you started playing? You're fine now, aren't you?"

"Didn't get drunk. You weren't even busy long enough for me to sober up, man. Must've been fast."

Silence. Christian breathed another low chuckle, one laced with danger and challenge. "Trust me, man, she was a happy camper. I don't leave a girl unsatisfied. Or is that what *you* do?"

"Fuck you." Logan rolled his eyes. "Whatever, let's go."

Christian caught up to him easily with his long legs. He overtook him and turned around, walking backwards, grinning at Logan. "I know what's wrong with you."

Logan forced himself to pick up the pace until his calves were burning. "Nothing's wrong with me."

"You're *jealous*. I can't believe you're jealous that I got laid."

It was as if a knife had gone straight through his chest. Logan glared up at him. It wasn't hard to be pissed off when Christian then picked up his pace so he was jogging backward, forcing Logan to push himself to try to pass him. "I'm not jealous!"

"Did you want her? I mean, it's not exactly my fault she picked me, is it?"

"She didn't *pick* you!" Logan's breathing was starting to catch, but Christian sounded as if he was completely comfortable with the pace. "You picked her! You just saw some girl, and you decided you had to have her."

"But you're jealous."

"I'm not jealous."

"Yeah, you are."

He was done with this conversation. He started running.

Christian whipped around with him, running right beside him with a laugh, as though this was *fun*. As if he wasn't rubbing in Logan's face how he could run as fast as him without breaking a sweat—that while Logan had to *push* himself, Christian glided like the perfect male specimen. "I'm gonna beat you to the dorm."

"No, you aren't," Logan gritted out. He never beat Christian, but his past track record didn't matter right now, not when he had a point to prove; he was just as good as him in every way.

Christian immediately started to pass him, and Logan grabbed his shirt from behind and *yanked*. Christian spun around with a sputtered gasp, flying off course for a second before he was coming back up on him. "Not cool! You could've thrown me in the street!"

Logan glared. "I don't play by the rules."

With their dorm building in sight, he pushed himself to the limit, sprinting as fast as he could go, his chest burning and his lungs barely able to keep up. And Christian stayed with him.

It took Logan a long second to realize Christian was intentionally not passing him. He was keeping pace with him only to make sure they got there at the exact same time. And that pissed him off.

He didn't think. He rammed into Christian's side, and his best friend stumbled over a concrete lip in the parking lot and tipped into the grass.

Logan didn't stop until his hands hit the door, and he whipped his head around to gloat. Except...Christian was lying on his face, not moving.

The fuck?

"Christian?" No response. Logan's hammering heart flew all the faster. "Fuck, fuck, dude, don't..." He stumbled over to him and leaned down to grab Christian's shoulder and turn him over. "Hey, are you—"

Christian's hand shot up, snagged him by the shirt, and jerked him down.

"Fuck!" Logan landed hard, wincing through the shock of pain, and he rolled away from Christian the second he started to laugh. "Fuck you!"

"Fuck *me*?" Christian turned his head and grinned at him. He wasn't the least bit put out. To him, this was nothing but a game Logan had been playing—as though Logan couldn't be pissed off if he tried.

Why am *I so pissed off?*

As Christian sat up gingerly with a groan, rubbing the back of his neck, Logan tried to parse through the anger—why it was there, where it came from, and why it had made him be an asshole. And try as he might, he couldn't find anything satisfying.

Christian had gotten laid. He'd found a gorgeous girl who liked him at least enough to fuck him, if not more, and Logan was throwing a hissy fit.

"What's gotten into you tonight, man?" Christian asked. He stood and held out his hand, and Logan hesitated before he pulled himself to his feet. "You got something you're really mad about, or is this just... *What* is it?"

Logan didn't have words to describe the tight bands around his chest, keeping him from catching his breath even though they'd finally slowed down. There was nothing but confusion and the overwhelming sense of something being *wrong*.

So, Logan shook his head. "I'm playing around with you. Don't be so serious."

Christian snorted and put his arm around Logan's shoulders as they walked toward the dorm. "Whatever. You won. Go jack off about it."

"I will. All over your sheets."

"Fuck you."

There was one thing Logan had been able to identify; Charlotte was the one who'd started all this weirdness. But she didn't seem to be a bad girl. Christian didn't want bad girls. He liked ones who got along with his friends and who were super chill souls, which meant Charlotte wasn't somebody who Logan should be pissed off at.

Logan clearly needed a girl of his own. And he needed her fast.

He cleared his throat as they waited for the elevator, his legs shaky. "So, uh…"

Christian watched him with his big brown eyes, still picking at the grass stain on his shirt. "What?"

"Does Charlotte have some cute friends?"

Christian smirked and rolled his eyes. "Man, I've gotta do everything for you, don't I?"

"Sure do."

The elevator doors opened with a *ding*, and Logan slumped against the cool metal wall inside as Christian hit their floor's number. "Fine! Fine. I'll ask. But you'll owe me, you got it?"

Already owe you everything. What's one more?

Chapter Three

CHRISTIAN

Sleeping hadn't been weird, really. Christian and Logan had been sleeping in the same room twice a month or more for the past twelve years. The bunk bed was a new addition, but once Christian got over the irrational fear that the whole thing was gonna drop on him, he slept as soundly as a baby. He'd had a good night, after all. He'd held someone new in his arms and checked an experience off his unofficial bucket list—sleeping with a girl the same day he met her—and he'd gotten a cute-ass good night text from her before he closed his eyes.

Waking up was weirder. There was some thudding in the kitchen. But Logan was quietly snoring, so he knew it couldn't be him. *Guy could sleep through a fucking explosion.* He envied it.

Still, if Daiki was going to wake him up, he might as well make him some breakfast too.

Christian crawled out of bed, pulled on a pair of soft flannel pants, and made his way out of the room.

The thing was, it wasn't Daiki.

Christian paused in the living area, frowning at the other guy's back. "Hey."

The guy whirled around with wide blue eyes and fumbled the bowl in his hand, barely catching it before it could fall to the floor. "Oh!" he squeaked and cleared his throat. "Uh, hi."

Christian stared at him. He then glanced over his shoulder at the front door, which was sensibly locked. "So, do you live here or am I about to have to beat your ass?"

It was a joke, but the guy didn't laugh. He set the bowl down too hard on the counter, the clatter louder than any other noise he'd been making. "No! N-no, I live here, I, uh, I just moved in today?"

Daiki's bedroom door was open, though he wasn't anywhere to be seen. Sure enough, there was a single new suitcase sitting on the bottom bunk in there.

"Oh." Christian rubbed his eyes and tried to force a smile—it was always hard when he first woke up. "Packed light."

"I live here, actually—in town. Figure if I need anything, I can run home, grab it, bring it back...won't be a really long drive or anything, and I'll still get to see my parents, and that'll probably make them pretty happy."

He's a rambler, excellent. Christian nodded slowly. "You got a name?"

"Oh!" The guy's cheeks flushed. He had a few spots of patchy facial hair, as if he still struggled with shaving, and the whiskers' russet hue brought out the pink of his skin. "I'm Noah! Sorry, I-I guess I'm out of it."

"Noah. Cool." Christian came toward the kitchen but slowed his steps when Noah backed up, like he was flinching away. Christian was used to getting such a reaction from extremely petite girls at home, but never from a guy. Maybe he wasn't used to meeting someone so tall? "You making breakfast?"

"Um." Noah thumbed over his shoulder. "Cereal?"

Christian caught sight of the box of Lucky Charms. "Oh, hell yeah, motherfucker." His smile turned genuine, and he slipped past Noah on his way to the fridge. "That yours?"

"Daiki's. He, uh, he said we could all have some—that's why he got the big box?"

"Man, fuck that, the whole box is mine." Christian picked it up, reached for one of the plastic bowls sitting on the counter, and then hesitated when he saw Noah staring. "That was a joke, dude. You look like you're about to shit yourself."

Noah burst out in a laugh as he pushed the carton of milk toward him too. "Sorry."

Christian shrugged.

By the time he'd poured his bowl of cereal and milk and grabbed a spoon, the bedroom door opened, and Logan emerged in a T-shirt and boxers. "'Sup?"

Logan popped his chin and grinned when he saw Noah. "Hey, new suitemate, right? I'm Logan."

"That's Noah," Christian called as he settled on the couch. "And I think he's scared of me."

"Aw, don't be scared of him." Logan started poking around the kitchen, pulling out the coffee filters as he settled in front of the brewer. "I know he's huge, but he's a fucking wimp."

"Shut the fuck up."

"Promise."

The two of them often had a calming effect on people around them, and Christian watched the magic happen as Noah relaxed against the kitchen counter. He didn't say much, apparently, but he also didn't look like he expected them to rob him anymore.

Christian had hoped they'd get away from that. Perhaps he'd been wrong.

"So where're you from?" Logan asked as he waited for the coffee to brew, all bright-eyed and bushy-tailed and apparently ready to make a friend.

"Oh, uh, here."

"From Fulton? Sweet! I've been needing somebody to tell me where the hell everything is."

Noah smiled tentatively. "Like what?"

"Like literally anything. I brought all this stuff from home because I was too scared to look for a grocery store out here." He shook his head. "Christian drove us to get here, and I *still* didn't see where anything was. I was too scared of him fucking up the car."

Christian had a mouth full of cereal, but he lifted a strong middle finger in response.

"Anyway." Logan turned his back to the living room, his full attention on Noah, and Christian wrinkled his brow. "What're you here for?"

"Writing."

"Really?"

Christian sat closer to the edge of the couch as Logan and Noah went off to the races, exchanging favorite authors and books and short stories and a world of things he didn't quite follow. He waited, itching for Logan to bring up something he could bust in on—plays, maybe, or movies—but they started off on the Louisiana Creole writing movement, and there was no coming back. Once Kate Chopin and Alice Dunbar Nelson were namedropped, Christian realized he was out of his depth, and he drew the shutters on the conversation.

He left his bowl on the coffee table and returned to the bedroom, taking himself through his daily routine to keep his hands occupied and his mind at a comfortable lull. Occupying himself helped him ignore the unidentifiable weird itch at the base of his gut.

By the time he was dressed and wandering out of their room again, Noah was beaming as he showed Logan some new gaming console, and Logan seemed about to jump out of his skin.

"Dude! This is awesome!"

"Right?" Noah grinned as he started hooking a mess of wires up to the TV. "Figured it might be hard trying to get work done if this was sitting around, but, I mean, we've gotta find a way to decompress."

"Whoa, bachelor of the year there. Some of us go on *dates* when we need to chill," Christian drawled, and Noah stayed silent, his lips thinning as he worked. Logan sent Christian a frown. *What?* Christian shrugged. "Logan, I've gotta get my textbooks, let's go."

Logan opened his mouth, closed it, then sat on the couch and put his bare feet on the coffee table. "Nah, man, Noah's gonna show me his way around *Starfox*. Ain't nothing you can offer to beat that."

Noah glanced up at him, smiling through the blush. "I-I mean, this isn't much." His voice cracked, and he cleared his throat as he went back to setting up the system.

"Whatever! This game is peak nostalgia! I wanna see it!"

There it was again, the crackling inside him, lightning curling out toward his fingers. Christian took a deep breath as he looked between them. "What, you got all your books already?"

"I'll get them later." Logan locked eyes with him.

There was a challenge there, plain as day. But Christian couldn't quite identify why. After a lifetime of being able to read his mind, Logan's face was completely cut off to him.

He didn't like it one bit.

"You can stay, if you want." Noah scratched his neck, not making eye contact. "You can go get your books together later."

"Nah." Christian ignored the peace offering in Noah's voice. There was obviously a reason Logan was sour at him. He usually avoided spending time with him if Christian pissed him off. But he didn't flout his annoyance by having a good time with somebody else.

Not a guy, at least. Maybe with a girl. But that was different.

Oh fuck, that's what this is, isn't it?

He narrowed his eyes, and Logan turned away first, grabbing one of the controllers and pushing it into Noah's hand.

"C'mon, man, impress me. Otherwise, I gotta kick your ass in some other game, don't I?"

Noah laughed and settled on the couch next to him. "Is that how this goes?"

"Yep."

Christian walked away in the thick of their good time, listening to Logan's laughter breaking high above Noah's before shutting the door behind him.

He stood there for a moment in the hallway, taking a deep breath to push down any latent frustration and then let his feet carry him toward the stairs.

Logan was throwing a hissy fit. He was pissed off that Christian had gotten a girl's attention so fast, and now, he was pouting. He was being a shithead instead of talking about why he was pissed off.

God forbid they talk when they were mad. God forbid they fix the issue instead of being macho and pretending it didn't exist and letting it affect their friendship.

Letting their friendship suffer wasn't an option. It never *would* be an option, as far as Christian was concerned. Logan was going to be the best man at his wedding. If he had his way, they'd get an apartment together after college while they were still figuring out if they were serious with their girls, and then they'd move into two houses on the same block when one of them got married, and their kids would grow up and be best friends.

The fantasy was something he couldn't bring up with Logan, of course—that was pushing the lines of being just a little too silly—but it was how life was going to be.

But they weren't ever going to get there if Logan couldn't sit him down and say, *"Hey, man, I feel jealous that you hooked up with a girl, and I didn't. I feel inadequate next to someone as handsome and talented as you, so if you could throw me some action when you meet one of Charlotte's friends..."*

All right, so maybe that's not *how that would go.*

He'd wait Logan's temper tantrum out. He thought Logan lashing out on their run last night was a joke. But if this was serious, then Christian would wait for Logan to man up and talk about what had made him so mad. And until then, he'd pretend nothing was wrong, and he'd text Charlotte and ask if she wanted to get coffee tonight, and, after, he'd come back and tell Logan all the details.

Nothing was going to fuck up their friendship. Nothing this small. He couldn't imagine a life without Logan, and he wasn't going to start now.

THEY WALKED THROUGH the misty warm morning together, Christian bleary-eyed and Logan bouncing as the caffeine hit him hard. They didn't talk. They didn't have to. Christian had gotten back late the night before, so late Logan was in bed and feigning sleep. He knew where Christian had been, and he didn't need to hear the sordid description of how he'd fucked her in her car.

Christian wasn't a morning person, and Logan relied on his silent exhaustion to keep from getting any details. There'd be time later, whether he liked it or not.

They stopped at a sidewalk in the middle of campus and peered at each other.

Logan swallowed hard and thumbed over his shoulder. "I've got my British Lit class over there, in McHenry."

Christian nodded. "I've got my math class."

Logan nodded back.

Silence.

"Which one of us thought 8 a.m. classes were a good idea again?" Logan asked.

Christian gave him a hard stare in response, crossing his arms. He didn't need to reply.

"Right." Logan ran a hand through his curls, cleared his throat and stared at the sidewalk. "So, uh, I'll see you for Freshman Seminar?"

"I guess."

"Yeah."

After a few seconds, Christian began to walk down the left fork of the sidewalk. "Later."

Logan waited, watching him disappear into the mist. "Yeah. Later." And then he turned on his heel and walked.

This is fucking weird as shit. He knew they'd both be making more friends as the year went on. Noah was turning into a prime gaming buddy, and Daiki was pretty cool all around. But actually saying goodbye and leaving him behind?

He shook the fear off. Just because they'd had every class together in high school didn't mean they were going to get hit by a meteor the second they were apart.

Right?

Logan had picked a *great* choice for his first class, and he knew it the second he stepped into the building. It was old as shit, with ugly wallpaper and a few missing ceiling tiles, and the warmth that hit him was one he recognized: radiators that had gotten turned on way too early in the morning chill. This was Georgia, which meant everyone would be wearing sweatpants and hoodies the second the temperature dropped into the sixties. But the building being so hot this early? Definitely a recipe for falling asleep.

He checked his schedule as he walked, comparing the class number to the doors he passed, and ran straight into a head of curls. "Oh!"

"Oh shit!" Those two words were in the thickest Southern accent he'd ever heard—more pronounced than his own. "I'm so sorry, I-I wasn't paying attention—"

"It's all right." Logan grinned down at the petite girl he'd run into. Her hair probably weighed more than the rest of her combined. One look at her screamed *debutante*. He hadn't seen many of them, but there was a pageant girl who'd transferred in during their senior year, all perfect smiles and makeup, and he couldn't help but think of her. "You okay? Lost too?"

She heaved a sigh—as if she was trying to project to the audience all the way in the back of a giant theater. *Yep. Pageants or acting.* Christian had pulled similarly expressive faces in the past, and they'd always cracked Logan up. This girl, though, had an expression that endeared him. Cute but familiar. "Yeah. I'm looking for room 120."

He lit up. "Oh! Me too!"

"Really?" She sent him a smile as bright as sunlight, and he basked in the glow.

"Yep! Brit Lit." He pointed down the hallway in front of them. "Something tells me if it wasn't where I came from or where you came from, it's probably right down there..."

"Well, look at you, being all clever." She tossed her hair over her shoulder and started walking. "You're coming, aren't you?"

"Guess there's no getting around it." The thrill of being coaxed and invited filled him with tingles, and he immediately walked side by side with her. She was taking her time, and he was happy to do the same. "I'm Logan, by the way. What's your name?"

"Kelly Anne. It's a pleasure to meet you."

"You too." He kept glancing toward her, studying the sharp angle of her cheekbones and the porcelain tone of her skin and the luscious brown curls too crisp to be real. He liked them anyway. "You from around here?"

"You can tell, huh?" She chuckled. "Athens."

"Really? That's only a couple of hours away from me in Greenbarrow."

She gasped. "I've got an uncle out that way!"

"Yeah?" He could practically sprout wings and fly right now. "What's his name? Bet I know him."

"Jimmy Smith?"

"Yeah, he owns Smith Ranch, doesn't he?"

Kelly Anne flashed him a wall of perfectly aligned pearly whites. "Yeah! I can't believe you know him!"

"C'mon, I know everybody at home." He chuckled. "Nothing happens that everybody doesn't know about ten minutes later."

"That's what he says. Always said I'd have been the belle of the ball if I came down there and stayed with him for a summer." She frowned. "He'd expect me to help out with the horses, though."

"Too messy for you?"

Her glossy lips curved into a dangerous smirk. "Now, I know you're not gonna make fun of a poor little lost girl you just met just 'cuz she doesn't like getting dirty."

"Who, me?" Logan grinned. "No, ma'am, I'm a gentleman."

"I bet you are." Kelly Anne came to a stop in front of the door for classroom 120. The way she tilted her head spoke multitudes, and Logan nearly dropped his books with how swiftly he moved to open the door. "Thank you, sweetheart."

"No problem!"

Sliding into a desk beside her was more natural than anything else in the world. They'd gotten there a couple of minutes late, and the teacher frowned as he passed them syllabuses.

A pity. He could've talked to her a few hours more without so much as stopping to breathe.

He fished his phone out of his pocket and sent a text under the desk.

Met a girl. She's cuter than yours.

The response from Christian came immediately. *Prove it.*

You know I'll get a double date.

You'd better.

ANYTHING WAS EASY to get used to if Christian put his mind to it. Living with a guy like Noah who was always in baggy sweaters and sweatpants as if it wasn't eighty degrees outside, for example, or listening to Daiki's phone conversations in Japanese every weekend. They were new things, but adjusting took time.

About the only thing not changing was the simple game of dating.

Kelly Anne was a sweet girl. She obviously needed all eyes on her all the time, just like Logan did, but she wasn't pushy. As thick as her accent was—which felt more like home than the languid, murmuring way Charlotte spoke— she always used perfect diction that Christian immediately recognized from his experience with acting.

He liked her. He liked how happy Logan was with her.

He liked Charlotte more, of course. Liked kissing her cheek and tangling their fingers together when they were studying in the library, and pulling her into his lap while Logan and Noah were busy with their video games.

And on a night like tonight, when he and Logan were strewn out on the couch with Charlotte and Kelly Anne on either side of them, he enjoyed being able to fit her against him with an arm around her shoulder, their bodies pressing together familiarly, their eyes on the TV screen as the movie played.

"Baby, stop!"

Mostly on the movie.

Kelly Anne giggled as she pushed Logan away, and Logan left three more kisses on her cheek. "What, are you shy now?" he teased.

"We are in *company*, baby, come on." When she shot Charlotte and Christian a look of amusement, Charlotte glanced up at Christian and surreptitiously rolled her eyes. "We've gotta be good," Kelly Anne insisted.

"You'd rather watch a movie than kiss me?" Logan asked. Christian turned toward the screen. He recognized the tone as a silly tease. If Kelly Anne let it rub her the wrong way, that was her fault. "I'm offended."

"I'm just saying, when a lady is on a double date, she doesn't start something she can't finish." She spoke with a practically theatrical primness, and Charlotte snaked her hand up Christian's thigh under the huge folds of her short skirt.

Logan sighed heavily. "Fine, fine."

Charlotte squeezed Christian's thigh, her sharp nails digging into the fabric of his jeans, and every bit of his attention diverted from the movie immediately. He glanced down at her. She glanced up at him. Her hand slid a little bit higher.

Oh.

Christian liked everything about Charlotte. He liked the familiar color of her eyes and skin. He liked the spark she got in her gaze when she wanted something specific and wasn't scared to wrestle with him to get it.

This was one of those spark moments.

He snuck his hand over and traced the edge of her fingers with his. The move was silent, but it was enough. Charlotte chuckled.

No one said anything, but Kelly Anne peered over. Christian caught the glance out of the corner of his eye and flicked his gaze between her and the TV as she glanced away, looked back, and sighed. "What's funny, Charlotte?"

"Nothing." She slid into Christian's lap at an angle, draping an arm around his neck, and flashed Kelly Anne a pretty smile. "Just didn't expect somebody like you to be so concerned about *appearances*."

Oh shit. This was immediately more interesting than the movie. Christian tucked his arms around her waist and studied Logan, who was watching them as closely as a tennis match.

"Oh?" Kelly Anne sat a little taller. "Why's that?"

"You do pageants, sweetie. Don't people like you get off on being watched?"

Kelly Anne scoffed. "You don't think that's a little bit rude to say? Some of us have particular morals, all right?"

"And some of us like to have fun." Charlotte trailed her fingers down the buttons of Christian's shirt, from his neck to his belly, and his breath caught hard in his chest. Her touch seemed to whisper that right now he was more of a plaything than a boyfriend—and he was surprisingly all right with it. He stared at Charlotte in rapture as she turned to straddle his hips, her thick thighs squeezing him tight, and leaned down to kiss him.

He sucked in a quiet breath as he ran his thumb down her spine. She liked being in control, and he wouldn't begrudge her that, especially when it meant she pressed her chest against his, her soft breasts almost spilling over the edge of her low neckline.

He heard Kelly Anne huff again, and Logan cleared his throat. As Charlotte popped the bottom button on his shirt, he got the sense they were in the spotlight—similar to the plays he'd acted in back home—and he slouched on the couch to let her be more comfortable, his long legs splaying out as she arched prettily.

If she wanted to put on a show so bad, he wasn't going to stop her. Not if he got to taste her sweet lip gloss like this.

There was a surprised sound beside him, and he peeked over through slitted eyes to see Kelly Anne holding

Logan's face and kissing him deeply, her tongue plunging into his mouth. Logan sank his fingers into her hair, twisting his back to Christian to kiss her all the better, and Christian grinned against Charlotte's mouth.

If she wanted a little competition, apparently she'd succeeded.

Charlotte broke the kiss with a low, throaty laugh and sat back, guiding Christian's mouth to her neck. "That's what I'm talking about," she murmured, her voice making her skin vibrate as he worshiped it with his lips. They'd done a hell of a lot of exploring since meeting only a month and a half ago, and he knew the exact way she wanted her skin nipped: with little marks only visible if someone knew they were there.

Kelly Anne glared at them, and Christian chuckled as he ran his hands up his girlfriend's spine, over the familiar bump of her bra clasp, finally squeezing the back of her neck. He hadn't realized they were playing a game of chess, but Kelly Anne scrambled into Logan's lap and pulled him into kisses that appeared more insistent than passionate.

Logan didn't seem to mind one bit.

They'd never done anything like this on any of their double dates, and a primal thrill lit right in Christian's gut. There'd always been some curiosity about Logan's technique—all the cheerleaders in school fawned over him. After Logan broke up with his pushy girlfriends, they'd flirt with Christian instead. Logan and Christian had kissed the same lips at least three times when that happened. Maybe the girls were attempting to make Logan jealous, not realizing how ironclad their friendship really was.

Either way, watching how Logan's hands cupped Kelly Anne's face so tenderly made Christian's grasp on Charlotte's neck loosen.

She wasn't a fan. She rolled her hips, and Christian gasped, tightening his arms around her as she kissed him roughly, all teeth and teasing sucks at his lips.

The sound called Logan's attention, and their eyes locked, both of them in the throes of kissing their girls. Christian froze, and Logan's hands, which had been running down the curves of Kelly Anne's waist, came to a stop.

Another buck of Charlotte's hips, and a shock of pleasure ripped through Christian and made him moan against her lips. Logan's eyes flicked downward.

I can't believe this is happening. The thought was tinged with fire as Charlotte shoved her hands up Christian's shirt, straining the buttons and the thinning fabric until they almost popped off. Her thumbs slid over his nipples—a new, surprising erogenous zone—and he squeezed his eyes shut, having to force them to stay that way.

He was curious. He couldn't help it. Kelly Anne let out a breathy sound next to him, and his cock twitched in his jeans.

"Hey, listen, Daiki could come back any second," Logan's voice was rough, positively ruined.

Christian thought of all the times he'd called him on the phone and heard a growl in his tone and wondered if he'd been out screaming in the fields or something. Nope. Apparently, he'd been making out with some girl. Nervous energy caught hold of his veins.

Charlotte broke the kiss, but her fingers tweaked his nipples as if they were the only two people in the room. "So?"

"So..." Logan licked his lips, glancing between Kelly Anne's heaving chest and Charlotte's eager attentions. "...so, where's this going?"

Christian stared at Charlotte—how she quirked her swollen lips, how she sat back and popped open two more buttons on his shirt, how she didn't adjust her skirt when the hem slid a little higher up her thighs. "I don't know. Where's it going, Kelly Anne?"

Even under her heavy layer of foundation, the blush trailed down her neck. "Well..." Kelly Anne chewed on her bottom lip, wiggling her hips, and Logan clutched his fingers around them. "...well, there's no reason we've gotta take up the whole couch out here, right?"

Christian and Logan snapped their gazes to each other.

"Not when there's a whole couch in their room, hmm?" Charlotte drawled.

Christian tried to telepathically ask Logan, *Is this really happening?*

Logan stared back, completely awestruck, stars in his eyes. *Fuck if I know,* he might as well have said.

Finally, Kelly Anne came to her feet, smoothing down her long shirt over her leggings. She picked up her purse, grabbed Logan's hand, and guided him toward the bedroom.

"What's in the purse, Kelly Anne?" Charlotte smirked. "Why do you need to bring it in the bedroom with us?"

"Never you mind." That primness fell around Kelly Anne like a cloak, and Charlotte laughed as she stood and brought Christian up with her.

So, this was happening. He wasn't sure what *this* was exactly, but his shirt was hanging half-open and Logan was adjusting himself in his jeans, which told him they were both on the same page.

And Charlotte? His exhibitionist girlfriend? The one who'd coaxed him into fucking her in a bathroom in the administration building? She certainly had something in mind. The one question seemed to be Kelly Anne, and he was more than curious what her trump card would be.

Maybe there wouldn't be one. Maybe things would keep accelerating.

And then what?

Christian locked eyes again with Logan as he brought up the rear and shut the door behind them—and, after a second thought, locked it. He wanted to bring Logan into the bathroom and have a pep talk, but he didn't exactly have the chance.

It wouldn't be weird to watch him fuck a girl, he was pretty sure.

Right?

Seeing them have sex would be like porn, that was all. Porn involving his best friend who he would die for without any hesitation. Not weird at all.

The four of them stood in the middle of the room. There wasn't a clear way to go about things, and Christian had never been the captain of any team. He gaped at the three of them until Charlotte rolled her eyes and grabbed his hand, pulling him toward the couch.

"Told you getting this couch was smart." Christian couldn't help throwing that out as Charlotte pushed him to sit and straddled him again.

"Shut up." Logan chuckled, but there was a nervous gleam in his eyes.

Kelly Anne shoved Logan so he sat a cushion away from Christian. She seemed to also be watching Charlotte for any indication of where this was going.

Charlotte nipped at Christian's ear and whispered so softly he wondered if he was making the words up. "You're okay with this, right, baby?"

"With what?" he murmured.

"If I fuck you in front of them."

If he wasn't hard before, he was now. His arousal was an afterthought, straining against his jeans, and he punched out a groan as he wrapped his arms around her. "I-I mean, if you're cool with it, then—"

"I'm gonna ride you harder than I ever have."

A full-body shiver broke over him, head to toe. He sank his hands into her plush hips. "Bet you won't make me scream."

Charlotte met his gaze, her eyes gleaming in challenge. Jackpot.

She descended on him like a viper, kissing him fiercely with her nails scraping over his scalp. The bite of pain drew something new and vibrant and *painful* to the surface, and he groaned out her name.

Slick sounds beside him brought a tantalizing image to his mind's eye—pretty Kelly Anne with her tongue in Logan's mouth, her back arching to show off the slight curve of her ass, and her nipples hard through her shirt. He could imagine it plain as day.

He'd had a love of porn for years. The videos were always a little too similar for his taste—the picture-perfect makeup, the long stretches of nothing but pounding, boring him so much he skipped ahead to the cumshot every time—but this was something he hadn't gotten to see among all the threesomes and orgies and gangbangs he'd watched in secret in his bedroom.

Two couples fucking each other in one room. Not touching each other. Just thriving on the energy of the other couple and competing with them to see who could make their partner moan first.

He was absolutely sure he was going to win that challenge. Logan was sweet, the girls around school said, but Christian was willing to bet he was gentle and took his time. That didn't always work.

Still, it'd be interesting to see…

Charlotte crept her hands up his chest, opening every button, and the cool air made goose bumps spread over his skin. He let his touch roam up her body until he was unclasping her bra under her shirt, and the way she grinned against his lips made his heart skip a beat.

She always teased him about going straight for her tits. But could she blame him?

His shirt came off first. He wasn't shy about his body. He'd been shirtless in front of Logan every time they had a sleepover. Hell, he slept in nothing but his boxers every night now, and so did Logan. Charlotte's tits, though…

He knew he was supposed to be jealous. He was supposed to worry Logan would stare at Charlotte and decide he wanted her and that he'd do anything to have her. But he didn't.

He wanted to show her off.

Charlotte peeled her shirt over her head and threw it across the room, and then she slithered out of her bra and dropped it behind her. Her tits bounced in front of his face, full and beautiful, from the plump one on the left to the smaller one on the right, and he made a show of reaching for them and thumbing over her nipples until they were as hard as erasers.

He glanced over. Though Kelly Anne was leaving marks on his neck, Logan was watching with wide eyes.

But he wasn't watching how Charlotte's tits fit in Christian's hands. He was watching *Christian.*

Those few seconds of eye contact seared him like a fire poker, and as he wrinkled his brow in confusion, Logan quickly looked away. Logan grabbed Kelly Anne and pulled her back for a deep kiss as he bucked his hips up, making her squeal and hold his shoulders as if she was riding a bronco. She laughed. She didn't seem to pay attention to Christian and Charlotte.

Am I not supposed to look? Christian bit back the question and leaned down to take one of his girl's nipples in his mouth. She gasped, letting out a shivery weak sound, like cool water trickling down his spine in the midst of a desert, and he focused on her.

Tunnel vision. That was what he needed. Nothing but tunnel vision.

And it worked, too, focusing on drawing quiet but needy praise out of Charlotte with nothing but his tongue and his fingers. He was *good* at this. He liked teasing her up until she was ready to throw him down and take what she wanted. Knowing he'd made her lose her self-control made him feel more powerful than any man alive. What man didn't want a beautiful woman to crave him so badly she nearly bruised him with how fast she had to get his dick inside her?

But then Logan let out a sound, and every cell in Christian's body lurched toward him a little more.

This new sound stopped him. He'd heard Logan swear and growl and throw a fit every time they wrestled and Christian played dead so he couldn't get the upper hand. He'd heard Logan cry over the phone once, when his grandma died and he couldn't sleep because he kept thinking about all the things he hadn't thanked her for. He'd heard Logan scream at the top of his lungs in the middle of the woods, off Old Man Yeargin's farm, because he was a powerful barbarian who didn't have to play by the world's rules ever again.

But he'd never heard such an aching sound come out of his lips before tonight.

Raw. That was what it was. Raw and honey sweet. Dew dripping down from the branches they walked under to go to school. The kiss of the first cup of freshly squeezed hot apple cider of the season.

He turned his head and stared.

As Kelly Anne rubbed Logan through his pants, her hand moving expertly over the swell there, Charlotte pressed her mouth against Christian's ear. "What're you looking at, sweetheart?" Barely any sound.

Panic flooded Christian. "Nothing," he whispered, twisting so he could get his mouth back on her.

"Uh-uh-uh." Her mouth moved against his lobe as she spoke, the heat of her voice warmer than the air she exhaled. "If you wanna watch, you can watch, baby. Don't act like I caught you doing something you weren't supposed to."

Fuck, how did I get so lucky with her?

He pushed one hand up her skirt, rubbing his thumb against her wet slit through her panties. "This get you hot too?" He kept his voice low so they wouldn't hear anything but a rumble on the other end of the couch. "Knowing they might look over and see me fucking you here in a second?"

"Oh, there ain't no *might*." She chuckled and pulled her skirt hem up so he could see the smooth skin of her thighs and the softness of the hair peeking out around the edges of her panties. He lit up at the teasing peek. "Don't seem all that shy now, do you, Kelly Anne?" she asked louder.

Kelly Anne turned her head, mouth open, but the words didn't come when she stared at Christian cupping Charlotte with his whole hand. "Shut up."

"No, I don't think I will." Charlotte gasped and wiggled against his hand. He knew she was being theatrical, but all her overblown reaction did was turn him on. "Fuck, baby, you make me feel amazing."

Kelly Anne had Logan's pants off the next second. She sat on her knees on the hard linoleum floor, and Christian didn't feel bad about glancing over and watching how she put her mouth around the shape of Logan in his boxers.

"Oh my God—" Logan whimpered, starting to sag into the couch.

As Kelly Anne ran her hands down Logan's legs, Christian swore phantom sensations sang on his own skin.

"Are we gonna let them win?" Charlotte bit his ear again.

He met her gaze. She grinned. He started tugging her skirt off the next moment.

Getting Charlotte stripped down to nothing was the best part of his day. She ran her hands down her body—the stretch marks on her breasts, the scar on her gut from her appendectomy, the freckles dotting her flesh—and he ate every inch of her up with his gaze. She stood and placed her knee between his legs and grabbed his hand, bringing it to his own mouth. As he sucked on his fingers, making sure they were dripping wet, he couldn't help himself. He glanced again.

Logan was watching him. Watching his *mouth*. And as Charlotte pulled Christian's slick fingers from between his lips, Logan's mouth dropped open, and his eyelashes fluttered.

Oh.

He didn't expect the kick in his gut at the sight—Logan watching so openly. Christian raked his gaze over his best friend's face, from the dusky rose of his cheeks to his swollen lips, and Logan didn't turn away either. Even Charlotte pushing Christian's first two fingers through her folds didn't take his attention away.

Logan cracked first. His chest shook with silent laughter.

This is funny.

It was less a natural thought and more a sentence Christian pushed into his brain. He grabbed Charlotte's hip and got with the program. He knew how she liked to be touched. A slow tease of his fingers through her inner labia could have her knees knocking in minutes, if he played his cards right, and he intended to. He dragged his gaze up her body and stopped on her face; she was already smirking.

Like she knew something he didn't.

He took Charlotte's leg from between his thighs and moved it to prop her foot on the cushion beside him. With her legs now spread, he had enticing access; he leaned forward and buried his nose in her thatch of hair, breathed in her musk and tasted her slickness. As he pushed a finger inside her, she clenched around him—another silent challenge. Her moan echoed through the air and had him straining painfully against his zipper.

Every sense was taken up by her, as it was supposed to be—normal and perfect and *necessary*—and he squeezed his eyes shut so he could focus on his drive to please her.

He kept pushing through the musical lilting of Logan's moans and the quiet filthy words Kelly Anne offered him every few seconds: "How's that feel around your cock, baby? You like it when I suck you off like a little slut?" He fought for tunnel vision, the same thing that got him in the zone on the field so he could get the last goal.

He wanted that brain fog. That heavy mist. That haze. He wanted to forget every confusing impulse in the base of his belly.

And it worked, all the way until Charlotte put a bullet through his plans.

"Kelly Anne."

"What?"

"Where's your condoms, Kelly Anne?"

Christian's eyes flew open.

Kelly Anne pulled back. Her shirt and leggings had been abandoned, leaving her in her bra and panties, and a glance farther away showed a drop of precum swelling on the head of Logan's dick.

Holy shit. If there was anything Christian didn't need to stare at, it was his best friend's cock, but he took in what he could—how hard Logan was, how the veins in his dick seemed like they were about to burst clean open, how he twitched as if aware he was being watched.

Christian looked away again.

"Why do you think I have condoms?" Kelly Anne came to her feet. "And why are you always using my name?"

"That's your name, isn't it, Kelly Anne?"

"So?" It could be she wasn't used to being teased. Maybe she felt as flayed open as Christian did. Either way, Kelly Anne grabbed her purse and started rooting around, and by the time she stood tall with two condoms tucked between her perfectly manicured fingers, Charlotte was coming up behind her. "Here they—oh!"

And then Charlotte was cupping her face and kissing her.

"Holy fuck," Christian murmured, his eyes wide enough to fall out of his head. Logan let out a sharp, surprised laugh, there and gone again.

Charlotte took command of the kiss, her hand on the small of Kelly Anne's back. Their breasts pushed together, hers bare against the vivid red lace of Kelly Anne's bra, and her toenails curled against the floor as she chuckled. What must've been only a couple of seconds felt like hours, and when Charlotte leaned away with a smirk, one of the condoms in her hand, Christian gaped at Logan.

Holy shit, Logan mouthed soundlessly, and Christian nodded.

"Damn. No wonder he likes you." Charlotte took slow backward steps, and Kelly Anne giggled as she stumbled into Logan's lap. "What's that, strawberry?"

"Mm-hmm." She peeked at Charlotte.

She grinned. "I like it."

Kelly Anne began wiggling out of her bra and panties without another word.

Charlotte held the condom between her teeth as she opened Christian's jeans and slid them and his boxers down at the same time. There was a sharp gasp beside him, but he didn't risk peeking, not when he was vividly aware of how his cock bounced to attention, hitting his stomach with how hard he was. He'd always suspected his cock would be longer than Logan's—he wasn't four inches taller for nothing—but with how lean his cock was, he didn't want to risk wondering if Logan's thickness got somebody off better than him.

Do people like a cock when it's thicker, though? Heat rushed through him. *Is a stretch…nice? Or painful? How do you know until you try? Is there, like, a way to test it out?*

Something about his thoughts made his blood boil, frothing until he couldn't focus. Any other time, he'd call the turmoil anger, but right now, he recognized it as the same drive he got before taking the field. It had nothing to do with being mad, and everything to do with taking what he wanted from the other team over and over again, making his performance look effortless, leaving everyone on his team satisfied and ecstatic.

Charlotte rolled the condom over his cock, pinching the tip as she worked, and that little bit of contact made him roll his hips to meet her. "You ready for me, baby?"

"You know I am." He opened his arms and welcomed her into his lap. "Gonna fuck you so good."

"Oh, no you ain't. I'm gonna fuck *you*. Gonna ride you 'til you don't know which way is up."

He didn't want to compete with her right now. He slouched so she could loom over him, tall and powerful, so he could feel small and could give her everything she wanted from him. She was the goddess here. He was just Christian. And he was bordering on overwhelmed.

Charlotte took him inside her with slow, teasing rolls of her hips, and he tipped his head back and groaned sharply. "That's my baby," she said.

He closed his eyes and focused on *feeling* her. She rode him as smoothly as a dancer with practiced movements, making him tighten his grip on her hips just to keep himself at bay. It was too much, hearing Logan and Kelly Anne gasp beside him as they started to rock together, feeling the couch move awkwardly with the conflicting rhythm of their hips.

Christian held Charlotte still for a moment and then guided her down to match the flow rocking through the cushions. *Perfect.*

As he gave her control, he itched to open his eyes, but he fought the temptation. His lids started to hurt—he didn't care. He couldn't risk peeking. He'd seen so much already.

Porn wasn't like this. Porn was impersonal. He didn't have a favorite porn star, unlike the ones guys would talk about sometimes in the locker room. He always found someone he'd never seen before, took what he wanted from that video, and moved on.

He couldn't do that here. He couldn't block out the fervent way Logan whispered Kelly Anne's name. He couldn't ignore how he murmured words that made her laugh so warmly.

What the fuck is going on with me tonight?

Something that was supposed to be interesting and fun was leaning into the realm of dangerous, and he couldn't identify why.

The couch shifted, Logan crying out in surprise, and Christian's eyes flew open as something tickled his bare thigh.

It was Logan's curls. Kelly Anne had tipped him over, his legs hanging awkwardly over the end of the couch and started to ride him hard and fast. Every little move pushed Logan's soft hair against his leg, until his head rested there instead.

For the life of him, Christian couldn't tell him to move.

"You feel so fucking good," Charlotte breathed, and Christian stared up at her, taking in how her breasts bounced with every movement she made. "I love this so much."

"Yeah?" His voice was rough, as raw as the inside of his chest.

"Mmm, God, Christian..." She opened her eyes into languid slits as she grinned at him. "You know what would make me feel even better?"

Anything to get my head back in the game. "What's that?"

She leaned down, her full lips spreading, a little more predatory with every inch. "Remember how me and Kelly Anne kissed to make you both a little hot under the collar?"

His heart pounded like a drum. "Oh, is *that* what that was?"

"You liked it, right?"

Of course, he'd fucking liked it. "Yeah?"

Logan wasn't making any sound beside him anymore. He wasn't even breathing.

"Well, you and Logan could give us a little show, too, huh?"

"No way." Christian shook his head, hands holding a vice grip around her hips. "No fucking way—you can't expect him to—without asking if that's cool or whatever, that's not—*we're* not—"

"Logan?" Kelly Anne asked breathlessly.

"Yeah?"

"Kiss Christian, baby."

"Yes, ma'am." Logan lurched up, twisting around, one of his hands around the back of Christian's neck, and he pressed a painful kiss to his lips.

Their teeth clacked together and sent a tremor through him, but tilting his head solved the problem, and Logan didn't seem too eager to let him pull away. He held him in place as they sank against each other. Christian tasted strawberries and cherries and yet another flavor under those, something he didn't have a name for.

I'm tasting Logan.

Every thought came to a dead stop, lost in the tight heat clenching around his cock and the teeth nibbling at his bottom lip. He didn't move. He *couldn't*. If he moved, everything would stop, and everything would change, and everything would *hurt*.

Logan trembled and fell away from him, swearing under his breath, eyes shut as Kelly Anne started a new, more insistent pace, and for just a moment, he rested his temple on Christian's shoulder. "Fuuuuck..." His hair itched over Christian's neck and cheek, smelling like the shampoo he always used to steal when he stayed over.

"Goddamn," Charlotte murmured, voice rich with lust. He tried to force his gaze back to her, but he couldn't quite succeed. Not when Logan sank down, his head pillowed on the edge of Christian's thigh.

Things sharpened after that, dragging Christian down the tunnel he'd craved so much. There wasn't an easy way out. There was only the slapping of bodies and the smell of sex and the slickness of Charlotte's clit when his fingers found it and the rocking of her hips as she drove him deeper and deeper into the tunnel.

And the way his eyes locked with Logan's—the way neither of them looked away—was what pushed him so far he couldn't find his way home.

His orgasm snuck up on him. One moment he was watching Logan's face start to shift, his brow furrowing and his mouth opening, and the next, Christian threw his head back and came harder than he had in a month. He didn't let himself enjoy it. He shoved through the sharp pleasure so he could focus on Charlotte, his mouth around her nipple and his finger cramping as he worked at her, and she came seconds after him with a rough groan, collapsing against his chest.

He held her, face buried in her neck, as Logan gasped and panted next to him. Something about the cry Kelly Anne gave when she came first struck him the wrong way, rough as nails scratching across a chalkboard. Logan being the last one, bringing up the rear with a moan Christian had goddamn memorized at this point, only made his frustration worse.

The sex wasn't the simple fun he thought it'd be. Charlotte kissed over his neck but didn't come near his mouth. The last thing he tasted was Logan's tongue and how it had brushed over his like a whisper before he'd moved away.

Like he'd done something wrong. Like Christian was going to punch the shit out of him.

Anyone back home would've. It didn't matter if they'd only kissed to get their girlfriends off—kissing another guy was a sin, one worse than anybody else could ever commit, even worse than taking down the Confederate flag or saying Andrew Jackson never did anything good for the South. Those things wouldn't get you sent to Hell, necessarily.

Christian didn't believe in Hell. But he *did* believe in his family pulling his ass as close as they could if they ever found out.

They won't. He rubbed Charlotte's arm as she shivered through her aftershocks, making no move to get her out of his lap. *They're never gonna know. Kissing was just a joke. We only did it to make Charlotte hot and heavy.*

He glanced down. Logan stared up at him through his eyelashes as Kelly Anne ran a hand up and down his lean chest.

Logan was frowning as if he was working through a math problem. Christian couldn't imagine the face he must've been making in return.

"Well, that was something, wasn't it?" Charlotte finally asked, chuckling. "What'd you think, Kelly Anne? Worth the risk? Worth not being proper every goddamn second?"

"It was all right." Kelly Anne grinned as she batted her eyelashes. "Not bad."

"Wanna do it again some time?"

There was a promise in those words, and Christian caught on immediately. He waited for the jealousy that never came. He and Charlotte were dating, but if she wanted to flirt with some girls, hell, who was he to stop her? Maybe she was only toying with Kelly Anne because she knew it would tease him up.

It *should* tease him up. It shouldn't involve him glancing up at them for a second before he stared at Logan instead. And when Logan stopped returning that confused gaze, Christian gave up.

Logan was thinking too hard, obviously, about whatever was going on in his head, and Christian didn't need to take his lead. Logan did the thinking for the both of them, and Christian did what he knew would work. And, right now, what worked was how perfectly Charlotte fit in his arms. So he held her tight and kissed her cheek and buried the rest of his confusion away.

Chapter Four

LOGAN

Logan slept hard. He always slept hard, and nothing was going to stop it, not even the weirdness of the evening.

A little fun. That was all the night before was supposed to be. A little experimenting to see how far he could get Christian to go. Eventually, he was supposed to laugh and take Charlotte in the bedroom and lock the door behind him, and pretend not to hear when Logan and Kelly Anne stood outside the door making gross noises to interfere with their fucking. But things hadn't gone that way.

No, he'd not only watched his best friend fuck his girlfriend, but he kissed him, whatever *that* meant.

Nothing had changed, of course. Why would it? As Christian walked Charlotte to her apartment, Logan simply kissed Kelly Anne good night and saw her to the door, then brushed his teeth and crawled into bed and slept like a baby.

The thinking came the next morning. And so did the changing.

Christian wasn't there, for one. Christian, as he often had in the past, left the bedroom without waking Logan, his sheets thrown messily around his bed and last night's boxers somewhere across the room.

This wasn't the first time Logan remembered exactly what pair of boxers Christian had been wearing, nor was it the first time he'd seen how they fit on him, but the image stuck with him all the same. There was a new weight to the fabric, lying haplessly on the floor, abandoned rather than put in the dirty clothes basket where they belonged.

More might've changed than he thought.

Logan crawled out of bed, ignoring the ladder and jumping to the floor instead, and he winced and limped only for a second before taking off.

Christian wasn't in the living room.

There was, however, the smell of baked goods.

Logan went into the living room and peered around, catching sight of Noah carefully placing cookies on a cooling rack. He liked Noah. Noah kept things clean, and he was always cooking and offering them food, and he didn't play music loudly or keep Logan up—but he wasn't the person he wanted to see right then.

It was too late. Noah opened his mouth to speak and then wrinkled his brow, skimming his gaze down Logan's frame. Logan had never much cared what he wore in the dorm, as long as no one but his suitemates were around, but he was now vividly aware of how his boxers fit on him and how much skin he had exposed.

Christian had stared so openly last night.

He rubbed his bare arms, chasing the goose bumps away. "Morning, uh—"

"Hey." Noah smiled and turned away quickly, the tips of his ears turning pink. "Good morning. Sleep well?"

"I...I slept." That would have to do. "Is Christian here?"

"Nope." Noah frowned down at the cookies. "He left, like, an hour ago? I don't know. Said he had warm-ups."

Warm-ups. Soccer. Just a standard thing, not an attempted escape.

Why did you think he was trying to get away? That's ridiculous. Nothing happened last night.

Nothing but the sex and the kiss and the ache leveled in his gut—

Nothing. Happened.

"Right. I knew that." Logan forced a chuckle. "That, uh, that was a test, okay?"

"Lucky me. Normally I don't do really well with those." Noah offered the last cookie from the pan. "I baked. Want some?"

"Are you offering me cookies for breakfast?"

"I absolutely am." Noah took careful steps toward him, hand held under the spatula to catch little crumbs falling from the morsel. "Chocolate chip. You can't tell me you're immune to a fresh, warm, homemade chocolate chip cookie."

Right now, all he wanted was to run down to the soccer field and see if Christian was tearing up the sod with his cleats...but that would be weird. If nothing had happened last night, there'd be no reason to show up.

And Noah wasn't a bad dude. Sure, Logan had only started spending time with him to lessen the inevitable ache of Christian surrounding himself with other friends, but Logan *liked* Noah. So, he shrugged and took the cookie. "Well, I mean...if you're offering."

Noah's grin widened. "I knew it." He slid the cookie into Logan's hand. "Cool Guy Logan Brown is actually just as weak to temptation as everyone else."

Logan laughed. "What does *that* mean?"

Noah shot him a look, then shrugged and went back to the pan. "Nothing. I don't know, you're *cool*. You're always putting off this air that you don't need anybody."

"*Me*? Have you *met* Christian?"

"I mean, he's worse, don't get me wrong, but it's a shared trait, I think. I feel like you guys probably started it in each other, didn't you?"

In all of the years of noticing exactly how he was different from Christian, he never really focused on how they might be similar. They always balanced each other. They came as a pair because they filled each other's deficiencies, and no one could imagine them apart.

But the same?

"I don't know what you're talking about." Logan shook his head as he leaned against the counter. "We're nothing alike."

"You kidding me?"

Logan didn't glance at him. He stared at the wall as he took the first bite of his cookie.

"Oh, buddy, let me count the ways."

Jackpot.

The cookie melted in his mouth. Absolutely perfect. Even better than his mom's, as hard as that was to beat— no one came between a Southern woman and her baking. "This is fucking amazing, by the way."

"No, no, don't change the subject!"

Logan turned his head, trying to hide his grin from Noah. "All right, fine, tell me how me and Christian are twins or whatever."

"I will!" Noah started washing the pan with fervor. "You have the same accent, first of all."

Logan pointed at him. "Cheap."

Noah's mouth quirked. "You didn't say I couldn't use cheap ones. Too late to impose rules. Two!" He continued scrubbing. "You're always looking at each other when you're trying to figure out what you're doing next."

"That doesn't make any sense."

"I mean you're both waiting to see who's gonna be the leader. Neither of you can start anything on your own."

That was a crock of shit, but it was still interesting. "Next?"

If Noah was annoyed with Logan goading him, he didn't show it. "Three, you both enjoy spiting each other."

"That's a fucking lie," Logan interrupted and took a bite of the cookie for emphasis. The warm morsel was soft and buttery instead of crunchy, and it didn't lend itself to the dramatic flair he'd intended. "He spites *me*, okay?"

Noah glanced over.

"What?"

"Really?"

"*What?*"

Noah laughed and pulled the pan out of the sink, grabbing a towel to start drying it with smooth, confident strokes. "You think I don't remember how we first met? The whole video game thing?"

His words were a shot to the chest. Logan narrowed his eyes and waited for Noah to look away, but he didn't. He held his gaze with confidence. "I thought it was cool that you had the system."

"You wanted to piss Christian off," Noah countered. "It's fine. I'm not mad, if that's what you're afraid of. I knew what you were doing, and I wanted to make a friend. It worked for both of us."

Logan broke the stare. He hated being so easily read.

"It's cool. I like you now. I think you like me too. We're fine."

"I *do*. You're a cool guy." Logan paused. "And not *just* for the free cookies."

"You think these are free?"

"Ha-ha." Logan deadpanned. "I'm not saying you're right. He does shit to piss me off way more than I do anything to spite him."

"Number five!" Noah slapped the wet towel on the counter and put the pan away, then crossed his arms. "You're both stubborn."

"I am not!"

Noah rolled his eyes and grabbed a cookie, a plate, and a napkin. He was careful, Logan noticed. Everything he did was deliberate, so he wouldn't have to come back and fix a mess behind him. Noah went into the living room, and Logan followed. "You're stubborn. Both of you. You want to pretend you're not, but the thing is, man, I'm not sure *which* of you is more stubborn. You both win that award. Congratulations."

Silence. He parsed through his thoughts, unsatisfied with them all. "Literally, no matter what I say, you can turn it against me right now and prove yourself right."

Noah flopped on the couch and tucked an arm behind his neck, grinning up at him. "You're gonna deprive me of winning? Really?"

Logan rolled his eyes, then stuffed the last of the cookie in his mouth and reached for the controller.

"You know that's just proving me ri—"

"Shut up."

Noah chuckled and grabbed the second controller.

As they loaded up the game, Logan chewed on the inside of his cheek. He knew he was stubborn. He knew

Christian was stubborn too. They both liked to win, and Logan was willing to admit, more often than not, Christian was the one who came out on top. They only admitted they'd messed up if there weren't going to be negative consequences for doing so or if they knew they could talk their way out.

Noah kicked his ass through two quick games before Logan huffed and twisted around.

"So, what, one of us is just supposed to *stop* being stubborn? Like it's easy?"

"I can't help you with that." Noah paused the game and turned to face him on the couch. "But has shutting down really not been an issue with you guys yet? After, what, how long? Twelve years?"

"I mean, we've fought, but we get over it."

"No compromise?"

Logan shrugged. "I don't know. We talk. We forget about being pissed. That's it."

Noah shook his head. "Typical."

Logan scowled at him.

"Never mind." Noah sighed. "Listen, not a lot of people have a friendship that lasts so long. Not even a lot of *marriages* last that long anymore. So, if you're asking me—"

"I didn't."

"You did, shut up. If you're asking me if only one of you should stop being stubborn, then, no. But maybe you can try giving in when he wants something."

A novel idea. It sounded more like relationship advice than advice for sustaining a friendship, though, and that thought made him squirm. "Well, maybe he should give in with *me* sometime."

"I give up," Noah said dully as he unpaused the game. "You stubborn ass."

"*Everybody's* like this at home, okay?" Logan focused on the screen, but his thumbs were clumsy. His game performance continued to tank. "Hell, it's probably the only way we're like everybody else."

Noah laughed. He delivered a solid blow to Logan's character, taking off health points in game and pride outside of it. "What does that mean?"

"You know." Logan gritted his teeth as he fought against Noah's constant onslaught. "We're not used to people looking like us in most places."

"What?"

"Black. You get me, right?"

"I don't follow."

Logan growled in frustration. With each hit he got on Noah, he received ten. He couldn't keep the sharpness out of his voice when he replied. "Christian and I are the only black kids at home. Hell, when I got lonely, sometimes I figured we were probably the only ones in *Georgia*. You know what I mean. FSU's fucking weird. The campus doesn't look like anywhere else."

Suddenly the tide turned. Noah's character stopped moving, as if his controller was unplugged, and Logan let out a whoop of triumph as he kicked his tail. Logan sat back and smirked at Noah, but hesitated to speak when he saw the expression on his suitemate's face.

Noah frowned, his bushy brows lowered. "You...you realize Georgia is incredibly diverse, don't you?"

Logan blinked. "What?"

"Have you ever, like, been to Atlanta? Or anywhere?"

Vacations were few and far between after his family moved to Greenbarrow. The workload on his parents was far too heavy to think about relaxing. "Not...not for a while." Logan searched his childhood memories, but no clear mental images of his six years before Greenbarrow came to mind.

Noah seemed more confused than anything. "I've lived in Georgia my whole life. My family moved around a ton when I was a kid. And believe me when I say there isn't a single city in this state that's *all* white."

His statement was interesting because Logan knew for a fact there was—he'd lived in it for years. "But..."

"Was...where are you from?"

"Greenbarrow," Logan replied thinly.

"Yeah, there. Was that all white...intentionally?"

As Noah's question sank in, Logan set the controller on his thighs.

"I mean, is Greenbarrow more like the Amish, where the town is isolated because they have a different culture? Or is it more like a suburb with a big gate they keep shut?"

Noah likely meant to clarify his thoughts, but the words slapped Logan's face.

As a child, Logan believed the whole country mostly looked like Greenbarrow. He knew from TV and the Internet that his assumption was false—but facts meant very little compared to living his own experiences. He'd gone through the stares and the questions about his appearance by other kids, and had his own curiosity about his background stifled by his adoptive parents.

Even as a teenager, he hadn't once considered his hometown might've been so homogenous by design—that he and Christian only received free passes because of their parents. And something about the realization crushed his chest.

"Why do you care?" Logan snapped, leaning on defensive habits.

Noah blinked. His voice went raw. "I know a few things about people who don't want you to be around them just because of how you are."

Logan didn't fully process the statement. He stared blankly at the paused game, lips parted, searching for words that would make more sense. But anything he thought only made him uncomfortable and angry, and for some reason, he couldn't get his parents' eyes out of his mind. He finally shook his head with a huff. "You're just trying to distract me so I can't kick your ass." He unpaused the game and started playing again.

And Noah let the words go, enduring a few more seconds of punishment before he destroyed Logan one final time.

"HEY."

Though Christian was walking with his teammates, he searched over his shoulder and grinned. "Hey, baby."

Charlotte beamed. "Walk with me?"

He'd just gotten done with practice, he was covered in a sticky sheen of sweat, and his muscles were still throbbing from the thorough workout. But it was Charlotte. How was he going to say no to her? "Sure, I've got a few minutes before I can't stand my own sweat." He popped his chin to his teammates and changed course, meeting her in the middle. She turned and started walking with him. "I get a hug first, right?"

"No."

"What?" He laughed. "C'mon, babe, what're you saying?"

"I'm saying I don't love you enough to rub your sweat all over my body," she drawled. "You're disgusting."

"Hey, you're the one who asked me out, if I remember right."

She frowned up at him but couldn't hide the twitching quirk of a smile threatening to escape. "Mm-hmm. I guess you're right. But no hug."

"Fine." He did reach for her hand, though, and she immediately laced their fingers. A spark of warmth blossomed in his gut, subtle but sweet. That was how things went with her. For once in his life, he didn't have to feel as if he was losing his whole mind over a girl, not now that the new relationship energy was wearing off. He could just enjoy *this*—the simplicity of holding her hand and walking with her and knowing she'd wanted to see him. "Missed you."

"I missed you too." She lifted his hand to kiss his knuckles. "I had something on my mind I wanted to talk about."

"Yeah? Nothing bad, I hope?"

"Nah, not bad. At least I don't *think* it's gonna be bad."

"Uh-oh."

"Shut up," she said, laughing.

She led him to the quieter part of campus, surrounded on all four sides with buildings and decorated with giant, broad trees. A gazebo stood in the center, and she took him there, guiding him to sit before she leaned against the banister. His legs welcomed the rest, and his gaze welcomed the chance to take her in from head to toe and bask in the cotton-candy sweetness.

She took a deep breath. "So. What we did. You, me, Kelly Anne, Logan..."

Oh. The realization kicked him in the gut, and he found himself filling his lungs up to the brim. The first seeds of tension floated away before they could take full root. "Yeah?"

"How'd you feel about that night?"

There were a million ways he could respond, and he wasn't sure which one she wanted to hear. "I mean, uh…"

Charlotte waited for a few seconds, until the silence started to turn awkward, before she squeezed his shoulder. "Geez, I'm not trying to get you in trouble here, Christian. I'm legitimately curious what you thought."

He risked a glance up, but he didn't find any answers in her face. "I-I don't really…know what the right answer is, though."

Her gaze softened. She rubbed her thumb over his shoulder, back and forth, lulling him into a more soothing state. "I'm not looking for the *right* answer. This isn't a trap, it's not a scientific study, it's only your girlfriend asking if you had a good time."

If she says I'm not in trouble, she means it. Charlotte doesn't play games. Christian sat up and rolled his shoulders back. "I thought the night was…pretty hot, actually."

"Yeah?"

"Yeah, I mean…" Now that he'd said it, the memories of the night flooded him, all novelty and curiosity. "Who *doesn't* wanna feel like they've ended up on the set of a sex scene, am I right?"

"Sure." She sat next to him and crossed her legs at the ankle. "Would you have been comfortable doing it if it had been some guy other than Logan?"

"Hell no." He didn't have to think about the answer. "Logan's my boy, y'know? He's got my back. I knew it wasn't gonna be weird if he was there."

"Why not?"

"I mean…" The words didn't come as easily this time. His mouth hung open for a few seconds before he snapped it shut.

"Like, I didn't know Kelly Anne at all until that night." She shrugged. "I only knew Logan from when you, me, and him hung out. It's not as if I was close to anybody but you, but I still had a really good time."

"I-I just, uh, I think…"

Charlotte lifted her eyebrows.

He exhaled sharply and slouched forward. "It'd be weird if there was another guy. I mean, what kind of guy wants to see a dude fucking somebody?"

Charlotte blinked. "Almost every man who watches porn."

"We don't watch porn for the guy. We watch for the girl."

"Okay, but listen, under your logic, you're saying you wouldn't care if we did that again with another couple as long as you got to watch the girl getting fucked."

"I'm not saying I'd wanna do that either!" The tension returned, pushing steel rods into his bones and making his jaw clench. "Why are you asking? What the hell is this? Do you have, like, a waiting list of people who you wanna watch fuck?"

"Hey, settle down there," she murmured. "I'm only trying to have a conversation with you, Christian. If I made you uncomfortable, I'm sorry, but you don't need to start accusing me of shit."

He bit his tongue until he feared it would bleed and made himself take a deep breath. "I know. I'm sorry, that was shitty of me. I just got…I-I don't know what you mean."

She touched his arm and rubbed his tight muscle, and he started to come down all over again—he'd never realized how grounding touch was before her. It seemed he'd gone his whole life with people trying to avoid touching him, and here she was loving on him as sweetly as a cat. As if she understood why he got tense. As if when he apologized, it made everything okay again rather than having his reaction held against him.

This was a different world, and he wasn't sure how to live in it. Nobody else had treated him like this before—none except Logan.

"What if we had Logan and a different girl? Would you be okay with that?"

He forced himself to think of the scene objectively. "Yeah, as long as Logan's there, I don't really give a damn who he'd be with."

"That's what I thought you might say."

He studied her suspiciously. "Why?"

"I'm wondering if you and him ever fucked people together before."

He breathed a laugh. "I'm pretty sure we established that as a no."

"What about the two of you alone?"

Two things immediately came to mind: *what does she know* and *what do I say?* The first answer would determine the latter. There were a handful of experiences as a teenager, locked so deep down inside him that sometimes he wondered if they existed. And if there was even a shred of possibility Charlotte somehow knew about them...

No, there was no way she could know. He hadn't told a soul. And, as innocuous as they were, he wasn't going to be talking about them today either.

"No," he simply said. The heaviness of his tone covered all possible bases.

Charlotte's gaze turned sympathetic, and Christian stared at her hard, trying to figure out if there was a chance she was pitying him, somehow. *For what?* The thought was idle paranoia, but it wasn't any easier to ignore. Especially when she slid into his lap and wrapped her arms around his neck.

"So, how about we try it again?" She nuzzled his temple, as if the contact would soften the suggestion. Like the only weight of those seven words was in their volume.

He tightened his arms around her and buried his face in her shoulder. "Why?"

"Because..." As she trailed off, he lost himself in the steadiness of her breathing, and he used the smooth flow to slow his down before he could get buried in frustration. "...because you seemed really happy when we were done."

He remembered the way he just about flew to walk Charlotte back to her dorm, wings on his shoes instead of the normal sluggishness of his afterglow. He'd thought it all had to do with how nicely their hands fit together.

Apparently, Charlotte thought his cheer was from something else. But, try as he might, he couldn't refute her belief.

He didn't have an answer to give her right now—at least, not one that would tie everything up neatly. So, he pressed a kiss to her neck and sighed. "Can I let you know?"

"Yeah, baby." She kissed the top of his head in return and let him rock her back and forth like a cradle under the pink glow of the setting sun. "You take all the time you need. We can talk whenever you're ready."

"About...?"

"Well..."

HIS FIRST LITERATURE test was when things came to a head.

Logan was a studier. He knew others thought he was naturally smart—as if he didn't have to work for the grades he got—but they were wrong. They didn't see the hours he put into making flash cards and taking and retaking notes until the information was drilled into his head. It was a good system, and it worked well.

Nights like tonight, though, when he buried his head in his textbooks, were the only times sleep was hard to find. His mind was filled to the brim with facts and dates and names, and they kept spinning through his head as he lay in the dark.

He'd been counting on falling asleep before Christian returned from his date with Charlotte. *Fuck.*

There wasn't anything wrong with Charlotte. He could admit to himself that his earlier jealousy about how Christian spent his time had been misguided, but just thinking about her felt awkward nowadays. He didn't want to have a discussion about her with Christian when all he could think about was how she'd been the one to get them to kiss.

What had she been aiming for in the first place? And why had she been so keen when the kiss finally happened?

He was still lying there staring at the ceiling when he heard the door open to their suite, and he sighed, rubbing his eyes. He'd sit up, maybe, and talk to Christian about whatever he and Charlotte had done that night. He'd listen to him talk about how great she was and how she was better than anyone he'd ever met before and...

The door opened, and, lo and behold, Christian wasn't alone.

Logan closed his eyes when he heard Charlotte's voice mixing with Christian's, the melodic flowing river of her words twisting around the warm flames of his. *Why is she here?* They went quiet in the doorframe, and then the door shut.

Maybe they'd left him alone. Maybe they'd—

"C'mon, you really wanna do this?" Charlotte teased, barely over a whisper. "He's right there."

"Boy can sleep like the dead. And I missed you, baby." There was the hint of a laugh in Christian's tone. It was the exact way he spoke when he proposed something ridiculous he assumed Logan wouldn't go along with. "You saying you didn't miss me?"

Charlotte hummed, Christian chuckled, and her heels clicked against the floor.

Closer. Closer.

The mattress beneath him squeaked, the frame shaking with their combined weight, and Logan's eyes flew open.

They're not gonna...?

There was a slick, wet sound that he took a moment to recognize. Kissing. They were kissing. Innocent enough. There was nothing to suggest they were going to go anywhere past that. He was safe.

Safe from what?

They'd established rules for what would happen if one of them was horny and the other was in the room when the beds were needed. One of them would come in, their girlfriend still in the living room, and quickly explain the situation, and the other, if at all possible, would relocate to the couch. Preferably with a pair of headphones. Once the alone time was finished, the intruder would buy the interrupted one something small—coffee or lunch the next day—as an apology, and would promise not to demand the room to himself again for at least two weeks.

They hadn't discussed what would happen if someone was sleeping at the time.

Logic suggested Christian should've left. Gone to the couch. Maybe taken Charlotte into the shower, if they couldn't hold themselves back.

Not the bed. Not their goddamn bunk bed, where every time one of them shifted the other felt the tremor.

Like now, when the frame shook, and Charlotte giggled. Logan's mind provided the mental image: Christian guiding Charlotte to lie on her back while his body met her from head to toe, cupping her cheek, kissing her deeply, intimately, romantically...

A soft whisper of a sound.

That was his shirt.

He knew that sound. He shouldn't, but he did. He'd heard the piece of clothing hit the floor a hundred times. It was intimate, somehow, picturing how Christian removed his shirt—pulling it over his head with a fistful of fabric, then tossing it into the pile of dirty clothes Logan hated so much.

A soft moan. Rich, heavy, like homemade whipped cream. Charlotte's.

Why did the sound of her moan grate on him?

There wasn't a reason to stay. If he was careful and deliberate, he could slip to the end of the bed silently and sneak his way into the bathroom. He could hide in there until he heard the bedroom door shut again. It wouldn't be weird. Christian would probably thank him for the privacy later.

But then another sound. Another low moan, this one as decadent as a thick, rare steak.

That one was Christian. And something about it chained him to the bed.

I don't wanna interrupt, Logan thought as he held his breath. *I can just...pretend I'm sleeping. It'd be an asshole move if I ruined the mood.*

There was porn about this. People fantasized about catching two people in the act and getting to watch them go at it, so there wasn't anything wrong with his curiosity. Besides, he'd already watched them in their most intimate moment, practically performing for him and Kelly Anne. And hadn't he done the same? Playing up his reactions a little more to see if he got a response from either of them?

This was fine. If Christian didn't trust him with this, he wouldn't risk letting Logan hear.

Holy shit, he wants *me to hear, doesn't he?*

Fire licked down Logan's body from head to toe. As their quiet sounds came more and more frequently, he strained to catch every last one of them.

"Mmm, fuck, Christian—"

"Shh..."

He didn't mind him shushing Charlotte. That broke the immersiveness, somehow, thinking about her as if she was an actress who was performing for the camera rather than drowning herself in her lover. All he needed to hear was how the springs began to squeak as they moved against each other, little by little. He could paint the picture himself.

Could paint Christian thumbing over Charlotte's nipples while staring down at her reverently, watching how her skin flushed with every little bit of attention she received. He could imagine how Christian's mouth would glide down her neck, leaving a slick trail behind, and how it would cool her overheated skin if he blew.

A drawer opened and shut. Logan had teased Christian about putting his desk directly next to the lofted bed—as if Christian was ever going to roll out of bed and immediately work on *anything*—but hearing the crinkle of the condom wrapper as it was taken out told him exactly why he'd wanted it there. Christian was a man of efficiency. He only took the number of steps he needed to take, and no more.

No wonder he was so focused during sex. He had a game plan to stick to, and he wasn't going to abandon it.

There was the condom wrapper being ripped open, and then a sharp groan that couldn't have come from anyone but Christian. Logan turned his head to hear him better.

More slick sounds. More quiet, deep moans.

She's blowing him.

The image sprang to mind immediately, how enraptured Christian was when Charlotte had taken him inside her on their couch. He'd look like that right now, wouldn't he? Subtly ruined, as though he was being burned from the inside out. As if this moment was the only thing he'd ever wanted.

He's gotta look beautiful right now... The thoughts came, and Logan didn't turn them away. He was too focused on the tightness in his boxers and the delayed afterthought—*holy shit, I'm hard from this*—that came right before he rubbed his cock through the thin fabric.

Christian would understand if Logan was getting off to this. It wouldn't be weird. They'd watched porn together once, when they were horny about anything and everything pretty. Logan was still flirting with being religious and had commented on how his folks wouldn't approve of what they were doing—how, if they were caught, they'd yank him up in front of the preacher to have a good talking to next Sunday. Christian had shrugged. Said that if those people didn't wanna be seen fucking, then they wouldn't have put the video online, would they? They were getting something out of it. Probably money. Christian and Logan were giving them money by watching it. Didn't everybody deserve support for what they did? For the toil they gave? For the services they provided? Christian and Logan, by jerking off to porn, were practically being patriotic.

It had been the most convoluted thing Christian had ever said, and Logan had been fascinated by it.

So here he was, his hand loosely cupped around his erection, his thumb resting at the base of his shaft where he swore he could feel his pulse pounding. Listening to his best friend getting blown. Making a decision, once and for all.

He made it. He slid his hand under his waistband.

He let out a shaky breath that he cut off quickly, and neither of them seemed to notice. He was in this now. With his breath held and his hand pumping slowly over his cock, he let himself drown in the filthy images.

Charlotte clearly knew what she was doing. The low litany of moans coming from Christian was impossible to ignore. With each little breath he took, a quiet sound followed, floating up to Logan's bed.

A quiet shift.

"Ready?"

"Yeah, baby, c'mon, fuck me."

And then two soft sighs before the mattress began to squeak rhythmically.

It was like being on a boat as the bed moved with the both of them. He was pulled into their sex, his body rolling with theirs through the slow waves of thrusting. Every movement made him buck his hips, fucking deeper and deeper into his tight fist as he slicked his palm with his own precum.

Christian knew what he was doing too. Would he have the same expression he'd worn when Charlotte had ridden him before? Or was his face different when he was in control? When he had someone under his hands, just waiting to be charmed?

He'd seen him like that once. When they were watching porn. When Christian had been so lost in the pleasure he'd been giving himself, his hand around his cock, jerking hard and fast as if he was running a race.

He'd looked incredible. And Logan remembered spilling in his own hand within seconds of starting to watch him.

He'd made a mess then, filthy and all over his jeans, and Christian had stopped touching himself, staring at him in surprise right before he'd started laughing. Had offered another pair of pants for Logan to wear home, so he could stuff his messy jeans in his backpack and sneak them into the laundry before his mom saw them and asked what he'd been doing. Logan hadn't been prepared to lie. He'd only been fourteen.

Luckily, Christian hadn't asked what had triggered him to come so hard and fast that he'd forgotten his own damn name.

It had been Christian's face. His sepia skin flushing a brilliant rosy shade. His cock so hard in his own hand, dark with his need. The shine of the precum that had spread to the head over and over again, like he was so hot he couldn't stop making slickness so he could touch himself more, like it was God himself keeping him from coming.

He'd memorized that face. And, after their little exchange with their girlfriends, he'd been able to add to his memory from four years ago.

It was fucking *hot*.

Logan covered his mouth with his other hand as he came, arching off the bed and squeezing his eyes shut as he muffled his ragged breathing.

There was no afterglow. Nothing after the quick jolt of searing white-hot pleasure shaking through him. The second he started to come down from coming all over his chest—which completely missed his hand, like an amateur—he forced himself to focus on the present again.

On the sound of Christian coming too.

He knew that sound now. He'd been cheated of it once. But that night with the four of them, the sound had been burned into his memory—the choked moan, as though he'd buried his face in someone's neck, and the quiet groan trickling into nothingness. A few more erratic thrusts shook the bed, and then Charlotte gasped so sharply he knew she was coming too.

He didn't focus on her. It wasn't her moans that echoed through his head.

No, it was Christian's.

Logan evened out his breathing and kept his eyes closed, his body cooling until the pool on his stomach started to dry. Disgusting. He'd never been a fan. But what could he do? He couldn't leave until they did. *God, please don't tell me she's staying the night.*

As he was finishing his thought, it sounded as if Charlotte was stretching like a cat, and the bedframe shifted again. "There. Happy?"

"Damn, baby..." Christian murmured, barely audible. "Wait, are you going?"

"Got stuff to do in the morning, sweetheart." There was the sound of a kiss. "I can let myself out."

"Are you kidding? You think I'm gonna make my own girlfriend let herself out of my dorm after the date? You think I can't walk you to the door?"

"You think your legs still work?"

Christian didn't reply, and Charlotte laughed. Logan's eyelids illuminated, and he peeked to watch the light from a phone scan the floor. Catching a hint of Charlotte's naked body from the glow made him turn his head away.

"See you tomorrow for dinner?"

"Yeah." Another kiss. "You sure you're gonna be okay to walk to your place alone?"

"Promise. I've got pepper spray, remember?"

"You are scary with that thing."

"Exactly." Charlotte chuckled, then kissed him again. "Hey, get some sleep. I'll text you when I get there, and you'd better not text me back."

"What!"

"You'd better be dead to the whole damn world!" Her heels clicked across the floor. "Bye, boo."

"Whatever. Bye. Be safe, gorgeous."

The door opened, then shut, and they were alone.

There were ways Logan could go about this that wouldn't be awkward. He could speak up right now and make a joke. As long as he was leading, Christian would follow in the same cadence, and they'd laugh the past fifteen minutes off and never talk about it again. He could wipe off his own jizz with, say, the corner of his sheet and wash his bedding in the morning so that for all Christian knew, he'd been asleep the whole time.

He didn't do either. Seconds passed, which made joking too late. And all he could think about was rolling over and waking up with his face glued to the sticky part of his sheet.

No, he had to take care of this in the bathroom.

Logan waited long enough for the air conditioner to kick off, then crawled out of bed and went to the bathroom. The second the door clicked shut behind him, he forced himself to take a perfectly normal leak, then washed his hands and scrubbed the living daylights out of his abs.

He'd come with the image of Christian's face plastered across his mind's eye. His orgasm hadn't had anything to do with Charlotte. Fuck, it hadn't had anything to do with Kelly Anne either. It was something about his best friend who just happened to be a guy.

Straight guys didn't have those thoughts, did they?

Logan leaned over the edge of the sink and took deep breaths. Even going through porn as a teenager, he'd known he'd be punished more for the videos with two or more girls in them than the ones with just a guy and a girl. It didn't matter that half the girls' soccer team was gay— they all knew and didn't discuss it—or that one of their older classmates, Ben, who always got the lead role in the school plays, was a gay man. The rumor had been confirmed when Logan was a sophomore. Ben's mother brought it up in the middle of a church service. She said that ever since Ben went to college up in New York, he'd started dating a man, and they weren't letting him come home until he repented.

Logan's parents hadn't spoken up. The preacher had simply extended his condolences and called people up to pray for Ben's parents. He remembered stiffening. He remembered glancing over at Christian. Their families all stayed seated, but Logan had the faces of the people who'd laid hands on Ben's parents burned into the back of his head.

Though Logan had stopped going to church when he was sixteen, his family hadn't. And that didn't bode well for any crisis he might have.

Is this a crisis? He tilted his head, watching the thin water layer in the sink drain away. Every gay movie he'd seen involved a crisis happening when someone realized they were interested in the same gender. It seemed as though a breakdown was somehow required.

But the fact remained this wasn't just a regular dude. This was Christian. This was his best friend, practically his brother, who'd been with him through thick and thin and never showed any sign he'd abandon Logan for any reason. So, if Logan was curious about seeing his dick, what was the likelihood the interest would somehow be the end of everything?

He wanted to have faith it wouldn't change anything. That Christian would love him all the same.

But it wouldn't matter at all—not when Kelly Anne and Charlotte were around.

Logan sank to the cold floor, his arms resting on his knees. These thoughts were trickier. He liked Kelly Anne. He was attracted to her, she made him laugh, and she lit something up in him every day that made him strive to be someone who was worth her time. So, was an attraction to Christian at odds with that?

She kissed Charlotte, didn't she?

Things were...open sometimes. Even as isolated as his childhood and adolescence had been, he'd had the Internet, and he was well aware of stories about people who weren't tied to just one person. That was what swingers were—they messed around in bed with other people, had all the sex they wanted, and then went home with their spouse at the end of the night like nothing happened.

Wasn't that what the four of them had done? They hadn't touched each other with more than a kiss, but they'd stared, all of them. He'd seen Kelly Anne biting her bottom lip as she watched how Charlotte rode Christian, and Charlotte had given Kelly Anne more than a few flirty smirks.

There wasn't anything saying they couldn't ever do that again. And what if they changed the boundaries up next time? What if they ran their hands all over each other? Charlotte intimidated the hell out of him. She seemed to know exactly what she wanted, and he was sure if he did something wrong, she'd scold him. But Christian could touch Kelly Anne, and...

Maybe they could *both* be with one of their girlfriends.

They could ask their girlfriends what they wanted to see Logan and Christian do, and then...

It was late, and he was delving into completely unfamiliar territory. Every straight man had a fantasy about a threesome with two girls, but one with a girl and another guy? No, that didn't seem as realistic.

Especially when in the five minutes of the threesome porn he'd clicked on with the two guys and the girl, the guys hadn't seemed like they were enjoying themselves—they had completely slack expressions and barely made any noise and appeared to want it all to be over. And Logan had clicked away because that was all he needed to know at the time.

No more thinking tonight. He huffed and pulled himself to his feet. *You've got an exam tomorrow. I don't care if you have to knock yourself out to sleep; you do it.*

He opened the bathroom door, and in the split second before he remembered to turn out the light, he caught a glimpse of Christian staring at him, and he hesitated with his hand on the switch.

Christian lay on his side, the sheets tangled around his hips, his chest bare, and a peek at his hipbone told Logan he wasn't wearing his boxers. He was naked in bed. Was he going to sleep that way?

"Can't sleep?" Christian asked, interrupting his thoughts.

Logan gulped as he snapped his gaze to Christian's eyes. "Nah, I just had to take a leak. No big deal."

"Mm." Christian nodded lazily. "You've got Johnson tomorrow, right?"

Dr. Johnson was one of the few professors they shared, but at different class times. "Uh, yeah."

"Cool. Tell me how the exam goes."

"You mean copy the answers and send you a picture."

"Duh." A smile quirked across his lips.

Logan flicked the light off and walked back to bed, feeling his way through the room. "I'm not doing that shit for free anymore, man. You've gotta pay up."

"Oh yeah?" Christian chuckled. His voice was throaty and a little ragged, like he'd been caught sleeping—or fucking. "And what exactly is the toll?"

Logan froze, one foot on the bottom rung of the ladder, his heart taking off as fast as a rabbit. "What do you mean?"

Silence. If Logan squinted, he could make out the whites of Christian's eyes gleaming in the few rays of moonlight. His eyes adjusted to the low light until Christian was nothing but a resplendent man, his dark skin highlighted by a shock of white sheets.

Christian sighed. "Nothing, man." His mattress creaked as he rolled over. "I'll buy you a coffee or something."

Logan's mind was off to the races again, moving so fast he couldn't register any of the thoughts, leaving him behind to stew in the first tastes of anxiety. "I don't want your coffee," he muttered as he started to climb.

"Too bad."

Logan landed face-first in his pillow and twisted around until he'd ruined the sheets.

I could still talk about it. He clenched fistfuls of his loose pillowcase. *If I bring it up right now, maybe we can air everything out before we go to sleep.*

But he didn't. He listened as Christian's breathing evened out and lay there for another hour waiting for his own to do the same.

FOR CHRISTIAN'S ENTIRE middle and high school career, he never thought another coach could stand up to Coach Glenn. He'd been tough, but he'd gotten results, and every time he yelled at them in the locker room, he lit a fire under their asses. Christian ran himself half to death just to win rare praise, and his efforts won him a star place on the team. Coach Glenn didn't joke like other people did—that he was playing the wrong sport, that some basketball team had gotten him and a wiry little forward switched up at the tryouts. He only demanded perfection from Christian, and he'd been more than happy to give it.

Coach Atkinson was different.

He was a former player himself. That much was obvious. The breadth of his shoulders and the way he handled a ball told Christian he'd probably been a damn good player himself. But he never bragged about what his record used to be. He didn't talk about his string of tournament wins, like Coach Glenn had. It didn't matter that he was past his prime—dark hair streaked with gray, blue eyes hidden behind glasses, and a curved belly under his shirt—not when he charmed something incredible out of his team.

That was the only word for it: charmed. Glenn had been rough. He'd scared the team into winning. Atkinson was never frightening.

Even when Christian turned eighteen, Glenn had treated him like a kid. But somewhere in the last few months, he'd apparently turned into an adult, if Atkinson was to be believed.

It was in the little things—how he opened the floor for discussions about how they thought they'd played at the last game, for example, rather than berating them for every tiny perceived flaw. He didn't talk over them when they were commenting on something he said, instead, waiting for them to finish their thought before he answered or reflected.

And he didn't yell. Not even when they were on the field. He used gestures that communicated clearly all the way to the corners, and there was an energy about him that always caught Christian's eye right when Atkinson had something for him alone.

It was as if he had some siren call that kept drawing Christian's gaze.

After practice, Christian had started to linger, waiting to see if Atkinson had some wisdom to impart to him.

Most days, he walked away with a personalized comment about his strengths or weaknesses.

Today, he waited, watching while Atkinson talked to the forward, Mateo, about his performance. He was relaxing after the cooldown—his heart rate dropping, his sweat lowering body temperature, his skin losing its flush. He wiped his forehead, took a deep breath, and let the air out gradually.

When Atkinson finally turned to him after sending Mateo off with a pat on the back, he overacted in feigned surprise. "Why, Christian, I didn't know you'd be there."

Christian rolled his eyes, but he couldn't hide his smile. "Yeah, sorry, I-I just wanted to know if you had anything to say about how I did today. How I could improve or whatever?"

Atkinson shook his head. "At this point, I think we've more or less hit on your points of attack. Listen, I know you're fighting to get moved forward from midfield, but until you've worked on the things we've talked about there's not going to be a whole lot changing unless one of the other guys breaks his leg or something." He paused. "That's not an invitation to go buy a bat, by the way."

Christian chuckled. "Okay. Yeah." He'd known Atkinson was going to say that; it was what he'd said for the past few practices, and apparently, Christian hadn't been putting enough change into his playing style or strategy to have anything shift.

He knew that. But he stayed anyway.

Atkinson quirked a brow. "Can I help you with anything else? It's getting kind of late. I don't want you to miss out on anything you've got planned."

"No," Christian said quickly. "I-I don't really have any plans tonight." He hesitantly turned his gaze from his shoes to Atkinson's face.

Atkinson opened his mouth for a moment, seeming deep in thought before taking a small step backward. "Well, I'm sure there are people who'd like to see you. You shouldn't spend your time standing around with me, should you?"

That stung, somehow, in a way Christian wasn't used to, and he stiffened. "No, I guess not. Sir."

"Good." As Atkinson nodded, Christian could read the relief there, and he wasn't sure what to make of it. He didn't have time. The relief bled away to a smile, like it hadn't been there in the first place. "Next practice, then, huh?"

"Yeah." Christian turned and walked away, waving absently behind his back. "Later, Coach."

"Have a good night."

Christian scooped up his bag and threw it over his shoulder. The gym was technically closer for him to shower at, but now all he wanted was to be in his dorm—somewhere safe and contained and more like home with each passing day.

He and Logan had set their room up nicely, mostly from Logan footing the bill to make the magic happen. After all this time, that part continued to rub him the wrong way. He'd never be able to pay Logan back for his new sheets or shorts or the one textbook he couldn't afford, and the awareness hurt more than he was willing to admit.

But it was okay. He'd find a way. And until then, their dorm room was a little nest he was reluctant to leave.

The shower there was better too. Better towels. Better toiletries than the spares he kept in his gym bag.

And Logan would be there. And Christian had a few things he wanted to say to him, thanks to Charlotte.

Though the elevator was on the ground floor, he climbed the stairs to the fourth one instead, his legs aching the whole way. The pain was visceral. Grounding. It kept him out of his head and in his body as a whole.

It was exactly what he needed before he went and proposed something ridiculous.

He let himself in, keys shaking in his hand, and tossed his bag down. "Yo."

Daiki popped his head out of his bedroom and gave a little wave before he returned to the phone conversation he was having. Noah was nowhere to be seen.

Logan didn't exactly greet him at the door either.

Christian carefully set his cleats aside and then kicked his flip-flops off before making his way to their shut bedroom door. No sock or anything on the handle. He checked his phone. No texts. With only the slightest bit of trepidation, he pushed the door open.

False alarm. Logan was only lying on his bed doing some homework, his thick headphones on under his curls.

For just a moment, Christian thought about discarding the whole conversation without having it. Their friendship was exactly what it needed to be. Nothing about it needed to change, even if Charlotte seemed curious about what would happen if it did. These past experiences he and Logan had—the porn, that long moment of fear in the congregation when Ben's parents needed to be prayed over to "heal" their gay son, and now the group sex—meant nothing in the grand scheme of things.

But his mind wouldn't rest until he brought his thoughts up, so he did the only sensible thing: he removed one of his sweaty socks, balled it up, and threw it right at Logan's face.

"Ugh!" Logan fell on his side hacking and gagging, and Christian bent over cackling as Logan knocked the sock away with his closed textbook. "You piece of shit!"

"You love me," Christian countered when Logan pulled his headphones off.

"I *hate* you. I'm getting a new roommate. Fuck you."

"Right." Christian threw his other sock on the nearest clothes pile and perched on the edge of the couch. "Hey."

"What?" Logan's nose was crinkled as though he continued to suffer.

What a whiny fucking baby. Christian shook his head and sighed. "I gotta ask you something."

Logan's eyes widened. "Oh?"

That's all you got to say when you make that face? Man, I know you better than you think. While Christian had been working through his shit, he hadn't realized Logan might've been going through some of his own. Maybe all his expression meant was that Christian had been less subtle about his thoughts. Either way, he was in too deep to back out now.

"So. Remember what happened with Charlotte and Kelly Anne and you and me...?"

Logan was a deer caught in headlights. "Y-yes."

"You sure?" Christian couldn't help but tease. "Or do you need to think about it for a second?"

"No, yeah, I remember." Logan sat up and pushed his textbook away, dragging his legs to his chest. He was wearing an ankle bracelet—a loose hemp thing that made his leg appear almost delicate compared to Christian's muscular calves—and Christian caught himself staring, running his eyes over the intricate light brown pattern as it fed into itself over and over again. "Why? Did something happen?"

Charlotte happened, he wanted to say. *Charlotte stuck her nose into my business and thought she knew some magic way to get me to start growing and shit. Hell if I know. It's like she wants me to be happy and comfortable with myself. Ridiculous, right?* But he didn't.

"Not really." He shrugged, as if the talk he had with his girlfriend hadn't been on his mind night and day. "Nothing bad, at least. Charlotte, uh, wanted me to ask if you'd be interested in doing it again."

Logan blinked. He was quiet for a little too long. "Charlotte asked that?"

Something hung in the air that Christian wasn't able to identify. He wasn't the thinker here—Logan was. He scratched behind his ear and rubbed his aching feet together. "I...yeah, she wanted to know if it was something you and Kelly Anne would be cool with doing" He tilted his head to the side. "It was...it was *fun*, right?"

"Fun." Logan grinned a little too slowly. "Yeah, man. Who knew you had such an exhibitionist?"

Christian snorted. "I did." He leaned forward. "So?"

Logan shrugged. "I've gotta talk to Kelly Anne, but...yeah, why not?"

Relief settled in his chest, as warm as the first sip of a mug of coffee. "Okay." And then he was buzzing and needing to move again. "Okay, awesome. Lemme know when you've talked to her. We can have a real double date. Not just a sit on the couch and watch movies kind of date."

"Sure. I'll let you know."

"Cool." Christian lingered. He wasn't in a rush to escape, and he couldn't remember why he had been. When he caught sight of his socks on the floor, he cringed at the tackiness of the sweat on his skin. "All right, well, I'm gonna take a shower."

"Mm." Logan pulled the headphones back on and rolled onto his stomach, returning to his reading.

That was fast. In and out. A proposal of double dates and group sex and gone again, as if it was perfectly normal—as if that was what this friendship was now.

As if he didn't spend the entire shower scrubbing himself raw and trying to forget how eagerly he'd let Charlotte convince him to fuck her while Logan was absolutely not asleep in the bed above him.

Chapter Five

LOGAN

There was no smooth way to present the possibility of another double date that might end with sex in the same room. How Christian had done it so easily—as though the suggestion didn't mean anything but a little fun—Logan still had no idea. He'd pondered his plan of attack the entire time as he finished his homework and then helped Daiki with his, sprawled out on the living room floor, while Christian ate an apple in the kitchen and watched silently.

How could Christian make it sound as if they'd been doing this for years? As if he wasn't nervous at the thought of Logan watching him and judging him?

As if he didn't feel anything when Logan watched him in the first place?

Either way, Logan couldn't ignore the proposal for long. He got through his Thursday classes and then answered Kelly Anne's text to meet him for their standard walk to the dining hall for dinner.

It was a chat he couldn't have in front of the rest of the student population, though. As he walked to meet her, legs moving so fast he was nearly jogging, he worked through the possible approaches he could take, but none of them felt right. No matter what he said to her, he'd be jumping through hoops trying to introduce the suggestion, and they all came with their own set of problems.

Why can't I just say "Hey, sweetie, do you wanna watch some people you don't know fuck again?" He rolled his eyes with a breathy chuckle. *Yeah, that'd go over well. "Hey, dear, wanna be the opposite of the center of attention?"*

He liked Kelly Anne. He really did. But they were so close to the surface—two teenagers getting to know each other, starting to learn what a future together might be. And it meant he didn't know the simplest way to get on her good side.

It was a shame people didn't come with an instruction manual.

He turned the corner, and there she was, standing in the setting sun, her brown curls lit a brilliant copper from the rays, and her lips painted in the most vibrant shade of red he'd ever seen. She was stunning. She was someone he wanted to *keep* getting to know—to learn the person under the surface too, if the sweetness she often spoke to him with was genuine. What was the likelihood he would lose that for asking?

She can say no if she wants, he reminded himself as she turned her head, caught sight of him, and waved. He waved back and then shoved his hands in his pockets. *There's no reason you actually have to go through with the whole group sex thing. No matter how curious you are. You're not gonna be missing out if she's not interested.*

She could say no, and he could say okay, and they would go back to getting to know each other just like they had been for the past couple of months. And that would be the end of it.

He wouldn't think about that night again.

"Hey, sweetheart," Kelly Anne said brightly as she kissed him on the cheek. "Ready for dinner?"

"Just about." He hesitated, tapping the toe of his shoe on the sidewalk. "Could you, um, walk with me? That way?" He nodded in the distance, where the sidewalk ended and turned into a vast green hill.

She blinked. "Sure." As they began to walk, she hurried to keep up. "Everything okay?"

"Yeah, totally." He shrugged—this was no big deal. Why *should* it be a big deal? Why did he have all this mire, thick in his chest? "I had something I wanted to ask you about."

"Okay..." She drew out the word, chuckling at the end. "You're not, like, proposing, are you?"

Though she was teasing, a spike of panic stabbed him. "No, oh my God."

"Good. You'd have to ask my daddy first."

"Right." He wanted to laugh, but somehow, the sound got trapped somewhere in his ribs. "No, I, uh, I wanted to ask about what happened with Christian and Charlotte—"

"Oh, that whole thing?" She laughed, chirping and lovely as a songbird. "Was wondering when you were gonna bring it up. We haven't talked about it since it happened."

"Yeah." Logan scratched the back of his neck as he turned to face her. "I was—"

"It wasn't a problem, was it?" She crossed her arms, her smile strained, somehow, as if she had to struggle to make the expression appear. Not normal behavior from her. "Just, like, a funny story to tell people one day. Dumb college stuff."

Logan quirked his brow. He wasn't sure how to respond.

"You know what I mean?" she continued. "People mess around in college and have those stupid experiences, and some of it's life-changing, and some of it's just stuff you admit when you're in your forties and playing drinking games."

This wasn't how he'd planned this going at all. That one night had been one of the most highlighted, fulfilling nights of his entire life so far—getting to open himself up and explore and study how someone he cared about experienced something so deep and intimate. How did someone shrug that off so easily?

Did...nobody else feel anything?

"Why?" Her teeth glared at him, too brightly white. "Did you feel weird about it? We can talk about what you felt if you like. Or do you want to forget it? We can pretend the whole night never happened."

"You, uh..." He shook his head to shake off the haze creeping in. "You seemed like you had a good time, though. You...you came pretty hard. You blushed when Charlotte kissed you."

Kelly Anne rolled her eyes. "Oh my God, it was all a game, baby. You know I did musical theater. You know that's what I'm majoring in. Sometimes you just put on a good show! And it was fun, but c'mon, we all know it was one of those heat of the moment things that's never gonna happen again."

He wanted to sit down. All he had was the sidewalk. If he sat on the sidewalk with no warning, what would she think of him?

Kelly Anne reached out and cupped his elbow, and something sick crept into his lungs, something he didn't know how to pull away from. "What's wrong?"

Don't tell her. Forget it. Just move on. Everything you've been thinking about is fucked up, and you know it. Don't. Tell. Her.

Those times he'd been in the shower thinking of Christian's face as Charlotte took him inside her. The night he'd been wide awake listening to them fuck and wondering if Christian wanted him to hear. The hours he'd wondered exactly how straight he was. None of it mattered. The importance of the memories was all in his head, a weird illusion, while nobody else around him cared. And he had to accept that.

He opened his mouth to tell her he agreed, and what came out was "They wanted to know if we could do it again."

Neither of them breathed. He couldn't look at her— he was too focused on his mouth's betrayal. He didn't see what her face did between the start of the silence and the five seconds later when she laughed and wrapped her hand around his arm, pulling him to face her head-on. "What?"

"Nothing."

"What do you mean, they wanna do it again?"

He squeezed his eyes shut and took a deep breath. "I mean, Christian asked if we all wanted to go on a double date, and said Charlotte was interested in us doing it again."

"Group sex. She was interested in us all having sex together."

What happened to the charming Logan Brown, and why couldn't he find him right now? "Yeah, I guess."

"Well, that's just not happening."

"Yeah?"

Kelly Anne shook her head. Her smile was twisted now, bordering on surreal. "I mean, I'm not a *slut*, Logan. Why would you even ask me? You should *know* what I'd say."

"Yeah, I-I, uh—"

"Why would I wanna take something so private and trot it out in front of them? Are you joking? What is this, a casting couch?"

"That's not what I meant—"

"I can't believe you didn't tell them no, straight out! What kind of girl do you think I am?"

"*Kelly Anne.* I need you to listen to me."

She reached up and touched his chin, her eyebrows lifting, her lips curving downward. "Of course, I'm listening."

For the first time he could remember, he didn't want to be touched by her, but pulling away didn't feel possible. He held firm and let the tightness take over his chest little by little.

"It's...hey, you don't, we don't have to do it, but you're not...you can't say Charlotte's a slut because you don't wanna do what she likes doing. That's not cool."

"I'm just saying." She shrugged, discarding any concern for Charlotte's feelings. "Anyway, it's a private thing. So, no, we're not doing it."

We. Logan took a deep breath. "What if it was only me?"

Her entire face froze. "What?"

"You don't have to do it. That's fine if you're not comfortable. But I could be interested, y'know? Maybe I had a lot of fun?"

"You are *not* having a threesome with them," she snapped.

"I'm not saying I'd do that." His tone was getting as hard as hers. "I'm not saying I wanna—"

"You wanna be with Charlotte? Is something wrong with me?"

"You're putting words in my mouth!" He pulled away from her, letting her hands fall away. "No, this isn't *about* Charlotte, it's about having fun and new experiences and seeing what other people like to do, and maybe I just wanna *watch* it. It's like porn, Kelly Anne, it doesn't mean anything."

"I don't think I want you watching porn either." She crossed her arms. "That's not...that's not okay. I don't know why you'd wanna watch other women getting naked and brutalized—"

"They're not," he shot back.

"Whatever. No, you can't. I'm not comfortable having you watch some woman having sex with someone else. Especially if you're there with them." The smile finally vanished completely, replaced with the thin line of her lips and faint wrinkles starting to appear at the edges of them. "You're on a downward slope. You realize that, don't you? I know you think it'd be fun to see or whatever, but...you'd be wanting in. You'd be wanting to have sex with her."

Charlotte was beautiful, but she wasn't someone he'd be interested in. "It's not about Charlotte."

"Well, what else would this be about?" she asked with an ugly laugh.

Silence. He stared at her.

"Is it about what I'm not giving you?" Kelly Anne shook her head. "That's it, right? You're wanting something from me, and you're afraid to ask for it. Listen, I knew from being around Christian and Charlotte for two seconds that they're...*kinkier* than me, but if there's something you really wanna try, we can. Just say it."

He had. And she'd already shot him down. And there was no reason to bring up the rest.

"Or is it..."

He snapped his eyes away.

"Oh my God," she breathed, barely a whisper. "It's him, isn't it?"

"Why would it be him?" If he had any doubt in his mind that this had everything to do with Christian, he put it all to rest now. He knew what trying to deceive someone felt like, and the lie crept through his gut, cold and icy.

"It is. Oh my God. You want...you're thinking of Christian, aren't you? Not Charlotte. You weren't kidding me."

Logan jerked his head up. "And what if I was?" He forced himself to hold her wide, stunned gaze. "It'd be a onetime thing, okay? To satisfy some curiosity. It wouldn't mean anything. One time. Me and him. Like when you let Charlotte kiss you."

"And what exactly would you let him do to you?"

He didn't know. He hadn't let himself get that far. One step down the rabbit hole would take him farther than he ever wanted to go.

"Logan, I let Charlotte kiss me because I wanted to get you a little hot under the collar. That was why I told you to kiss Christian too." She shook her head. "Never in my life did I think you'd actually do it. But you didn't question it. You just...went right for him, faster than the first time you kissed me, didn't you?"

He clenched his jaw, his hands curling into tense fists.

"Don't look at me and tell me it wouldn't mean anything. The fact that you had to ask...my God." She shuddered. "If you're wanting to do it, that means you're not as interested in me as I thought you were."

"What the hell do you mean?"

"It means if you wanted to be with me for real, you wouldn't look at anybody else. Not Charlotte. And especially not Christian. Because you—if—if you even *think* about him like that, you know it means you're not straight."

"I can be bi." It was the first time he'd said it, and just tasting the word on his tongue opened a new door he hadn't known was there. "I know bi people. I've seen plenty of bi people around campus. I could be bi and still be with you."

"See, that's the thing." She pursed her lips and sighed. "Eventually, you'd break up with me for a guy. And I'm willing to bet you'd choose Christian."

"What are you *talking* about?" He spread his arms wide. "I like *you*, Kelly Anne! I picked *you*! I didn't have to go out with you, but I liked you—I still do—and I wanna be with you! Me being...*curious* doesn't have anything to do with our relationship, and you and me both know it."

"No, sweetie. What I know is that if you're wanting to mess around with him right now, you're never gonna forget that. And, one day, it's gonna happen. And I'm not gonna stand around waiting until the day you break my heart."

He was nauseous. The acid brewed deep inside him, thick and poisonous, settling until he didn't know how to spit it out. "So you're gonna break mine instead. For something that won't happen."

Kelly Anne gave him a perfect smile—as dazzling as any leading woman of the stage could muster. "Logan. My whole life when I get out of college is gonna be about uncertainty. And the one place I want some stable ground is with my husband." She shrugged one delicate shoulder.

"And now I know I can't trust you. Even though I wanted to."

Just that easy. As if it didn't matter—like *he* never mattered. Like he was a shirt she could shrug off and donate to charity. "So that's it?"

She stepped forward and pressed an acidic kiss to his cheek. "Bye, Logan." She turned and walked away.

He watched her for a few steps. And then he stared down the hill, listening to her heels click until they faded in the distance.

So, this was what happened to people realizing they'd lived so much of life without really knowing who they were. They had something good going for them, and they lost it because they wanted to take a chance and figure out a part of them they'd ignored for years. Someone important to them would make painful assumptions that weren't fair instead of choosing trust over fear.

Questioning his experiences wasn't worth it after all, was it?

I need to go running.

He wasn't much of an athlete compared to Christian. He'd always let Christian take on that mantle—the dinners, the award ceremonies, the fanfare that came from being a black man in an all-white community who stood out for another reason. He'd felt the burning spotlight too. He'd been the smart one. The bright one. The one who had people sneer at him about *equal opportunity* when he got a spot at FSU with parents more than happy to foot the whole bill—as if his grades had meant shit and the essay he wrote about finding his identity in a white family had meant nothing. But he'd always been a runner. It was the only thing that kept him moving sometimes, running so fast that nothing could catch up to him.

Numb and cold, he went to his dorm room, pulled on his old, beat-up running shoes, and took off down the stairs, out the door, and through the streets.

His legs knew where they were going, though his mind didn't. He let them carry him. He didn't entertain a thought. He simply focused on the ache in his legs from running without stretching.

At this point, he'd welcome a cramp. It'd feel more real than the burn in his heart.

This wasn't even about Kelly Anne, really. As conservatively as his parents had raised him, he knew enough about himself to recognize he didn't *want* to fit into the status quo. That was the entire reason he'd followed Christian to college in the first place.

They'd dreamed about ending up in California, somewhere they could pursue careers in entertainment. Sometimes, Christian fancied going to New York, and Logan would've gone with him too. He hadn't wanted to think too hard about where he was going; he just wanted to be by Christian's side.

Preferably writing.

Christian had been performing in church and school plays since he was a kid, but he'd missed his chance at a lead role for years. Though no one said the casting had anything to do with the Phantom or Mr. Darcy or Tom Wingfield not being black, Logan always believed it had. But being an impressive swing and understudy meant Christian's bad luck couldn't last forever. One night, in eighth grade, the actor playing Romeo had broken his ankle. A few hours later, Christian was in a new costume, with new lines rolling off his tongue.

Logan had been enraptured. He'd gone to every single performance—even the ones he refused to admit to

Christian—and had eaten up his best friend's unusual eloquence and confidence as he commanded the stage. The night of the final performance, Logan hadn't been able to sleep. He'd sat in bed, staring out the window, thinking of the words Christian had spun more masterfully than he'd ever commanded a field.

And he'd had an idea, all at once, of other words Christian could say. So, he got out of bed and began to write.

The first play Logan wrote was shit. The second one he wrote was shit. The third one, though? It wasn't half bad. Even his freshman year English teacher said so. And he'd written more and more and more, from monologues to one-man shows, until one night in his sophomore year, he'd walked to Christian's house in the dead of night and thrown rocks at his window until he snuck him in.

Christian had made an exhausted Logan sleep at the foot of his twin bed, and when Logan woke to the familiar smell of oatmeal, he found Christian watching him.

Without any warning or greeting, he'd opened his mouth and begun to quote the monologue, word from word, perfectly phrased and memorized. The recitation was the most beautiful thing Logan had ever heard. On Christian's tongue, the amateur sentence structure prettied itself up, until it was something they could both earn a Tony from.

That was where the dream had started. For the first time, Logan had something going for him besides his fantastic mind for studying and the lucky charm he had when he spoke. Writing was something he wasn't born with, perhaps, but a talent that he could develop—that he could go to a great university to sculpt until it was perfect.

And Christian would come with him, he'd reasoned. Christian would become a tremendous actor, and Logan would write every play he would ever perform in, and they would take the world by storm and make it their own. Just two black men changing the face of art.

It hadn't happened.

Logan's parents would only pay for college if his major was sensible. Christian's parents couldn't pay for college at all. He had to miss acting in the play his last year of school so he could work his ass off on the soccer field, trying to catch the eye of the few scouts who came through their small town. And Logan had compromised with his parents until his degree was something small and busy and, for him, soulless.

Teaching English literature. Teaching words rather than writing them. Pretending his mind for studying gave him patience for tutoring. That he could hope to capture someone's mind and show them the passion he had for the written word.

Fulton State hadn't been high on the list, but it had been the only place that offered Christian a full ride if he played for them, and so it became the only place. Acceptance letters from their two top dream schools were a slap in the face when they came with a fifty-thousand-dollar tuition each year and almost no scholarship money.

Fulton State wasn't bad. But it hadn't the edge of California or the sharpness of New York. And so it would never be good enough.

A dream demolished rather than deferred—that was what Logan's entire life was shaping up to be. No passions to follow that wouldn't bite him in the ass. A lifetime of compromises.

In a few years, he'd teach a roomful of bored middle schoolers and go home to his pretty wife and kiss her lips and hug his kids and that would be all. He wouldn't trouble himself with learning what it would feel like to kiss a man. He wouldn't write a play again. He'd sink into mediocrity, and if he was lucky, his children would outlive him by decades.

How are people so easily satisfied with that? Why doesn't life reward people who take risks? Who chase their passions?

He slid to a stop and leaned forward, hands on his knees, trying to catch his breath. He hadn't realized where his feet had carried him until he glanced up and saw the house where he and Christian had gone to their first college party—tall and innocuous and lovely in the daylight.

If Christian hadn't met Charlotte, none of this would've happened.

But that wasn't fair.

Charlotte had been a catalyst, but she hadn't been the only one to make his life take this path. Regardless, he still would've met Kelly Anne, he still would've been interested in her, and he probably still would've dated her too. He'd *liked* Kelly Anne. Part of him still did.

And Charlotte was good for Christian. A man like him deserved to be cherished and admired, just like he treated her. Logan didn't have to be in the room to feel their regard. They respected each other, they weren't afraid to live their own lives apart and meet somewhere in the middle, and, as far as he knew, they weren't waiting for the other person to fill up some hole deep inside.

He couldn't make her a villain, no matter how easy it might be. He wouldn't disrespect her like that.

No, one day down the road, whether Charlotte or Kelly Anne or any other woman was involved in their lives, he'd take a good long look at Christian and recognize why his chest got tight sometimes when he was close to him. Why sometimes he had dreams about watching porn with Christian's hand around his dick instead of his own. The discovery might have happened. Just might've taken a few more years.

Could've been worse. Could've realized this whole thing was going on after you both had already gotten married.

Since Kelly Anne hadn't wanted to be up-front with him, they wouldn't have lasted very long together anyway. What sort of woman did something one time for fun and then never talked about it, assuming it wouldn't happen again? That it wouldn't come up? That Logan wouldn't be curious about trying it once more? He knew the ball had been in his court too—he could've brought his curiosity up a hell of a lot earlier—but for her to *assume* they were both on the same page...

Logan had always been curious about where the edges of the envelope were so he could push them, and, eventually, he would've ended up in a situation like this— where one moment of shared intimacy would lead to him wanting another. And another. And another. It was better for him to get used to not having those experiences now.

He'd been alone before. And as long as he had Christian by his side, he wouldn't *really* be alone if he didn't have a girlfriend. He didn't have to run to Kelly Anne and beg for her to take him back, or go out to a club and find some loose and eager girl to get on his arm. He could be by himself. He could figure this out.

He could dream and explore his thoughts so deeply he wouldn't have to feel them in real life.

He walked into his dorm and allowed himself the pleasure of taking the elevator. He'd punished his legs enough, and now that he'd burned off his frustration and despair, he didn't want to break them. When he let himself in this time, however, he was vividly aware of Christian in their bedroom.

Logan took a deep breath outside his range of sight before he stepped around the corner and toed off his running shoes.

"Hey, man." Christian turned the page of his notebook and glanced up, pencil held tight between his fingers. "'Sup? You been running?"

"Yeah." Logan shrugged. "Sometimes you need to get out under the sky and just…just *go*."

"I hear you. But some of us actually remember to change into clothes made for working out."

Logan glanced away. So, running in jeans and a T-shirt had been stupid, but the temperature was cooling outside, and it wasn't as if he'd been tempting heatstroke. All he'd risked were some chafed thighs and pit stains. "Whatever. I wasn't out for long anyway."

Christian closed the notebook and sat back in his chair, looping his arms behind his neck. "That sounds interesting."

"What do you mean?"

"Look at me."

Logan immediately snapped his gaze up, meeting Christian's. He tightened his jaw at the probing gleam in Christian's eyes—as though he was an experiment under a microscope. Like he couldn't hide what was going through his head.

"Yeah," Christian murmured, narrowing his eyes, his long eyelashes distracting. "That's what I thought."

"What the hell are you talking about?" Defensiveness swelled in Logan's chest as he dug through his dresser to find some clean clothes. He needed a shower; it would give him respite from being right there where Christian could read him.

"You've got something really shifty in your gaze, man. Like there's something you don't want anybody to see."

"You're looking at exactly what I don't want you to see." Logan scoffed. "I just got back from running. I feel like shit. You're not exactly a model when you get back from practice either, buddy."

Christian chuckled. "You're defensive too. That's cute. Real cute."

Something about his words pricked Logan, and he pressed his hands into the edge of the drawer he was leaning over, squeezing tightly. He almost wished he could splinter his hands to get him angry about something useful.

"Are we gonna play this game today?" Christian's tone was light and teasing, not a care in the world. "Or are you gonna tell me what you're pissed about so I don't have to guess?"

"I'm not pissed about anything," Logan snapped. He pulled out a pair of boxers and a T-shirt and tossed them on his bed, then started searching for clean socks and shorts. "I had stuff on my mind, so I went for a jog. It's normal human behavior, man. I've been doing it for years."

"Not unless something's got you down."

"People change." He slammed the drawer shut, grabbed his clothes, and headed toward the bathroom. "I'm gonna take a shower."

"You talk to Kelly Anne yet?"

Logan froze with his hand on the doorknob. *So, it'd come up that fast, huh?* Lying wasn't an option and talking his way out of this wasn't one either. He might've been able to take somebody else for a ride, like Daiki or Noah, but not Christian. Never Christian. He wasn't gullible, and he'd always seen right through him. *Shit. Fuck.*

"Logan?"

Logan heaved a sigh. "Yeah, I talked to her. She's not really into the idea anymore."

Silence. "Oh."

"Yeah." Logan's grip loosened on the handle. "That's that."

"Did she, uh..."

Logan glared over his shoulder. "Did she what?"

"Nothing. I was just wondering if you two had a fight, like, if we needed to go on an emergency trip to get some flowers."

She probably would've loved that—Logan groveling at her feet—and for that reason alone, he discarded the thought immediately. "Nope, no flowers, it's fine."

"No flowers? Girls always want flowers. What's wrong with her if she doesn't want flowers?"

Logan crossed his arms, clutching his clothes. "No, it's... *God,* you're so *stupid* sometimes..."

Christian laughed. "What? C'mon, what is it?"

"Just..." He gave up. "Uh, Kelly Anne and I aren't seeing each other anymore."

There was the sound of a sharp intake of breath, and when Logan hesitantly glanced up, he saw how Christian was squeezing the arms of his desk chair—how he'd gone rigid as he stared at Logan without blinking. Like Logan had a secret he was trying to dissect.

More microscopes. More reading him. More invading his right to privacy because he knew him well enough to pick him apart.

"Oh." Christian cleared his throat and let go of the chair, reaching up to scratch his jaw. "So, uh, did she break up with you, or did you—"

"She broke up with me, yeah." Logan stared at the linoleum floor and focused on how cold it was through the thin fabric of his socks.

"Was it because of the double date thing? Or something else?"

Logan snorted. "She didn't wanna be some slut who kept fucking her boyfriend in front of other people."

"Excuse me?"

"I already gave her shit on Charlotte's behalf," he murmured. "You don't need to go after her."

"I mean, I figured you would've—I know you, and I know you're not gonna let somebody shit on someone like that—but what about you? You were interested, weren't you?"

Logan shrugged.

"So, she called you a slut 'cuz you wanted to let somebody watch you fuck somebody else. Like it's a big fucking deal."

"Yeah, well, whatever. It's *not* a big deal. I'm single again, and it doesn't mean anything. We weren't gonna last long anyway, and I think I always knew it."

Christian's chair squeaked as he stood. "I mean, sure, but you don't have to pretend like you're fine in front of me if you're hurting, man. It really pisses me off that she did that."

"It was her prerogative—"

"But she didn't need to leave you feeling like shit. She could've actually tried to talk through it with you instead of, what, pretending she was better than you? 'Cuz she tried something once and didn't like it?"

"It happened. It's over. I don't really wanna talk about it anymore." *I wanna go back to living my life and remembering where you fit in it. Maybe I'll try jerking off while thinking about you sometime. Who knows? Live big, right?* He thumbed over his shoulder. "I'm just gonna go shower and do my homework and forget I have to see Kelly Anne in class next Tuesday."

"Did you like it?"

Logan froze.

"When you got to watch me and Charlotte have sex." Christian tilted his head to the side as he took a few steps forward. "When you...when we got to watch you."

Dangerous questions. Status quo or not, Logan knew better than to answer those. "It's fine, dude," he said, forcing a laugh. "You don't have to pull me in or whatever. That'd be weird, wouldn't it?"

"You're not answering my question." Christian's voice dropped until his tone was nice and quiet, and he glanced toward their bedroom door before meeting Logan's gaze. "Did you like it?"

Fuck this. "I'm gonna go shower." He touched the doorknob and turned it.

Christian's hand slammed into the door above his head and kept it shut. "Will you stop avoiding the goddamn question?"

"Yes! Okay!" Logan glared at him. "Yeah, I liked it."

"What part?"

"All of it?" Logan shook his head and pushed at Christian's chest, trying to get some breathing room, but

Christian didn't move an inch. "Stop it, dude, I'm done talking about this."

Christian leaned down. "So, you can still come. You don't have to do anything. You can sit there and watch us. It'd be funny, right? Like, it'd be a really funny story later. And between you and me, we both know how Charlotte gets when she's being watched, like—"

Just a fucking funny story to tell when we get a little too drunk on wine one day. Logan ducked under his arm. "All right, you know what, fuck you, I'm gonna go use Daiki and Noah's shower."

Christian grabbed his arm and pulled him back, then got in front of him. "I'm not done talking."

Logan scowled. "Well, I am."

Christian would always have the height difference and the more athletic build, but Logan was wily. He feigned moving to the left around him and then bobbed to the right, sliding past him and getting a hand on the doorknob. But then he made the mistake of smirking over his shoulder in a moment of triumph, and that was all Christian needed to yank him down by the shirt.

They grabbed each other, searching for a shirt or a belt loop or an arm, dragging and pulling and wrestling for dominance. Logan gritted his teeth and tried to push Christian to the floor, but he dug his heels in and pushed back, thudding him against the door for a moment before Logan was twisting around again.

Sharp breaths and grunts peppered the air as they moved—a leg between the other's to try to trip them, a hand around the back of a neck to pull them down, and a tug at the belt to unsettle their balance. It was rough. Messy. It was a miracle neither of their clothes got torn.

Logan lost his footing on the slippery floor, though, and he finally went down, crying out at Christian's solid weight slamming into him a second later.

That was where things always went to shit—why should he bother fighting? The full weight of Christian's muscular body was enough to keep him down, and whenever he tried to shimmy away he was held still.

"You're still not telling me everything," Christian murmured, his warm breath ghosting over Logan's neck. "I know you're not. You look goddamn scared, man."

No, I don't. He let the lie echo around his head as he tried to jerk away, and Christian pressed his hips down against Logan's ass to pin him there. "I don't wanna talk about it."

"I do."

"I don't care!" Logan threw his head back, hoping he might clip him in the chin or the nose, but he didn't get any satisfaction. "If I don't wanna talk, then we're not gonna!"

"Nah, we are, though." Christian got a little more comfortable, pressing the air out of Logan little by little. "We can talk about it now, or we can talk about it when you finally give up and realize that I was right."

"I pick later, then. Get the fuck off."

"I'm comfy. I think I'll stay."

Logan rested his cheek on the cool floor and let out a shaky breath, trying to focus on anything but the way Christian was squeezing the tension out of him, or how he had his nose resting so intimately against his neck, or why Logan's skin boiled hotter and hotter with each passing second. He clenched his jaw, but his secret escaped anyway. "She didn't...she didn't break up with me about the...double date."

"Mm?" Christian's chest rumbled against his spine. "I figured she didn't. So, what was it, buddy? What sort of trouble in paradise do you have going on?"

Logan bit his lips shut.

"Still not gonna tell me?" Christian huffed. "That's fine. I can just take a nap here."

God, please don't. Every cell in Logan's body was focused on the weight right against the cleft of his ass.

"I don't have to go anywhere. And you can settle in and tell me when you're ready."

Logan started to shake, his body jumping through hoops to betray him. As if being honest wasn't going to ruin their entire friendship and throw whatever future Logan had always dreamed of with Christian at his side out the window. As if it was *easy* to say why she'd really broken it off with him.

"You trust me, right? You know I can take whatever it is. And then we can go and tell Charlotte and she can go fuck Kelly Anne up for us and—"

He couldn't wait anymore. "Look, she fucking broke up with me 'cuz I said I wanted to mess around with you, and it pissed her off, okay?"

Silence.

Logan's breath trembled as he exhaled, his nails scraping over the linoleum beneath him. "Sh-she said nobody would ever fucking let their...that they...she wouldn't ever..." He couldn't find the words to make her poison sound neat and pretty. "She said if I was fucking thinking about guys, I'd cheat on her or leave her o-or, that I wasn't even *trustworthy*, like..."

The steady warm breath tickling over his neck hadn't stopped. He hadn't moved an inch.

"She broke up with me 'cuz something is wrong with me. That's what it's really about. So, fuck you, all right— Is that what you thought you were gonna hear? That my girl fucked me over because I'm nothing but shit?"

Languidly, the tip of Christian's nose brushed a path down one of the tendons in Logan's neck, a treacherous warmth that lit up every cell in his body with an aching frustration. "That's not what Charlotte said."

Logan scoffed. "What the hell are you talking about?"

"When I asked if I could mess around with you."

His heart stopped. Logan jerked his head painfully, trying to see Christian from the corner of his eye. "What?"

Christian lifted his head, his lips pulled into a frown and his eyes a warm, bright brown. "She said we could."

Logan stared at him for a long moment, trying to find out how to breathe again. Had he hallucinated what he just heard? He shook his head. "No, dude, that's not funny. No girl's gonna let their boyfriend play around with another guy."

Christian's gaze trailed down to Logan's lips, as if it was his fingers on him instead, and lingered there. Christian furrowed his brow as he studied Logan's mouth. "I wouldn't joke with you about this. You know it."

"But..."

The hand on his shoulder moved and buried in his hair pulling Logan's head back with a sting to his scalp that lit a wick inside him.

"Look at me." Christian leaned in an inch. "Do I seem like I'm kidding?"

There wasn't a right answer. Logan's whole body trembled against the floor, his pulse beating too hard and too fast until he was dizzy. He was terrified to move.

Christian rocked forward, grinding his hips against Logan's ass as he kissed him.

"Mm—" Logan tried to twist on the floor to reach him better, his hands shifting helplessly, and his shoulder digging into Christian's chest as he melted against his mouth. But no, he was stuck. He was left right where Christian wanted him. For a long moment, neither of them moved again—their lips quivering against the others. And then Logan tilted his head slightly, welcoming him closer, and Christian growled.

He readjusted his body, and for the first time, Logan felt the swell of his cock against him. There was nowhere to hide. As Christian worked his mouth against Logan's— parting his lips and inviting him to do the same—Logan scrambled to hold his awkward angle.

He didn't want to move. If he stopped, everything stopped. If this ended, they'd have to talk about it, and they'd have to discuss what was going to happen next.

Christian's hips jerked one more time, and Logan became vividly aware of his own hardness as it crushed painfully against the floor. He pulled away with a gasp and turned his head when Christian chased him like a tidal wave. "Hurts, dude, hold on."

"What?" Christian let his hair go but didn't try to move away. "What hurts?"

"This, I'm..." Logan's face lit on fire. "I'm hard, man, you've, you've got me—"

"This?" Christian ground against him, and Logan buried his face in his forearms, crying out at the bite of overstimulated pain. "If I let you up, are you gonna run?"

He didn't know the answer to that. He'd just tasted Christian, after years of not knowing that he wanted to, and he couldn't guarantee he wouldn't jump straight out of the window.

"Logan?"

"I-I'll try not to."

Christian huffed and touched his mouth to Logan's neck, more lingering than a kiss. "Now, how the hell am I supposed to mess around with you if you don't stand still for me, brother?"

"Fuck—" Logan arched his hips as best as he could, crushing against him, burning from the hot pressure of his cock.

Christian sat up, looped one of his arms around Logan's torso, and pulled him up too. He crept his other hand up Logan's chest and wrapped it loosely around his neck as he nibbled at his earlobe, drowning Logan in too many sensations to keep track of. "C'mon. Forget about Kelly Anne. Let's have some fun, huh?"

"You gonna fuck me?" Before he spoke, Logan didn't know it was something he'd even wanted, but now all he could think of was the dizzying rock of the bed frame in the darkness, listening to Christian's sweet moans, feeling almost as though he was swaying from the press of his cock inside him.

Christian's hand tightened around his throat, enough to make Logan's breath hiss as he inhaled, and then he touched his other hand to his hip, holding him still as he rocked against him. "Yeah?"

Logan gasped. "Oh my God..."

"I bet you I could fuck you real nice if you wanted me to."

He'd spent so many years being held down under Christian until he submitted to him, his skin too hot and his voice ragged and his words ashamed as he called uncle. Doing it again in Christian's bed, their bodies naked and slick with sweat...he couldn't imagine that'd be any worse to try at least once. "You wanna?"

Christian's chuckle was unsteady against his ear as he stood, dragging Logan to his feet. "We'll see."

He hadn't fantasized about this. He'd come back to the dorm with the express purpose of getting the shower and touching himself to the thought of Christian, yes, but he hadn't had a chance to really probe his curiosity and see what he wanted beneath the layers of nerves. Having Christian handle him so easily—a hand splayed across his stomach, and his muscles barely tensing when he pulled Logan to stand—only added to the sense of unreality.

There's no way this is happening.

And yet Christian was turning him around and hauling him forward by the belt loop and kissing him again.

Eagerness rushed through Logan as he scratched his nails over Christian's scalp. He groaned against his lips, and Christian ground forward—was it in response to him? Was there something about Logan that lit him on fire too?

Curious, Logan rolled his hips back, and two hands guided him until their cocks were flush together in their pants.

"Fuck," Christian whispered as he broke the kiss. He pressed his forehead against Logan's curls as they moved inexpertly together, rocking back and forth on their heels, chasing the sparks that shot off every time they met in the middle. "Shit, dude—"

"Yeah..."

It seemed like they'd given up on talking or figuring out exactly what was going on. There was no room for logic or indecision about what was going on. They hadn't spoken a word about being interested in each other, yet, here they were, both separately asking their girlfriends for an opportunity to check it out?

It was nonsensical. And somewhere deep inside, Logan knew this wouldn't happen again—so he had to get everything out of his system all in one night.

He kissed Christian's neck fleetingly and yanked at his shirt. "C'mon, dude, bed's right there."

Christian charged forward like a bull, pushing Logan backward until his legs hit the edge of the bed and he tipped under, his hair grazing the edge of his bed above him as he fell. Christian's hands touched his inner thighs, pushing them apart, and Logan got a perfect view of his best friend raking his gaze up his body from his hips to his eyes. Wildness simmered there.

They didn't have a rulebook for this, and it showed. Christian stared at him for one moment of searing heat before he crawled between his legs and slid his hands up Logan's shirt.

Slowing down wasn't an option. Logan yanked his shirt off and then tugged Christian's over his head too, taking in his finely muscled torso. He was more lean than muscular on top—built for speed rather than brute strength—and the fine hairs on his skin seemed almost like an afterthought, as if a painter had added a few fine brushstrokes at the last second. It wasn't the first time Logan had seen his bare chest, and it sure as hell wouldn't be the last, but never before had his cock twitched as he stared.

It took him a few seconds to realize Christian was staring at him just as openly.

Logan touched first, before he lost his drive, his hand drifting up Christian's abs and admiring how his fingers spanned the tight valleys and mountains of his muscles little by little. "Goddamn."

"You like?"

Logan grunted in response. Was it weak to admit he did? Would he give off the wrong vibe? If all this was only the two of them sharing a once-in-a-lifetime opportunity, then he didn't want to make it too serious by implying he'd been *wanting* a chance to touch him like this.

He vaguely remembered something, and he bit his bottom lip as he trailed his thumb over the swell of Christian's pectoral. "Charlotte, she..." He stopped at the edge of Christian's nipple, watching his chest heave in rapid breaths. "...I remember that she..." *She touched you a lot here.* As he thumbed over Christian's nipple, he flicked his gaze to his face and watched his lips part in a quiet moan. *Sensitive, huh?* Logan didn't let himself blink as he traced over the pebbly skin again and again, feeling it harden with each pass.

A glance down showed him the thick swell in Christian's pants, and he licked his lips as he tweaked the nipple between his thumb and forefinger, then watched Christian's hips move in response.

He wants to fuck something real bad, doesn't he?

It wouldn't hurt, would it, if he let Christian do that? If they took their time? Logan had never done anal with a girl before, but he'd taken the time to research the best method just in case. He'd wondered as he read about it how it would feel—having one, two, maybe three fingers inside—and he'd been careful to keep his nails trimmed and smooth from that day on. He'd reasoned that he wouldn't want someone's jagged, raggedy-ass nails scraping up inside him, so there was no way in hell he'd do that to a girl either.

Now, he realized his obsession with being prepared might've been fueled by a different drive.

Christian took his hand and gently pushed his wrist into the mattress by his head. He licked his lips as he admired Logan, looming over him, leaning bit by bit until their bare chests were flush together. Breathless, Logan couldn't speak if he tried.

Christian tilted his head to the side, his gaze going intense as he stared at Logan's mouth. His other hand trailed down Logan's side, lighting little paths of fire in the wake of his touch, until he reached the most sensitive part that had Logan squirming and breathing a chuckle. Christian grinned. "Well, well—"

"Don't you dare."

Christian laughed and ran over the arch of his hipbone, the waistband of his boxers, and the loops of his jeans. Hesitation. Logan held his breath.

The brush of Christian's fingers over his thigh dragged more anticipation through him than the first time a girl had knelt between his legs. There'd been expectation there, and knowledge of what would happen from a few years of watching porn, but now, there was nothing planned. There were no conventions telling him what had to happen next. For all he knew, Christian would laugh and pull away and say he'd changed his mind.

For a moment, as Christian rolled onto his side, blocking Logan in against the wall, he thought that might be what was going to happen. And then Christian cupped his hand over his hardness.

Logan tipped his head back with a ragged gasp, closing his eyes in rapture as Christian rubbed him with leisurely strokes. "Oh, fuck, Christian…"

"Good?" The bedframe rocked as Christian shifted, and when Logan opened his eyes, he was lying on the pillow right beside him, ravenous.

Logan nodded, terrified to move or shift or even *breathe*.

"Yeah..." Christian glanced down as he pressed the heel of his palm against him, trailing down the seam of his zipper. "Gonna chafe after a bit, though."

There was already a hint of pain right at the edge of his senses, dotting the haze of pleasure.

"Maybe I should..."

Pressure relieved as Christian popped his button and tugged his zipper down, and Logan covered his face with both hands, trying to hide his expression. Kelly Anne teased him every once and a while for how desperate he was when she took her time undressing him and refused to let him touch her until she was ready. Christian's careful movements were ten times as agonizing.

"Logan."

Goose bumps exploded over his skin, standing every hair on end at the shock of hearing his name spoken so desperately. "Mm?"

"Look at me, baby."

Baby.

He curled his toes, viscerally shaken by that one word, and so incredibly eager to hear it again. He dropped his hands on his chest and swallowed hard before he caught Christian's gaze.

"Yeah." Intensity rolled off Christian in waves. "That's it, let's just..." His cool fingers brushed along Logan's flushed skin, parting through his treasure trail, and slid under the waistband of his boxers. "Let's see if that cock's as pretty as I remember, huh?"

"Fuck—" Logan shut his eyes at the first touch of Christian's fingers along his shaft, and then they flew open a second later. *He wants me to see.* He kept his eyes on Christian's like a staring contest as his calloused fingers caressed up and down his cock in slow, careful movements. When he thought he'd burn up inside if he was teased for a second longer, Christian twisted his wrist and brought Logan out of his boxers and jeans.

Christian's eyes widened when he peeked downward, and he immediately pulled Logan's boxers and jeans down together. He dragged them all the way off with Logan kicking helpfully, then dropped them over the edge of the bed and started opening his belt.

He's gonna fuck me. Logan bent his knees, pointing one at the sky and the other at the wall, sitting up on his elbows to get a better look at Christian's stumbling fingers. Christian fought with the belt for a few seconds before finally getting it open and shoving his jeans and briefs off.

With the two of them stripped down, hidden in the shade of the top bunk, it was almost like being kids in a secret fort, exposing their deepest and most tender secrets because they couldn't see the other's face. But this was a far more intimate secret than Logan ever dreamed of sharing, and as Christian trailed his fingers up his calf, he realized there would be no pretending this never happened. It wasn't like the times he'd seen Christian cry and then acted like he hadn't seen a thing. No, this was the two of them pressing close, stretching their bodies out beside each other, trying to fit in a twin bed as though they weren't two grown boys pretending to be men.

As Christian pulled him in again, burying a hand in his curls, leading the charge through his lips and the questing of his other hand, Logan refused to lie there and pretend he wasn't as eager for this as Christian was. There wasn't room for fear in this bed. Not after all they'd been through.

Logan rolled Christian onto his back and broke the kiss, leaving a trail of them down his chest instead. He welcomed Christian's full body shudder when he laved his tongue over his nipple, then sucked at the hard flesh with just the barest tease of his teeth grazing over the tip. He groped his other pectoral, relying on old habits—searching for a tit to love on—and fought how flustered he became when there was nothing but a taut muscle for him to grab—hard as a rock.

Don't fuck this up. If you fuck this up, he'll laugh and make fun of you. He'll make this into a joke. You'll never be anything but the guy that gave him bad sex.

"You're gonna fuck me, right?" Logan breathed and then flicked the tip of his tongue to distract Christian from the nerves in his voice.

Christian groaned, his fingers massaging Logan's scalp. "Not today. Don't have...the stuff I need."

He leaned up a little taller on his belly. "Stuff?"

"Lube." Christian wrinkled his brow. "You know I wouldn't fuck you dry."

There were two things Logan took from his expression: one, Christian's *not today* meant there would be more potential times in the future; and two, Christian was about to start laughing at Logan thinking he'd fuck him without proper prep.

The first one was immediately overshadowed by the second one, because he *Couldn't. Let. Him. Laugh.*

Logan immediately slid farther down. Messy kisses traced over Christian's torso, through the neatly trimmed trail downward, and then...then he was there.

He knew Christian's cock by sight now. He'd seen it when it was hard and tucked in Charlotte's hand before she began to ride him. He'd stared a little too long—longer than he'd stared at most pussies in his life—and he'd thought about it the night after, when he was getting out of the shower and studying his own physique in the mirror. Comparing, he'd told himself. Only comparing his equipment to Christian's.

Now he knew better.

He wrapped his hand around Christian's cock, giving a few slow tugs, and his heart set easier in his chest. It was like grabbing his own dick, from the velvety smooth texture to the darkness of his skin. Thick veins rose out against his thumb, and a shiny drop of precum waited on the head.

"Have you been tested recently?"

"Yeah." Christian jerked his head toward his desk, breath coming shakily. "I, uh, I've got my results in the drawer with the—the condoms, so—"

"I trust you." Logan forced himself to hold his gaze. "Are you negative?"

"Yeah. Negative for everything. So's Charlotte. We just got tested together two weeks ago."

"Kelly Anne and I did too. Do you want me to put a condom on you?"

Christian twitched in his hand. "Not if you don't want to. Charlotte doesn't care either."

"Okay." He stared at the dick in his hand and took a deep breath. *I can't believe I'm doing this.* Logan licked his lips. "Can you do something for me?"

"What's that?"

His cheeks heated. *I can't* believe *I'm* doing *this.* "Could you call me *baby* again?"

Christian's abs tightened as he exhaled sharply, and he buried his fingers deeper still. "Are you gonna suck me off, baby?"

"God," Logan whispered, his eyelashes fluttering. Warmth spread through him—a blanket in the thick of winter—and he breathed out an inch from the head of Christian's cock. "You want me to?"

"Fuck yeah." Christian tugged his hair again. Did he do that with Charlotte? Or was he just obsessed with how Logan's hair felt in his hands? "Bet your mouth'll feel amazing around my cock, won't it, baby?"

Every single time he said that goddamn word, something knit tighter in Logan's chest. He was throwing himself to the wolves with his lack of experience and hopes and prayers that he'd do something worthwhile.

Before he could second-guess himself any further, he dragged the flat of his tongue up Christian's shaft.

"Fuck!" Christian arched his back, hips lifting off the mattress, and Logan pressed them down again before he could gag.

If you fuck this up, you fuck the whole thing up.

Logan focused on the sharp taste of Christian's skin as he inched upward, until he could swirl his tongue over the head of his cock—

And immediately pulled away.

"Holy shit," Logan said, pressing a hand to his mouth as he sat up. "Oh my God, Christian, do you have any idea what precum tastes like?"

Christian immediately burst out laughing, covering his face with both hands.

Fuck, fuck, *that was what we were trying to avoid here.* But try as he might, he couldn't forget the bitter taste on his tongue; it was unlike anything he'd ever tasted, and he hated it. "Oh my God."

"You're fucking incredible!" Christian cackled for a few seconds more, reaching up for him with grabbing hands, and Logan shamefully let him pull him to lie on his side. "Holy shit, you should've seen your face. You went from the fucking hottest thing I've ever seen to the most disappointed, horrified...holy shit."

He'd messed up, and now he'd be nothing more than a laughingstock. "Sorry."

"Hey. Hey." Christian rolled onto his side too, gazing into his eyes with a slow smile. "Don't be sorry, dude, you don't have to blow me if it's gross."

"I think I could. I just..."

"Hey," he whispered again, then leaned in and touched a kiss to his forehead. Logan's heart skipped a beat. Was it not over yet? How was that possible? "C'mere; let me."

"Let you—*oh*!"

Christian wrapped a hand around Logan's cock and brought his hips forward until he could use his long fingers to take hold of his own dick in the same grip. "Fuck...saw this in a video once..."

"A video?" Logan choked out. How did he manage language when his mind was zeroed in on his hardness pressed so solidly against Christian's?

"I mean..." Christian breathed another laugh and slowly began to move his hand. "Can't tell me you never watched gay porn just 'cuz you were curious or something."

The mental image of Christian touching himself to two men kissing and fucking was too much for Logan to handle. He grabbed Christian's arm and pressed his face into his neck, his breathing shallow and frantic as he drowned in his touch.

It seemed like a crime not to see his face right now, but Logan knew himself. The second he took a good long look at Christian, he'd be coming way too fast. And would that be enough for him? Having this once and never again?

"Fuck…"

"Yeah," Logan whispered, shivering. "Fucking good, isn't it?"

"The *best*."

He shouldn't have been as pleased by that as he was.

Memorize this. Everything from Christian's solid grip to his other hand on Logan's hip patterned itself on his mind. *Don't forget anything.* Christian's mouth touched Logan's forehead for a moment, his heated breath brushing against his skin, and then there was a fleeting kiss that made Logan moan. *But don't let him know how much you need this. Don't make him think you're gay. He'll get weirded out if you're gay. This is just playing around, remember?*

Christian's hand glided over them faster and faster, catching precum at the heads every time and slicking them up. Logan tried to hold his breath so he could hear every sound coming from Christian's lips, but he couldn't handle it—he had to let the air out on a moan.

"Close?" Christian asked in a raw voice.

"God, yeah." He'd barely been holding himself back the entire time.

"C'mon, then, baby, come for me."

It was like a depth change yanking Logan straight underwater. He threw his head back with a cry, squeezing his eyes shut, white-hot pleasure raking through his entire body as Christian practically stripped his cock bare with his hand. He was floating out of the bliss when Christian pushed him onto his back and planted his other hand on the pillow beside him, and Logan jolted from his aftershocks with wide eyes.

Christian hovered over him, teeth gritted, his gaze laser focused between them, as he moved his hips wildly, fucking against Logan's spent cock like a man possessed. His grip tightened around Logan's oversensitive skin—too much, *too much*—and Logan bit into his own arm to restrain his pained whimpers.

He wouldn't tell him to stop. Wouldn't even *dream* of it. Not when every little burn of pain somehow felt so *good* in the back of his mind.

He'd fuck me just like this. Just this hard, this fast, this passionately... Logan couldn't stop staring at the veins swelling on Christian's neck or the sharpness of his eyes. *God, let him last forever, holy shit.*

The next few seconds stretched out, Christian's breathing ragged, before a long moan slipped from his lips as he came on Logan's stomach. His hips jerked spasmodically, teasing out every last sensation, and then he tipped forward, catching himself with a slick hand on the sheets by the pillow.

Christian glanced up at him, his thighs still squeezed tight around his hips, still panting. "Hey."

It was over. Logan blinked a few times, trying to come out of the haze, feeling very much as though he'd lived through a dream—a whole fantasy he hadn't known he had. He looked away. Until Christian moved, he was trapped.

Christian did move. He rolled onto his side, and Logan immediately started to pull away.

"Hey, no." Christian held him down with a hand on his chest, then reached over the side of the bed and picked up a discarded T-shirt. Christian had worn the soft blue shirt two days ago, and the fact that Logan knew that so quickly shook something inside him.

Logan didn't move a muscle as Christian wiped up the mess on his stomach and then tossed the shirt away as he lay down. *What the hell is happening?* They both couldn't fit on the twin bed—hell, just one of them barely fit. So, when Christian shifted his weight and rolled over, Logan was forced to move with him until he was on his side.

Without looking, he rested his head on Christian's chest, his other arm awkwardly wrapping around his waist. Christian's heart was beating faster than a hummingbird's. It was...nice, actually. Soothing.

Christian's chest rumbled as he hummed—his pleased hum, the one Logan memorized years ago when they were still kids—and tossed an arm over Logan's waist to pull him a little closer...until they were cuddling. Like this was normal or something.

They were two best friends who were still naked and had just fucked. Logan swore he could feel the stickiness of his release. Christian was sweaty. *Is this weird?*

"Is this weird?" Logan asked not even a full second after having the thought.

"Only if you make it weird." Christian replied, as casual as if they were grocery shopping.

"Huh." He wasn't sure that made sense, but if Christian wasn't pushing him away, then there was no reason to go.

The weight of the day was catching up to him—the fight with Kelly Anne, the exhaustion from the unplanned jog, and the frantic wrestling before they'd ended up in bed together. He thumbed over Christian's abs one more time before deciding he'd close his eyes only for a second, only to rest them.

Logan thought one more thing—*I've gotta get Charlotte a fucking medal or something*—before he was out like a light.

Chapter Six

CHRISTIAN

Logan fell asleep.

Of course, he fell asleep. Logan had been falling asleep in strange places for years. Christian once had music blaring as they worked on homework in middle school, and Logan still passed out face-first on his notebook, drooling all over the page he'd been working on.

And I just tired him out, so...

He was...smug, really. Cocky. When he'd been the first to come during their little escapade with the four of them, he'd been a little sour. Real men could last. Real men got their partner off first. Real men didn't leave their partner to finish themselves off, when everything was said and done, unless they were practically dead on the bed from being ridden like a fucking stallion—*thanks for that, Charlotte.* There'd been a moment of reclaiming pride when Logan lasted only seconds after he got his hand around the both of them.

And now, Christian had to think about what he'd gotten himself into.

The pride trickled away little by little as he ran his hand up and down his best friend's waist. *Best friend.* As far as Christian understood, that implied something platonic with unbreakable boundaries. Maybe everyone else around campus was less inhibited than he was, but he'd never thought about himself getting off with *just a friend*. Any girl he'd fucked had become something more within a few hours. As free loving as Christian had always been—his eyes on any number of people when he was single—he tended to zone in on one person and keep them in his sights until their relationship eventually ended.

He couldn't let that happen to Logan.

Relationships ended. That was how life was. Unless it was moving toward marriage, a relationship would end at some point, and that wasn't where he and Logan were going. Their lives were parallel, not necessarily crossing. They ran as close together as two lanes on a road with a dotted line separating them, and never did they merge into one lane.

Except for the events that had led them here. And now, they had to split into those two lanes again before they crashed into a wall.

Logan had wanted to play around. And they had. And no matter how fucking phenomenal the experience was, there was Charlotte to consider—his beautiful, amazing girlfriend who'd put the suggestion in his head in the first place. She'd known more than Christian how good he and Logan could be together, and she'd mentioned she'd messed around with her friends when figuring out her bisexuality. That it hadn't had to mean anything when they were queer girls who enjoyed getting off together.

Is that what we are now?

Two less-than-straight boys who'd enjoyed getting off together. And who were now going to transition right back into a platonic friendship.

God, I wish I knew what I was fucking doing. He rubbed his face and sighed. *How do you search for info about this online?*

Logan shifted, his bare leg rubbing against Christian's and lighting a trail of tingles over his skin. As Christian watched, Logan blearily opened his eyes, blinked up at him, and drew away an inch as he frowned.

It was over, then. It was time to fit themselves into their separate lanes. "Morning, sleeping beauty."

"Oh fuck, is it?"

"Nah." Christian chuckled. "You've been out for, like, fifteen minutes, tops. No big deal."

"Oh." Logan sat up, glanced down at Christian's body, and looked away just as quickly. "Shit, I meant to take a shower when I got back."

"And then you got distracted." He couldn't help but tease. "Shower's open, dude. Clothes are probably still on the floor over there."

"Yep." Logan started to stand and banged his head on the underside of the top bunk. "Fuck!"

Christian burst out laughing. "Holy shit!"

"Shut up!" Logan rubbed his head as he started across the room. Christian's gaze slid down the sharpness of his spine and over the curve of his ass. "I'm not used to being down there like you!"

"You're stupid." He sat on the edge of his bed and watched a little too closely as Logan leaned down to scoop up his clothes. *He wanted me to fuck him.* Christian chewed on his bottom lip, swollen from their kisses. *I wanted to have him too. Fuck, why didn't I have any lube around?*

"I'm *sleepy.*" Logan whined the words. "I might just shower and go to bed."

Christian frowned. "What, no dinner?"

"Not hungry. I don't know." Logan held his clothes strategically, Christian noticed, right over his junk as he walked toward the bathroom. "Go ahead to the dining hall. If I feel up to eating, I'll catch up with you."

"Okay. You sure?"

"Yeah." Logan opened the bathroom door, searched his face, then blinked and hurried inside, leaving Christian alone and with no idea what had just happened.

He hoped the mood wouldn't be tense, that Logan, as enthusiastic as he'd been about getting his hands all over Christian's body, would've been calm after the experience. That was what Charlotte said had happened with her and her friends—they didn't have to *try* to be relaxed.

Maybe we're not as compatible as they were? There weren't any clear answers, and the more he sat there and tried to think, the hungrier he got. He'd always been voracious after sex.

He tugged the nearest dirty clothes on—a T-shirt and pair of shorts—and slid on some flip-flops as he grabbed his keys, wallet, and cell phone. The shower cut on right as he touched the doorknob, and he hesitated, wondering if he should linger.

And then he didn't.

Noah and Daiki's room was still unoccupied, so he headed out and down the stairs. It was fortunate that their dorm wasn't too far from the dining hall, given how often he found himself eating.

He swiped his card at the door to charge his meal and went inside, hands shoved in his pockets. It was a perfectly normal night now. He could walk in as if he hadn't just rolled out of bed with his best friend. As if he hadn't gotten curious about the taste of semen the second Logan pulled off him, gagging.

He shook his head and tried not to laugh in front of the hundred students eating. He was used to protecting an image by now. With a few thousand white eyes on him at home, in addition to the laser focus of his coach demanding perfection, Christian had worked to groom himself into someone who was as spectacular and yet unremarkable as possible.

Spectacular on the field. Forgettable everywhere else.

Well. Almost everywhere else.

Christian filled his plate with turkey and mashed potatoes and corn and, as usual, tried not to think about the stage. He'd tripped into his first play—a kid's play at his church for Christmas, where he ended up playing Joseph and getting a lot of strange looks he hadn't understood at the time—and he'd been caught up in acting ever since. It wasn't as if a jock couldn't exist at the same time as a theater kid, but a lead role hadn't really been possible as team practices and games frequently interfered with rehearsal time. Those precious moments on stage with actual lines to speak were perfection in and of themselves.

He wasn't going to have that again, but at least he had the memories.

He was used to not having something again once he'd experienced it for the first time, whether it was an expensive beer or being at his dad's house for a few weeks over the summer. Most of those things he had no desire to try again.

The handful of things he craved...well, he could spend his time forgetting about them.

As he wandered, searching for somewhere to sit, soda in hand, his eyes fell on Noah and Daiki sitting alone at a table with cards spread out in front of them, their empty plates stacked to the side. Since the few classmates he'd started to click with were nowhere to be seen, he figured he might as well give his suitemates the pleasure of his company. "Hey, guys."

Daiki was mid-laugh and waved at Christian, and Noah sat back in his chair, grinning. "What's up, man?"

"Nothing." He sat and sipped his soda and then furrowed his brow when Daiki looked away, cheeks flushed, covering his mouth with his shoulders shaking. "The hell'd you do to him?"

"Cursed him. Laughing curse. Easy enough."

"Right." Christian glanced down at the cards. He knew they both collected some from a trading card game, but they didn't make sense to him. The art was pretty, at least. "Did you...do something cool with the game, or—"

"I used a loophole to kill him on the first turn, and he's taking it better than I thought," Noah said brightly, resting his elbows on the table while Daiki put his head down and snorted. Noah smirked, then winked at Christian. "He never had a chance."

Christian took a bite of his food. "Man, as long as he's happy."

"Exactly." Noah peered around the room, his smirk fading. "What, no Logan tonight?"

Christian stiffened, but Noah was still scanning the room. *He doesn't know. They weren't in the suite when we fucked around. It's okay.* "No, he's, uh, not feeling well. Sort of tired, I guess. Said he was just gonna take a shower and go to bed."

"Mm. Hope he doesn't have some bug going around."

"Me too." Lying came easy; he didn't have to look away to sound sincere. He cut his piece of turkey into individual bites before he started to eat them one by one.

Any other time, he'd try to make conversation, but Daiki started shuffling the deck, and both he and Noah were immediately distracted. Neither of them noticed how quickly Christian ate, his eyes always on the door of the dining hall, waiting to see if Logan would end up walking in.

I should bring him something. Stuff some food in a napkin and just...I don't know. I could make him a sandwich. Get him a drink. Anything. They had food in their kitchen, but it wasn't a lot, and Logan had always been helpless with cooking anyway. Christian had gotten used to making himself dinner as both his parents worked full time—sometimes overtime, in his stepdad's case. While they could rely on fast food or freezer meals, Christian had to stick to a diet plan to keep in shape as he'd hoped to start on the team.

Maybe I'll cook him something instead. Make him a plate and keep it in the fridge until he's ready to eat.

It was better than nothing.

"Hey, c'mon, don't—"

"What?" Noah laughed, and Christian glanced over.

"Don't do it again, don't, don't!" Daiki grabbed Noah's wrist, pulling it away from his fanned cards in his other hand.

Noah threw his head back, losing it as he and Daiki weakly batted at each other, acting as if he was just as half-hearted about whatever he'd threatened to play as Daiki was about stopping him.

For one crystal clear moment, their fingers loosely intertwined, and Daiki pinned Noah's wrist on the table, holding it there as he snatched Noah's cards out of his hand. "No!"

"I'll do it!"

"No, c'mon, man!"

They were so casual about their contact, but so fleeting—as quickly as they'd touched hands, they were pulling away.

Noah managed to get his hand back, then laid each card down one after the other until Daiki buried his face in his shoulder and screamed. Noah cackled as he rested his temple on the top of Daiki's head.

Are they...?

"You're a fucking asshole," Daiki snapped, but the smile on his face said the words were all in good humor.

"And yet you're still my friend!" Noah announced proudly.

"I don't know why. I'm getting ice cream. You've ruined my life."

"Oh! Get me some too?"

"Fuck you!"

Noah grinned and separated their cards, then neatly stacked his own before glancing at Christian. Their eye contact lingered for a long moment before he put his deck away.

Christian came to his feet abruptly, plate empty.

"You done?" Noah blinked.

"Yeah. I'm, uh, worried about Logan. Gonna go see if there's anything I need to run out and get him." Even as Christian was speaking the lie, there was a brief glimpse of vulnerability in Noah's gaze, impossible to miss. He couldn't have him being scared of what Christian had just seen. "Hey, you need anything? Or Daiki?"

"Don't think so."

"Cool." Christian gave him a thumbs-up. "Text me if you do, okay?"

Noah relaxed in his chair. "Yeah, will do."

"Awesome. See you later?"

"Sure."

Christian delivered his plates to the bussing area and set off for his dorm. He got halfway there before realizing he hadn't searched for Charlotte in the dining hall. Guilt bit at him. He stopped and leaned against a tree, pulling out his phone and dialing her number.

The line rang twice before she answered, loud music being turned down. "Hey, baby, how are you?"

"Good. You?"

"Good! Finishing up my homework."

Christian closed his eyes, welcoming the sound of her voice. He liked her. He really did. Probably more than he should, honestly, since he couldn't imagine bringing her home to his family with all of her piercings and two tattoos. His family had enough trouble with *Christian*, much less someone who acted a little too much like him. "Just got done with dinner. Didn't see you there. Thought I'd give you a call."

"I appreciate it. Yeah, I grabbed a really late lunch. Think I'm gonna throw something together in the microwave."

"You sure?"

"Yeah." She paused. "You sure you're okay too? You don't ever call me only to talk. Thought something had to be wrong."

He could hold back what was on his mind. She hadn't requested a check-in, but... "I, uh...Logan and I just finished..."

Her chair squeaked in the background, and then there was the sound of a door shutting. "You did it?" Her voice echoed—she must have been in the bathroom.

His cheeks warmed. "Yeah. We did it."

"How was it?" She was breathless, excited, and for a second, Christian wondered if all she cared about was hearing the dirty details. He tried to let the thought go. If he was ever going to have a threesome that included another guy, no doubt Logan would be the one he'd pick. But Charlotte had already sworn she wasn't interested— that she'd only invite him for Christian's sake.

Maybe she was proud of him. And that made him feel sheepish. "Good, uh, it was good."

"Good?"

"Really good." He made sure no one was around him. "Jesus, Charlotte, you want details or something?"

"If you wanna give them to me, sure!"

He *did* sort of want to go over the highlight reel with someone, but not in the center of campus on his goddamn cell phone. "I didn't...we didn't, like, fuck. You know what I mean."

"You didn't put your dick inside him."

"Yeah, that." She spoke so casually—like it was something he did every day and not a new terrifying experience. "We didn't have the stuff we needed."

"Oh my God, do you really not have any lube there?"

"No! Why would I need it?"

"Baby, *I've* got lube! You've fucked me in the ass like three times now! What were you gonna do if I ended up in your bed wanting anal? Make excuses? Tell me to hold on for fifteen minutes while you run to the drug store? C'mon!"

He was sure his cheeks were bright red now. He swore people could hear her. "Will you stop! Oh my God, I'm sorry. I wasn't prepared, holy shit."

Charlotte sighed. "We've gotta get you some lube, then."

"Why? Bring me one of yours."

"I'm not giving you one of my expensive-ass bottles of lube for you and your little boyfriend to stick fingers in each other's butts." While Christian caught up with that mental image, she went on, "We'll run down and get you some the next time you come over, okay? Hell, I'll buy it myself if you're too nervous."

"I-I'm not nervous! I just didn't know…"

"What?"

He tensed, his shoulders nearly at the level of his chin as he ducked his head and mumbled, "I didn't know you'd let me mess around with him again."

Charlotte sighed. "Baby, do you know who you're talking to? Who do you think I am? You think I've got this pretty tattoo on my forearm for nothing?"

He blinked. "What tattoo?"

"The…the fucking…the hearts, the two hearts and the infinity symbol. Do you know what it is?"

He hadn't paid much attention. Apparently, there was more to the image than being a nice design. "Not really?"

"It's a tattoo to show I'm ethically nonmonogamous."

That was new. "What?"

"We've talked about it before. At the party where we first met."

"Charlotte, listen, you're sweet, but I didn't hear a thing you said at the party until you asked if I wanted to go make out."

She burst out laughing. "I can't believe you."

"I'm serious! Music was too goddamn loud, and I was too lost in your eyes—"

"All right, lover boy, settle down. Now, what the tattoo means is that I'm not monogamous, okay? I like dating and hooking up with people… If that's something you're not cool with, I can totally commit myself to you until we figure out what you're comfortable with me doing, but I'm the last person alive who's gonna be pissed off if you're interested in your best friend, okay?"

"I'm not, I, uh…y'know, messing around was just for fun, right?"

Silence. "Right." She drew the word out, as though she didn't believe him.

"Listen, you're throwing a lot of stuff at me. Are there friends you wanna go hook up with too?" He should be jealous. He knew he should. But, somehow, the thought didn't elicit any strong reaction inside him. He'd seen Charlotte checking out other people, and he'd thought it was funny when she pointed out a hot girl and asked him what he thought. She was so different from what he was used to back home that somehow it made *sense* she'd be different in this way too.

"I mean, sure, but I'm with you right now, okay? And since you apparently didn't hear me go over the whole ethical nonmonogamy thing *before* we started dating, that means we should probably sit down and iron out all the details before I start scoping out some cuties to kiss. Deal?"

At the very least, he had questions, even if he didn't feel worried about her lifestyle. "Deal."

"First things first, I'm gonna pick up your own bottle of lube tomorrow."

"Oh my God—"

"Some new condoms too, some that are better for anal."

"Do those *exist*?"

"I mean, I know I have *my* favorites."

"I can't believe you're trying to get me laid with somebody who isn't you."

"Hey." Her voice lowered, softening and smoothing the tension until he was relaxing against the tree. "Listen. I want you to be happy, even if it's different from what you're used to. And call me crazy, but there's a certain way you look at Logan that I can't exactly ignore. It's the whole reason I said you could make a move on him. So, if I can make it all a little easier by buying you some lube and condoms so you know you have my blessing, then I'm gonna. Okay?"

What was he supposed to say to his girlfriend of only a few months being so excited at the self-exploration he'd done? He hadn't thought a girl like her existed, but here she was. It was possible there was a whole population of people like her out there.

Maybe he wouldn't go home to that repressive, thick atmosphere. He might keep exploring and opening his boundaries until he was a Christian Daniels he could be proud of, from head to toe, inside and out.

"What if he changed his mind?" he asked. "Like, there's no point in getting any supplies if he's not interested in trying it anymore."

"Did you make him come?"

"I mean, yeah."

"Then, good, that's one point in your favor—you gave him a good time."

Christian rubbed his eyes, trying not to laugh. It would only encourage her. "Charlotte..."

"*Talk* to him, baby. That's what you've gotta do in situations like this. You can't expect to read his mind. He's been your best friend for so long. Surely, you can sit down and talk to him."

Easier said than done. It was one thing to talk about where they wanted to get lunch and another thing entirely to ask if Logan was damn sure he wanted to be fucked up the ass.

"Talk to him. Promise me you'll talk to him."

"I can't promise you anything."

"Why not?"

"What if the conversation goes badly? What if he gets uncomfortable that I asked again?"

"Then you do what best friends do, and you talk about *that* too, until you're both on even footing again. God, it's like you two are in kindergarten."

Christian rolled his eyes. "I'll try. That's all I can say. I'll try."

"Good. Because if I spend my money on nice lube and you don't use it because you're too scared to ask him if he liked what you did, I'm gonna be really pissed off."

"Noted." He turned his head when he heard footsteps and moved away from the few students he saw coming his way. "Listen, I've gotta go. But uh...thanks."

"You're welcome, sweetie. You'd do the same for me."

He would. He really would. Realizing that was nice, honestly—knowing he had someone in his corner other than Logan, someone he would protect and help too. *Maybe dating isn't just about having sex with someone and having a good time.* Fancy that. "I'll talk to you later, Charlotte."

"Bye, baby."

As Christian hung up, he considered returning to the dorm, but he knew the second he stepped foot inside he'd feel the pressure to ask Logan about everything he'd just discussed with Charlotte. *I'm not ready.* He tipped his head back and stared at the sky. *Things are up in the air. I'm not gonna make them weird this fast.*

A walk would do him good. When he was finished, he could go back to their bedroom and be completely normal with Logan. Easy.

It sounded awful. All he wanted was to curl up beside Logan and learn sensual secrets about his body—but things would be better this way. *Everything's gonna be fine.*

LOGAN PACED. HE didn't like it, and being restless made him look like a fool, but he didn't know what else he was supposed to do after the experience he and Christian had. Though he'd scrubbed himself in the shower, he still swore he smelled Christian on him, and...he *liked* it. His body was bruised from their painful wrestling, and he spent five minutes after his shower staring at the mirror in fascination. He was marked by Christian, and though the aftermath wasn't anything new, each purple spot was far more intimate.

The real question was what would happen when Christian returned from dinner. *Is he gonna just lay a wet one on me when he enters the room? Will he grab my ass? Will he say it was all a mistake?* There was no way to tell, and the vastness of the possibilities terrified him.

He never thought he'd see the day when he was scared of Christian.

The door unlocked, and Logan jumped and stared guiltily at it. But when the door opened to reveal only Noah and Daiki, he deflated and held back a sigh. "Welcome back."

"Hey!" Noah smiled as he went past. "Feeling better? We asked about you at dinner."

Shit, Christian, what did you say? "Yeah, I'm fine. Just needed to rest for a while."

"Good." Noah touched his arm, squeezing it, and walked by. "I'm going to start on homework. Come get me if you need anything."

"Sure." Logan gave a half-hearted wave. Daiki sat on the couch and turned on the TV, and Logan took it as an excuse to go to his room, where he immediately resumed the pacing he hated.

There were more things to consider now—the shape of Christian's lips, the agility of his tongue, and the whisper-thin sounds he made as he got close to coming. They occupied him for minutes more until there was an unexpected sound: not the door unlocking, but a knock instead. Logan came to his doorframe, then froze when Daiki opened the front door and revealed Kelly Anne.

She fixed Logan with a gaze sharp enough to slice him open and lifted her chin. "I left my Spanish textbook here a few days ago."

He couldn't meet her eyes. Running from the scene of their breakup and going straight into Christian's bed hadn't been his plan. But everything she'd accused him of, like selfishness and a desire to cheat, was far too real.

He'd done exactly what she predicted. She'd been right all along.

He found the textbook, turning red when he located it beneath one of Christian's shirts on the floor, and brought it to her. From the doorway she hadn't moved from, she took the book wordlessly and left, and Logan wallowed for a few seconds in his own pain before shutting the door behind her.

"What's eating her?" Daiki piped up.

"Nothing." The word was sand on his tongue. His mouth was gritty and his mind frustrated with how he couldn't open up to anyone about what happened—no one except Christian. Kelly Anne had filled Logan with an inescapable shame, and he was bound to overflow eventually.

Daiki tipped his head upside down over the back of the couch, staring at Logan. "She didn't wanna stick around?"

"She's not gonna be around anymore, man," Logan said with a huff. "We broke up today."

"Seriously?" Daiki scrambled for the remote and turned off the TV. "Didn't you guys get together, not that long ago?"

"Yeah, well, shit happens." Logan took quick steps toward his room. If he didn't cut off the conversation now...

"What happened?"

Logan stopped on a dime. He closed his eyes, his back to Daiki, and took a deep breath. "She thinks me and Christian are...too close."

Daiki scoffed. "Come on; he's your best friend. Is she one of those people who gets jealous and tries to get in the middle?"

"No, she thinks we're..." *Please don't notice how bad I am at not telling the whole truth.* "She thinks we wanna fuck."

There were a few moments of quiet before Daiki burst out laughing. When Logan whipped around, Daiki held up both hands and shook his head. "Okay, so?"

Logan opened his mouth and then closed it again. That was the last thing he expected to hear. "No, I mean, she says..." The truth was right on his tongue, and he bit it back. "She's afraid if I was bi or something, it'd only be a matter of time before I cheated on her with a guy."

All humor faded from Daiki's expression. Instantly, he turned cold, eyes unblinking on Logan's face. "She did *not* say that."

"She did." Logan shrugged. Given how confident she'd been when she spoke, he could only assume the statement was a tried and true fact—but Daiki was visibly furious, and Logan took a step away. "You okay?"

"I should give her a piece of my mind." Daiki came to his feet and raked a hand through his hair. "We *both* should. We should TP her dorm, break her favorite heels..." As Daiki's gaze settled on Logan's, he paused. "You didn't believe her, did you?"

Was she wrong? Logan blinked, unsure how to respond.

"Or did you *already* believe it before she said anything?"

The steely tone of Daiki's voice made Logan immediately begin shaking his head. "No, I-I just assumed she knew what she was talking about. I...man, I've never been close with anybody who was bi."

"You are, though." Daiki crossed his arms. "You live with me."

Oh. Logan exhaled quickly.

"And I'm here to tell you that what she said was fucked up." Daiki shook his finger at Logan like an angry mother, his other hand on his hip. "That's a disgusting misconception, and I *hate* it. Just because I like genders the same as me *and* different from me doesn't mean I'm going to go off and cheat on somebody! It doesn't make me *selfish*! It makes me a goddamn human being!" He jabbed a finger at the door. "She's just as likely to cheat on somebody as I am! God!" He collapsed on the couch and rubbed his face, groaning. "Logan, people are so gross sometimes."

Logan couldn't stop staring at him. Wordless applause came from Noah in his bedroom, making Logan wonder if this was another fundamental lesson everyone learned—something he missed growing up where he did. "So, she was wrong?" he asked softly.

Daiki dropped his arms on either side of him and nodded. "She gave you the most popular excuse in the book—and the worst one too. We hear it all the time, and it's wrong. *She's* wrong."

She's wrong. Logan nodded. He hugged his stomach and hung his head, processing the information. Nothing was wrong with him if he *was* bi. He knew and trusted somebody else that was—and they were telling him to his face that everything Kelly Anne said was a lie.

Maybe it was silly, but Logan was more inclined to believe the actual bisexual man in front of him than a girl who tried to tear him down.

Thank you. He couldn't bring himself to say the words, but the gratitude rattled in his bones. He swallowed hard and searched for something less awkward—less *revealing*—to say but was only fixated on one other thing. "Didn't you used to be a shy, nervous kid the first week I knew you? Who's this asshole yelling the roof off the dorm?"

Daiki returned instantly to warmth, flashing all his teeth as he threw his head back and laughed. "Freshman jitters. I had to relax around you first. Now you're stuck with loud, opinionated me."

"You're a force of nature, Daiki." Logan couldn't help but smile back.

Daiki shot him a pair of finger guns.

Logan relaxed afterward. He went in his bedroom and began homework without a second thought, and it wasn't until Christian arrived halfway through the assignment that Logan remembered he was nervous in the first place. "Hey," he said, putting his notebook aside.

Christian brightened. "Hey. Hard at work?"

"One of us has to be, right?" Logan teased.

Christian snorted. He shut the bedroom door and removed his shorts, but before Logan could stare and wonder what he was intending, Christian pulled on a pair of pajama pants. "Mind if I join you? I've got a hell of a lot of reading to catch up on."

"Sure."

"Cool." Christian sat on the bottom bunk with a textbook and flipped it open, angling so his back was against the wall beside Logan's desk. When Logan stared for a few seconds, Christian glanced up, flashed him a broad grin, and returned to the pages.

Logan expected either to be ignored or for them to transition into something hot and heavy—but this was a good compromise. The physical closeness of Christian and the comfortable silence meshed into a fonder version of how they often treated each other.

It gave Logan time to adjust to whatever their friendship was now—and he hadn't realized how badly he needed the reassurance.

Logan gave himself three more seconds to drink Christian's profile in, strong and handsome, before he returned to his own homework. It was a good start.

LIFE WENT BACK to normal over the following month. Logan deleted Kelly Anne's number from his phone and changed seats in the class he had with her. Fortune smiled on him when the teacher didn't pair them up for projects. He was polite and learned ahead of time about Christian's dates with Charlotte so he could make himself scarce. He settled into his friendship with Noah and Daiki—driving them where they needed to go, grabbing dinner with them when Christian was busy, and helping them with their homework.

He could almost ignore the weird things.

He and Christian had been changing in the same room for years, but now there was a different weight to it. When Christian came out from the shower with only a towel wrapped around his waist, Logan would only have enough time to track the few droplets dripping down his skin before Christian lost the towel and rooted through his dresser butt naked.

He'd stare at a hickey on Christian's neck until Christian ran his fingers over the mark, as though feeling Logan's gaze.

Being squished on the couch between Christian and the arm of the couch was arguably the worst to normalize, though. There wasn't enough room, and he was never sure where his arms should go. Christian would loop an arm behind his shoulders—to have stretching room—and Logan would realize at the last possible second that he couldn't lean into him. Their thighs would press against each other and Logan would remember the strength of Christian's legs, tight around his hips as he fucked against his cock, his face a storm of intensity.

He could get used to almost anything. But adapting to how his body reacted when they shared space now was more difficult than he anticipated.

Everything was going to come to a head if he didn't pull himself together. They'd have to have a difficult talk. He'd have to pretend he wasn't eager to do everything again. If he couldn't act as though he was just Christian's best friend, eventually it would become a problem.

And I am *just his best friend. Charlotte is his girlfriend. I'm practically his brother. There's no real comparison. They get along perfectly. What's the likelihood he's gonna break up with her when they're such a good match?*

Besides, he didn't know what Charlotte thought about him. He was avoiding her, but what else was he supposed to do? Go shake her hand and thank her for the opportunity to fuck her boyfriend? Like she owned him?

Thinking through all of it was too much sometimes. If he couldn't lay out a logical way to forget little things—like the two dimples on the small of Christian's back or the weight of his lips against Logan's or how curious he was about how their hands would fit together—then there was no game plan. On nights like tonight, he'd sit at his desk staring at his laptop screen while the line cursor of his word processor blinked over and over, waiting for him to finish his essay.

It's no use. Logan blew out a frustrated breath and pushed away from the desk, then got out of his chair and went to the living room. *I'm not doing shit. I've gotta get my mind off this and come back and finish my work later.* He'd stay up all night if he had to.

Daiki and Noah were locked up in their room talking and occasionally laughing. Christian was watching some soccer game on TV, and though Logan didn't have a huge heart for sports, he understood enough of the game to drop onto the couch with a huff.

"What's up?" Christian got up. "I'm getting a soda. Want one?"

"Sure." Logan laced his arms behind his neck and slouched, putting his feet on the coffee table. "Essays suck ass, man."

"I bet." The fridge opened, then clicked shut, and Logan told himself to keep his eyes pinned to the TV. He failed. As Christian crossed the room, his lean hips cutting through the air and his broad shoulders swaying, Logan glanced up and stared, taking him in from head to toe. "Don't suppose you wanna write mine for me either."

"Fuck you."

"Figures." Christian smirked as he sat next to him—*right* next to him, no breathing room, their legs pressed together—and offered him a can. "Get some caffeine in you. We'll knock it out together."

"Yeah." Logan sighed. He hoped Christian read the weary sound as exasperation for his essay and not from Logan trying to forget the desire to bury his face in his neck. "How's the game?"

"Fine. It's halftime."

"Yeah."

Silence. Logan opened his can and took a long drink of the cold soda, welcoming the bubbles that popped down his throat. It was a distraction—something sensory he could focus his attention on—and better than drowning in the heat rolling off his best friend.

"Daiki and Noah seem busy," Logan finally offered.

"Yeah."

"Wonder what they're doing."

"Group project. Won't be out for a while."

The lilt of his sentence peaked Logan's interest, and he shifted, not sure if he wanted to press closer to Christian or move away. "Oh."

The announcers continued their discussion of the game proceedings. Logan started to regret the soda as his adrenaline kicked in with every second of sitting quietly with Christian.

This used to be easy. I used to know nothing was going to happen. I didn't even think about it. And now I'm being desperate as hell. He took a deep breath and let it out carefully, resting his soda on his leg, letting the condensation soak through the thin material of his jogging shorts. *Nothing's gonna happen. You need to learn to live with him again like this. If he's not getting married right out of college, you two are probably gonna share an apartment. And nothing's gonna—*

Christian put his hand on Logan's thigh. "Can I ask you something?"

Oh my God. Logan jolted, a little soda splattering out of the can and landing on his leg. He was both horrified and desperate for the hand on his leg to move. "Yeah?" His voice cracked once, and he cleared his throat. "Yeah, man, what's up?" *Better. Perfectly normal.*

Christian didn't move away—evidence to support it perhaps wasn't a mistake that he'd grabbed so high up on his leg his knuckles were about to start playing a tiny xylophone on his balls. "I've just been thinking about..." He paused and then gently squeezed his thigh. "Do you mind my hand being here?"

"Nope!" Logan's cheeks flamed. "No, dude, that's fine, uh, what's up, brother?"

Christian quirked his brow. Logan bet he could practically read his face—*man, dude, brother, really?* But Christian only ran his thumb over the outer edge of his thigh, barely more than a tease. "So you remember that thing we did, right? The messing around thing."

Logan nodded quickly, on the verge of being frantic. "Yeah, that night, that, that was a night, you're right." *Being fucking smooth as silk here.*

"I wanted to know if you wanted it to happen again."

He made the statement sound so simple. Christian could lay out an invitation to fuck as though he was asking if he wanted to go four-wheeling. As though there wasn't anything weird about asking.

Christian coughed. "'Cuz I know I really enjoyed it, personally. I guess if you didn't have such a good time, then we don't—"

"I enjoyed it," Logan blurted.

Christian leaned forward until he could lock gazes with Logan—as though he didn't care that Logan was trying to avoid his eyes. "Oh, yeah?"

"Yeah." Logan leaned forward too, putting his soda safely out of reach. "Is, uh... What does Charlotte think about it, though? I don't wanna do anything to mess up a good thing."

Christian chuckled. "You couldn't if you tried. She's cool with it. We've been talking about not exactly being exclusive—that sort of thing."

Logan stared at him, eyes widening. "Why?"

"Well..." Christian scratched his neck, wincing as if Logan was quizzing him on physics and not on a simple conversation he'd had with his girlfriend. "...you know, sometimes, people just wanna have fun, even if what they do looks a little different."

Fun. Christian had drawn a line in the sand, and the casualness of what he wanted stung Logan, grateful as he was. He knew where they stood now. What this could be and where they couldn't go any further. Fucking was fun, and that was all it was.

"I don't know. I wanted to ask if you'd be interested." Christian shook his head and laughed again, glancing at Noah and Daiki's door before he leaned closer and dropped his voice. "She, uh, got us some lube and condoms and..."

Charlotte, you are my favorite person ever.

"...I don't know, dumb shit like that. So if you ever wanted...?"

Logan made himself nod with as neutral an expression as he could. "Then we could...?"

"Yeah."

Make it look as if you're thinking about your decision real hard, man. Don't be too eager. Don't get too excited. Be cool. "So, if I wanted to...right now."

Christian squeezed his thigh again, his fingers inching higher on the sensitive inner edge. "I mean, not everything *right* now."

Disappointment struck him. "No?"

"No, I, uh, I meant to grab some lube when I was with her last time, but I forgot, so..."

Logan stared. Christian stared back. And every bit of coolness Logan had was neatly bundled up and tossed out the window. He started to stand.

"Wait, where're you going?"

"We're going on a field trip to Charlotte's to get the lube," he said very calmly.

Christian pulled him back down. Logan landed awkwardly, legs splayed out, half sitting and half lying, and Christian put one hand on his thigh and the other on his waist. "There's other things we can do, you know."

His heart was going to explode in his chest. "Y-yeah?"

"Yeah." Christian glanced over his shoulder one more time before moving his hand, dragging it up Logan's leg and pressing against his crotch, lighting him aflame. "Lots of them."

Logan whimpered and slapped a hand across his mouth to hide a shaky groan. *Okay. Okay, this is happening.* As Christian leaned down and left three hot kisses on his neck, his knee pressing between his legs, Logan gave up all hope of not seeming overeager.

He wrapped his arms around Christian's shoulders and shivered, eyes falling shut as he ground against the leg teasing at his balls and cock. Christian must've liked his reaction—he grabbed Logan by the hips and pulled him down to lie flat on the couch.

"Noah, Daiki," Logan whispered in panic as Christian laved his tongue over his Adam's apple. "Th-they could—"

"They're not going anywhere." Christian's voice was deep in his chest, a beautiful timbre that only stoked the flames building in Logan. "And neither are you, baby."

Logan grabbed him behind the neck and pulled him to kiss, letting out a weak moan against his lips.

He didn't know what it was about Christian that made him like this. Maybe it was because he was young and experiencing things he'd never done before. Maybe it was something intrinsic that made him react to the pheromones stirring in the air. Maybe it was simple lust. Either way, he rode Christian's thigh with desperation, fucking the thick muscle hard and fast, pushing past the ache of chafing for the chance to tease Christian's tongue with his own.

Christian's hands slid under Logan's shirt, and he gasped, breaking the kiss, a frisson of sparks crackling over his body. "Gonna come fast, man."

"No, you aren't," Christian growled, pulling away so suddenly Logan whined and covered his eyes. "Stop that." He left Logan's body for only a second before he thudded to his knees on the floor. He held Logan's waist and turned him so he could kneel between his thighs as they faced each other. "Gonna take care of you. Gonna let you come when I'm ready."

"Yeah?" Logan caught a glimpse of Christian leaning forward as he pulled his shorts and boxers down. "Are you...holy shit, *Christian*..."

Christian licked the precum off the head of his cock, then took him in his mouth effortlessly—as if he'd fucking done it before, the bastard—and glanced up at him as he bobbed his head languidly, inch by inch.

Logan cupped Christian's face, keeping his touch as gentle as he could. He was used to girls whose hair he could play with, but Christian's was trimmed short, barely a fuzz against his palms. It made him all the more careful not to grab him or force him down—only to knit his fingers behind his head and let his arms go slack so Christian could keep whatever pace he wanted.

Giving into the slow tempo didn't matter, really. Seeing how Christian's full lips fit around his cock, how inexpertly he took him halfway down his shaft, was enough to make Logan's balls tighten.

"Can I come?" He'd never asked permission before, and his voice trembled—he was past the point of no return, and there was no stopping even if Christian said no.

He didn't pull off like Logan expected. Instead, he rubbed his balls between his fingers and went down an inch more, eyelashes fluttering, and Logan was gone, coming in his mouth and biting the back of his arm to muffle his inarticulate curses.

Nothing about this night made sense. That was why he wasn't surprised when Christian leaned up and kissed him, the taste of his own cock still on his tongue.

Logan blinked up at him. "I taste disgusting."

"I mean..."

"I taste *disgusting*."

Christian chuckled. "Okay, yeah, you do a little, but it's fine."

"I-I can't believe you *did* that."

Christian shrugged, his eyelids drooping, a sexy smirk on his lips. "I always go above and beyond, man, c'mon."

That was a challenge if Logan ever heard one. He glanced down, taking in the sight of Christian hard in his pants, and then tilted his head to the side to look around him.

"What're you doing?"

Well, since they're still not coming out... Logan slid his hand down Christian's shorts and grabbed his cock.

Christian's hands trembled against the couch on either side of Logan's hands. "Fuck," he whispered, his voice quaking at the edges.

It was a power surge, knowing he could take someone like Christian—popular, talented, athletic, handsome—and have him trembling from one touch of his hand.

Christian had always won in any physical battle with Logan. *Always.* If Logan ever got the better of him, it was more a stalemate than a true success—but he could make up for all the losses right now by learning the feel of him in his hand.

Not very different. Not strange, in comparison to his own dick, but a new and awkward angle to jerk him off from. He peeled the waistband of Christian's basketball shorts down little by little, until he could get a look at him, and licked his lips, watching how he reacted to those slow, subtle tugs.

Christian hung his head, biting his bottom lip hard enough that it turned white around the edges of his teeth. A rough sigh slipped free. His knees shook, knobby and weak.

All from just a little touch. What'll he look like when he fucks me?

It was going to happen. There was no pretending it wouldn't now. No matter what he needed to do, Logan would get his hands on that lube and those condoms, and he wouldn't rest until he'd been fucked. What was there to be afraid of? Girls did it all the time. Hell, *other guys* did it all the time. He'd never heard any complaints.

Besides, there was something incredibly tempting about finally winning over Christian—rocking down on his cock with Logan's hands pressing down on his chest to keep him still and making him beg to come.

It was a new power move, and the mere idea made his mouth water.

He tugged at Christian's cock, abandoning his slow tease. "You like that?" Logan breathed, flicking his eyes up. "That feel good?"

"Fuck…" Christian groaned the word beautifully, color spreading down his neck. "Yeah, don't, don't stop…"

"Not gonna." He grinned, every cell in his body vibrating from his blowjob.

Christian had made them both come. Now it was Logan's turn.

He slid his leg out farther, pressing it warmly against Christian's, and the little bit of connection grounded him like a handhold. They were together in this. Nerve-wracking and new the experience might be, but they were both 100 percent present and focused—no pretending someone else was touching them. No acting like Charlotte was sliding this simple pleasure through his veins. It was intoxicating.

"Next time, you'll fuck me."

Christian banged his fist against the couch once in that little way he had—burning off energy when he was feeling overwhelmed. "Logan—"

"You'll fuck me so good. I'm gonna be tight as hell around your cock, dude."

Christian's mouth fell open, and he tipped his head back, eyelashes fluttering against his cheeks as he gasped. "You'd really let me have that? You want me that bad?"

"Oh yeah," Logan growled. "Yeah, I fucking want you, Christian."

"Shit!" He hissed the word as he came in Logan's hand, spraying across his shirt and dripping down his forearm and wrist—a searing hot mark that was claiming, somehow, as if the two of them were still rutting for dominance.

But are we, really? Or are we both figuring it out together?

Christian didn't let him linger. He pushed Logan's hand away with a mumbled apology and yanked his shorts up as he peered over his shoulder. Noah and Daiki's door stayed shut, not a sound to be heard. He stood tall, legs visibly shaky, and chuckled. "I made a fucking mess, holy shit."

"Asshole." Logan held out his hand. "You like the taste of jizz so much, motherfucker, you clean it up."

Christian gaped at him, eyes wide open at the challenge, before he laughed again and shook his head. He cupped Logan's forearm and dragged his tongue over his skin, licking up a thick line of his release.

Something in Logan's head fizzled and went out, leaving him stammering, and Christian patted his cheek— almost a slap—before he pulled away. "Hey!"

"Clean up the rest yourself." Christian tossed the words over his shoulder, as though he hadn't eaten his own jizz without a word of complaint. "Cover yourself up, asshole."

Logan dropped his head and then swore under his breath as he pulled his boxers and shorts back up. He took a long look at his relaxed body from head to toe and followed Christian.

He waited until he'd shut the door behind him to speak up. "Are you forgetting about the game?"

Christian jolted and then immediately started making his bed. That was suspicious in and of itself—Christian didn't believe in making his bed. "I mean, my team was losing, so—"

"Which team was that?"

Three seconds ticked by before he replied. "I mean, the, uh, the team was..."

He doesn't know who was playing. Logan moved until he could see Christian's profile. "You were sitting out there for...what?"

"Nothing." Christian picked up the pile of clothes on the floor and walked to the laundry basket. "The game."

"Okay, either you're sick or possessed or lying to me, because I don't think you've done laundry once in your whole damn life." Logan picked up a shirt from the top of the pile and wiped his arm off to try to get a rise out of him. None came. "Were you waiting to make what just happened...happen?"

Christian dropped the clothes in the basket. "What do you want me to say, man?"

Logan stood directly in front of him. "The truth."

Christian stared at him. When he reached out, his fingers delicately trailed over Logan's face, as gentle as a breeze. He cupped his cheek and leaned down to kiss him, quick and fleeting, then pulled back as if he hadn't taken Logan's breath away—as if staying close enough that Logan could see every individual eyelash didn't make his heart stop. "You've got homework to do, man."

Goddamn refractory periods. Logan huffed. "I hate homework."

"Yep." Christian sauntered away, and Logan's eyes lingered on his ass as he went. His concentration was broken when a binder slapped him in the chest. "You've gotta do mine too, so..."

"Fuck you!"

Christian burst out laughing and dropped onto his bed, eyes sparkling. "I'll make you a deal. You come do your homework down here with me on my bed, and I'll do my own shit for once."

Logan frowned. There had to be a catch. But when he didn't get anything but a beguiling stare, he grabbed his textbook and notebook and crawled up next to Christian.

Nothing bad happened. Christian grabbed him by the back of the neck and pushed his head toward his own knees—Logan's eyes fluttered shut at the strength of his fingers and the promising squeeze—and when he eased him back again, there was a pillow behind Logan, between him and the wall. He watched as Christian settled himself in the same position, close enough that their thighs were touching.

"So, you're gonna wear that gross-ass jizzy shirt the whole time we're doing homework, huh?" Christian asked in a soft as satin voice.

Logan pulled the shirt off and tossed it aside. Christian's gaze openly took in his body from neck to feet. "Better?"

He licked his lips. "Yeah."

They settled in a little closer—so that every time Christian turned a page or wrote in his binder, his elbow grazed Logan's bare skin. Oddly enough, it took twice as long for Logan to get his homework done, though he refused to admit to himself why.

Chapter Seven

CHRISTIAN

Charlotte's roommates were saints. Christian didn't know what she told them so they'd be gone long enough for a good fuck every time they saw each other, but they'd never been walked in on, and as far as he knew, the girls didn't complain either. It made for these idyllic moments after, when they were naked and catching their breath, when Charlotte would snuggle against his bare chest and pull the sheets up with her toes so they were both warm.

It was nice, especially since they didn't get to see each other much anymore. He wasn't sure what was taking the most time in his life—soccer practice, homework, or hanging out with Logan—but either way, he spent more time missing her and not enough remedying it.

Weekend afternoons like this were nice, though. He had to get ready for a game tomorrow, and that meant finishing all of his homework tonight. But for now? Being able to rest here and remember every wonderful thing about her? He was content. He could pretend the next hour would stretch out forever.

He caressed her arm, unhurriedly rubbing her sweet-smelling skin, and when he glanced down to see if she was starting to fall asleep his eyes caught the tattoo on her arm. It seemed strange, somehow, that the mark on her skin didn't have texture. It always seemed as though the image should be rough under his fingers.

Christian traced the smooth lines with his fingers. "Can I ask you something?"

"Sure, baby." She sounded exhausted, but she opened her eyes and smiled at him.

He pressed his thumb against her tattoo in significance. "You said we'd talk about this. The whole... what did you call it, ethical monogamy?"

"Nonmonogamy." She grinned and stretched with a squeak. "Ethical nonmonogamy. Pretty much the opposite of monogamy."

He quirked a brow. "You saying that monogamy isn't ethical?"

"I'm saying that when I see less marriages and relationships end because of cheating, I'll give it another thought." She rolled onto her stomach, her curls springing out when she shook her head, and then held her arm out so he could see the tattoo better. "So, you've got these two hearts connected to each other, right? Overlapping. And then you've got the infinity symbol on top of them as well. Basically, a secret code about how I've got the capacity to love multiple people."

Christian frowned. "We've all got that capacity, don't we? That's how cheating happens."

She shrugged. "I've met people who can only have feelings for one person at a time. Whether that's their choice or something genetically encoded, I can't really say, but I know I've always been nonmonogamous. If you could read my diary when I was seven, I had a list in there of the reasons I had a crush on every single boy in my class." She paused. "A couple of girls too. But that realization came later."

He chuckled. "All right, so you were a lovestruck seven-year-old. Was that when you knew?"

"Nah. Not so simple." She sighed and rested her chin on her forearms. Her gaze became distant. "I guess I was in high school when I really started figuring it out. My sophomore year, me and my best friend liked this guy, and we joked around about having a competition to see which one of us he might like. She ended up being the one who got asked out, but I remember teasing her about sharing him. And though I was kidding, I couldn't stop thinking about the whole thing. I went to bed thinking about our schedules. I had weekly volunteer sessions at the local science museum twice a week, and she had volleyball practice on the weekends. It occurred to me that we could both have dates with him—she could see him on Tuesday and Thursday nights, and I could see him on the weekends—and we'd each get our fair share of time. She and I could even still hang out together on Mondays and Wednesdays to do our homework."

He fanned his hand over her hair, pushing it out of her face so he could trace the shape of her profile. "Always a planner."

"You know me. Obviously, it didn't work out that way. I tried to explain my thoughts to her the next day, as a joke, and she got so pissed at me that I didn't bring it up again, but...it made sense. If we liked him and if he liked both of us, then there wasn't any real reason why we couldn't both have a relationship with him. And when I couldn't stop thinking about it, I did some Googling, and what do you know? There were other people like me. They called themselves polyamorous, and I failed a test the next day because I stayed up until four in the morning reading every blog post and article I could get my hands on."

What she described was a whole new world, one filled with vocabulary he didn't recognize, but getting a peek inside it was warm and welcome. It was like having a veil lifted to a secret part she didn't show many others. He appreciated her openness. "But you call it ethical nonmonogamy, not polyamory?"

"That came later. See, there's this whole world of lifestyles that fit under the ethical nonmonogamy banner. It's just what it sounds like: people choosing to live in a nonmonogamous way but doing it ethically. No cheating. Everybody is aware that their partner is interested in other people or going on dates or being in another relationship or having one-night stands. It's not a big deal, and it's not a secret. No one's doing anything wrong as long as everybody agrees they're okay." She studied him. "You still with me?"

"I feel like I'm in a calculus class, but I'm managing."

She laughed and put an arm around his waist, snuggling close. "You're doing good. Anyway, being polyamorous is having a focus on beginning new romantic relationships with other people, especially ones that will last for a significant period of time. Not everybody wants to do that. There's swingers, for example—"

"Goddamn, finally something I know about!" He beamed.

"Good for you!" She kissed him in reward, and when he pretended to swoon, she chuckled and rubbed his side. "So, swingers are a couple who'll have sex with other people, but their time together is typically not gonna become romantic, and the sex mostly involves the couple together rather than apart. And then there's relationship anarchy, which is when people don't assign a term to any relationship they're in—no girlfriends, no boyfriends, no friends with benefits. It helps them keep from assigning expectations to things, and they're able to have a flexible experience with everyone they meet. Really freeing lifestyle."

The second the terms started flying around, Christian felt as if he should be taking notes, but he nodded anyway. She described things he didn't know existed, yet in such a clear way, he couldn't help but feel like he'd known about them all along. Wasn't that the way guys always pretended they wanted to live? Being able to flirt with whatever girl they wanted without their own girl getting mad?

He tossed the concept around in his head—seeing Charlotte flirt with and dance up on some other guy at a party—but the way the image came together in his mind was strange. Sure, she was dancing with some faceless guy and letting him put his hands all over her, but when he pulled the picture away, little by little, he saw *himself* sitting on a couch with his arm around Logan.

Whatever that meant, he didn't feel like analyzing the image too hard, especially since he wasn't sure this impromptu lecture was over yet. He rubbed their noses together and kissed the tip of hers. "So, which one of those do you identify as?"

She wrinkled her nose in thought. "I mean, for a while, I identified as solo poly—oh, that's when someone doesn't have one primary relationship, but has a lot of relationships they're involved in."

"Primary?"

"Primary, like, uh..." She rubbed his side. "You'd be my primary partner, I guess. If I ever got married, my spouse would probably be a primary partner. Basically, it's the person you spend the most time with and who has the most influence over how you spend your time. If I got married, I'd probably spend more than half of my time with my spouse rather than with another partner simply because we'd be living together, and our finances and futures would be more intertwined."

A little burst of pride popped in Christian's chest. "So, I'm that primary, huh?"

"For now." She flicked his side, and he feigned dramatic pain to amuse her. "I don't know, man, you caught me without me realizing it was gonna happen. I wanted something with you, no matter how it ended. The thought made me happy."

"You make me happy too."

Her smile softened. Though Christian hadn't let himself think of a future with her yet—it was all still too new, too soon—he warmed to how she already considered him so important in her life. "And Logan makes you happy?"

That was a different can of worms, one he kept pushing further and further away so he didn't have to see what was inside. "I mean, he's a piece of shit sometimes, but he's cool."

She laughed. "Cool like I'm cool?"

The discussion had taken a sudden turn, and he wasn't sure he liked where it was going. He narrowed his eyes in suspicion. "Just cool."

"Okay." She rolled her eyes. "I'm only trying to figure out how you identify is all. Monogamous? Nonmonogamous? What's it all mean to you, man?"

"I mean, before I met you, I didn't know there was a way to live besides having one partner. I don't know if I've had enough time to really figure out what I am, but..." He forced himself to think of the same mental image—Logan under his arm, Christian giving Charlotte a thumbs-up from across the room when she was going in for a kiss with a faceless party guy. "...I mean, I'm not mad at the idea of you seeing somebody else. As long as you have time for me."

She heaved a sigh and traced her fingers down his chest, her gaze going unfocused again. Something was clearly on her mind, and he wished he could reach inside and pull the thought out so she wouldn't have to be so careful where she put her feet, walking through this conversation. "Time's a big factor. You're right. That's the whole reason I wanted to be solo poly in the first place—being able to make my own decisions about how often I saw my partners. You end up feeling as though you're neglecting somebody."

He touched her cheek. "Do *you* feel like that? Is...is there somebody else you've been wanting to spend more time with?"

"No, that's not it."

"Then where did this come from?"

She blinked, and a slow smile crossed her lips. "Nothing. It's just somewhere my mind went."

"You sure?"

"Yeah. Don't you worry, baby." She pulled him close again. "That was a lot I threw at you. You got any questions or anything?"

He needed time to digest everything, for sure. Maybe things would come to him later, but not now. Not when he only had a precious forty-five minutes left to hold her close before he had to be a productive adult. "Can I let you know if I have questions later?"

"Absolutely. What about a little nap?"

Christian groaned and kissed the top of her head, wrapping his arms around her so there wasn't a breath of air between them. "God, you have the best ideas."

She giggled. "Yeah...yeah, I guess I do sometimes."

"HEY THERE!"

"Hey, Mom." Logan sat on the bench outside his dorm and settled in for a long chat. His mother was nothing short of wordy. "How're you?"

"I'm good! It's about time I heard from you. I was starting to think you were dead."

He rolled his eyes. Though her tone was teasing, an underlying passive aggressiveness lingered. "Weirdly enough, college is busier than high school. Who knew, right?"

"Well, I bet your roommates find time to call their parents, don't they?"

Daiki talked to his family three times a week. Was it because he was a dutiful son? Or did they guilt him into calling too? *Or does he actually like talking to them?* "Ha. How's work?"

"Fine. Slow right now. But flu season is starting up, you know—have you gotten your vaccine?"

Going from talking about corpses to his own life would've been dizzying for most other people. Not Logan. "Yeah, Christian and I got ours two days ago at the campus clinic."

"Good. Can't imagine how his family would be able to pay for his hospital stay if he caught it, bless their hearts."

And so the conversation slid into its usual territory. Logan stared at his new sneakers—bought a week ago with the money his parents transferred to his bank account— and thought of the holes he saw in almost all of Christian's socks. "I'd help him out."

"Oh, you're sweet, but that's not your job."

"Mom—"

"He has to learn how to take care of himself sometime. How's your girlfriend? What was her name? Kelly?"

Finally, just hearing her name didn't hurt his chest anymore. He leaned forward and rubbed his eyes. "I broke up with her, like, two months ago, Mom, remember?"

"Oh, right!"

There were reasons he didn't call home. Monthly phone calls were about all he could manage, and he tried to make them as short as possible. There was inherent judgment in everything his mom said. His dad barely tried to hold a conversation with him, whether he was watching a game or taking care of the pharmacy or milling around doing nothing. It was like pulling teeth to connect to him. And his mom? She didn't know anything about Logan.

She couldn't. He wouldn't risk her hearing his secrets. Not with how eager she was to tear down Christian's family—even if he *was* his best friend.

"And the other girl Christian's seeing?"

"Charlotte."

"Right, that's her name. I guess they're still an item?"

Yesterday, he'd caught Christian coming into their room to change his shirt and spritz on cologne, flowers in hand. "Yeah, they're fine."

"Wedding bells, you think? An elopement before he comes home?"

"Jesus, Mom, it's been like three months."

"Well, he's always moved fast, sniffing up those trees. Won't be long before he's moving on and starting a family!" She chuckled. "We'll have to put an ad in the paper to find you a new best friend—I don't think I've ever seen you two apart."

Oh, fuck you. "He's not gonna stop being my best friend when he gets married—"

"He won't exactly have time, sweetie. I know you like him a lot, but it's natural for friends to drift apart when they start new lives."

"It's not gonna happen!" Logan snapped. He refused to think about their friendship ending. He had enough nightmares about Christian waking up and realizing he deserved better—or that he was outright tired of kissing Logan in the first place.

But it had to happen, didn't it? Eventually, they'd get married. And it wasn't as if they could do any messing around then. They'd have kids. They'd have new couple friends. What would people say if they saw them together?

"Don't you take that tone with me, Logan Brown."

"Just...just stop. Charlotte's great. She's really nice to me." His cheeks flushed. "She never tries to keep me and Christian from...hanging out. Okay?" *If only you knew the truth. You'd piss your pants.*

"Well, every girl's nice in the beginning. I was nice to your dad's friends too. But things change. And if a wife can't know for sure that she's the first thing on her husband's priority list..."

He couldn't keep doing this. He checked his watch. Five minutes. That was enough. He was done. "Mom, I've gotta go."

"What? We only just started—"

"Homework. Love you. Tell Dad hi." He hung up.

The phone vibrated in his hand immediately as she called again, and he silenced it.

Logan leaned forward, elbows on his knees, and dragged his fingers through his hair. He couldn't stand this tension. Couldn't stand his family. They were his— they'd chosen him when he was a baby, before he knew what adoption was—but there were days he wished they'd picked anybody but him.

But then he wouldn't have met Christian. His life would've never taken the path it did.

Things happen for a reason. And they love you. And you have to love them back. Even when Mom's being a bitch.

He took a deep breath and centered himself. Then he stood and made his way into the dorm, where he could put the entire talk behind him.

THEY HAD A nightly ritual now—one that Christian looked forward to—working on homework in his bed with Logan. Though they hadn't had sex since their stolen few minutes on the couch, they got away with accidental contact here and there: their thighs squished together, one of them not wearing a shirt while he did laundry so he could feel the teasing brush of the other's arm, or one of them slouching so low they could get away with resting their head on the other's shoulder for a few seconds.

They were playing a game, seeing which of them was going to crack first. It didn't matter that there wasn't a reason to hold out. Neither of them could get in trouble— they were adults, and he had permission from Charlotte to touch as much as they wanted, and they were living on a thriving queer campus in a liberal town. But they'd never done things easily. They waited things out, whether it was a discussion or getting ready for an event like prom or completing their college applications. They waited until they were *both* ready to do something.

And besides, it was more exciting to see how long they took to break.

Eventually, they might fuck. Eventually, they'd touch and kiss and learn what the other person liked. But until then, they could thrive on the thrumming energy right beneath their skin every time one of them "accidentally" brushed against the other's stomach.

During one of those homework sessions, Christian's phone buzzed. He glanced at the screen.

Are you free?

It was a normal enough text from Charlotte, and he replied with an affirmation before returning to his essay.

"Everything okay?" Logan asked.

"Yeah. Just Charlotte." He shrugged. "Think she's gonna stop by for a sec. I need to get away from this essay anyway. Running out of ideas." He glanced over, batting his eyelashes.

Logan didn't look back. "I'm not writing your paper for you."

"Fuck you."

"Yeah, I know you love me, buddy."

Christian rolled his eyes, cheeks flushing as he returned to typing. They didn't speak again—they didn't have to fill every bit of empty space between them, and they hadn't had to for years now. He liked how they weren't afraid of silence. Now, if only he could be more talkative around other people. Logan had spoiled him into keeping his thoughts to himself long ago, especially with how he could practically read his mind.

Christian had gotten barely another paragraph written when there was a knock at the bedroom door. He got up and opened it, leaning down to give Charlotte a quick kiss. "Hey."

"Hey. Hope you don't mind that Daiki let me in."

He glanced up as Daiki scuttled back to his room like a baby turtle. Daiki always seemed to be a little more nervous around Charlotte than the rest of them—as though she was too pretty to be ignored. Christian had pity on him, but not much. "She looks cute today, doesn't she, Daiki?"

His suitemate stopped and gave Charlotte a stare of clear pleading. "Uh—"

"Ignore my fuckface of a boyfriend." Charlotte waved him off, and Daiki melted right before shutting his door.

Christian chuckled as he backed into the bedroom, dodging one of her patented swats at his arm. "Hey, hey!"

"Asshole." She hugged him and then stuck her hand in her pocket. "Hey, I brought the thing you keep talking about."

"What?" He barely got the word out before she'd pulled a fresh unopened bottle of lube out of her pocket. "*Charlotte!*"

"What?"

He snatched the lube away from her, trying to hide it against his stomach as he glanced over his shoulder. Logan was frowning, brow wrinkled, craning his neck and obviously trying to see, and Christian shuffled over a few steps to his dresser before opening a drawer and shoving the bottle in. *Smooth.*

"You're fucking incredible." Charlotte came up on her tiptoes. "I'm sorry about him, Logan."

"Me too!"

"Will you both shut up?" Christian caught Charlotte's hand and interlaced their fingers. "Did you just come here to make fun of me or...?"

"Nah." She grinned. "Wanna go for a walk? Leaves are starting to change. It's gonna be gorgeous."

Anything was better than the two of them making fun of him together. It wasn't fair for a man to be ganged up on like that. It gave him ideas about them ganging up on him in a different way. "Sure. Lemme get my shoes."

As she waited, Charlotte leaned against the doorframe and started talking again. "Looking forward to Thanksgiving break, Logan?"

Christian thought it was sweet of her to make conversation with his best friend. She didn't have to, but something warmed inside him—he'd had enough girlfriends who preferred to pretend Logan didn't exist, like they wanted to take Christian away from him instead.

Logan smiled. "Yeah, it'll be great to get more than, like, two days off."

"You didn't go home for fall break, right?"

He shrugged. "Didn't seem to be much of a point. I had a big essay to finish up. Would've spent all my time in my bedroom anyway."

"Fair enough." Charlotte tilted her head. "Y'know, if you end up staying in town for Thanksgiving, my roommates and I are having a meal at a friend's house. Should be about twenty of us there? There's gonna be a lot of home-cooked food, card games, booze... We'll have a good time."

As soon as Logan began to talk, Christian glanced up from tying his shoes. "We'll have to see, I guess. Christian and I can talk about what we're gonna do and get back to you."

Christian blinked. It was pretty interesting that his best friend would be telling his girlfriend they'd make their decision together—as if Christian hadn't intended to have the discussion with her instead. But before he could say anything, Logan's eyes widened, and he glanced back and forth between them a few times. *Yeah, man, what gives?*

"I-I don't know," Logan finally said with a chuckle. "Uh, *I'll* see. It sounds fun."

Christian stared at him as Logan returned to his essay. "Yeah, uh. Yeah." That sounded like a conversation the both of them needed to have too—but later, maybe, when Charlotte wasn't standing there waiting for him. He stood and grabbed his keys. "Anyway, we'll probably grab something to eat while we're out, right?"

"Maybe." Charlotte peered down at her feet. Perhaps she was embarrassed about the awkwardness in the air too.

"Cool." He tucked his wallet in his pocket and waved at Logan. "Work hard, brother."

"Yep. Have fun."

They held hands as they left the room and headed downstairs, comfortable in their silence until the crisp air hit their cheeks. Christian breathed the cool breeze in.

"Always feels like I'm walking through a whole other world when Fall gets here. Like every door outside is a portal to some new universe or whatever."

"Me too." Charlotte squeezed his hand, then let it go, sliding her hands into the pockets of her hoodie. "My favorite season."

Normally, they'd take a walk around the very edges of campus, letting the sidewalk lead them in a giant square before they ended up in front of Christian's dorm again, where they could cross the street for fast food. But today, Charlotte curved them toward the grounds. The last time they'd spent time there, Charlotte had suggested they mess around with Logan and Kelly Anne again, and the memory made him catch his breath.

She's got something on her mind.

He didn't try to engage her as they walked, but he stared at her profile, brow furrowed, waiting for her to be ready. She didn't seem *upset*, but from the frown she wore, he could tell she wasn't speaking her mind. Something to do with her roommates? A fight she'd had with her family? Trouble with homework? The possibilities were endless. They hadn't yet run into a situation where he had to be her shoulder to cry on—they were still in a very young relationship, more like friends with benefits than romantic lovers with deep, expansive plans—but the prospect made him nervous. *What if I fuck taking care of her up?*

She led him straight toward the gazebo they'd occupied last time, and she sat and flashed him an almost convincing smile. "Sit with me."

He didn't want to, but he made himself do what she asked. When she turned on the bench to face him, his heart began to thud.

"Can I ask you how things are going with Logan?"

Oh shit. A million things ran wild in his mind—she'd brought the lube over, which meant she intended for him to use it, but these last words sounded otherwise. *But she's not manipulative. She's not a bitch. Stop.*

"Uh..." He cleared his throat. "It's going pretty well, I guess."

"You guess?" She grinned. "Not sure?"

"I mean, like..." He shrugged. "We've both been pretty busy. There's been a lot of homework and projects, and I've got my soccer practice, and I've got my dates with you, like... W-we haven't really had time to figure anything else out, I guess."

She hummed in understanding and touched his knee. "I'm sorry you've been so busy."

"It's fine. It's life, right? This is how busy my whole life's gonna be from here on out, and the sooner I start getting used to that, the better." A bird flew by and perched in a nearby tree, shaking the orange leaves and giving him something to focus on. "I mean, I miss hanging out with him without having to do homework at the same time. And I sort of miss being able to go out and get food with my team when I've got a test to study for the next day. But...it's all right, y'know? Things will get easier."

The bird trilled like sunshine breaking through the courtyard, and Christian reached for Charlotte's hand again. She didn't take it. Instead, she stood, knotted her arms behind her head with a sigh, and paced away a few steps.

Oh no. "Everything okay?"

She spun around and beamed at him, but there was a distance in her gaze he didn't recognize. The expression was something he hadn't had time to learn yet. "I hate that you've got so much going on."

Alarm rattled through him. "I mean, I could shift some things around, spend more time with you—"

"Christian..." She breathed a quiet laugh, more regretful than happy.

He stood and held his hands out, and then pulled them away on second thought. He already towered over her; he didn't want her to think... "Listen, I don't need the stuff with Logan, okay? That's fun and whatever, but it's not like..."

She hugged herself now, but to her credit, she didn't back away from him. She wasn't scared of him. She simply looked like she was facing a firing squad—with grim focus and determination and the belief she'd done everything she could leading up to that moment.

"He's my best friend. But that's all. Okay? You're my *girlfriend.*"

Charlotte sighed. "I know. I know I am, but..." She slowly shook her head. "...I don't think he's *just* your best friend."

His palms burned and his legs ached and every bone in his body wanted to run to her and kiss her and keep her from talking, but he couldn't. He was rooted to the ground. "What are you saying?"

"I'm saying—"

"You *told* me to experiment with him, Charlotte." He didn't mean for the reminder to sound as sharp as a knife. "You *told* me to mess around with him and see what happened."

"I know I did." She searched him with open, honest eyes, her smile lingering, and he was at a loss for words. "And I'm proud of you for doing it. I know it wasn't easy with how you grew up, but I really think being with him made you happy, didn't it? Getting to see another side of yourself—and the same side of him, I guess—and knowing at the end of the day that what you did was a *good* thing and not a mistake. That all makes me so happy."

"But?"

"But..." She sighed. "Christian. I like you a lot. But I feel like you're not really getting a chance to figure out what you are with him. I think you're focusing too hard on you and me. And it's such a heteronormative concept, you know? That you need to make sure your relationship with a girl is thriving instead of figuring things out with another guy, and I—"

"You said you were open. You said I could do both."

"And I'm not saying that you shouldn't have." Charlotte came toward him and finally took his hand, squeezing it between both of hers. "I'm saying I want you to have more time to figure out this thing between you and him."

"There's nothing between us." He touched her chin with his other hand, tilting her head back so he could see her face. "Charlotte. There's *nothing*. We're just two guys messing around. He doesn't like me the way I like you."

Her curls bounced when she shook her head. "That's where I think you're wrong. I think he likes you every bit as much as you like him."

"I don't—"

"Don't lie to me." She grinned, flashing her teeth at him like she was about to laugh. "This is something you should be happy about, okay? Why do you keep thinking you have to run from what you feel?"

He dropped his arms to his side. "Because you're about to tell me that I have to make the choice between a relationship with you and a *chance* at a relationship with him."

"Oh no." She took a deep breath. "No, I'm not letting you make the choice. I'm making it for you right now."

There it was. A bullet right through his chest. Something crumpled inside him, something he couldn't articulate. It wasn't like every other breakup he'd had. She'd taken his agency away in a deep betrayal—as though he wasn't strong enough to balance the two of them at the same time.

"You didn't do anything wrong. I promise this isn't a bad thing."

"If I didn't do anything wrong, you wouldn't be breaking up with me."

"Baby." She touched his arms and came in closer, staring up at him. "I'd love to go out with you again when you get this figured out with him."

"You mean when I fuck things up with him too?"

"No. Stop." She gripped his wrists. "You've only ever been monogamous. You've only ever been in a relationship with a girl. And I can see you've got something with him that has the potential to be *incredibly* powerful—but listen to what all you told me. You don't have time for yourself. You don't have time to hang out with your teammates or your other friends. You barely have time for homework. And making you feel like you have to carve out time every week both for me *and* for Logan? Do you know how selfish of me that would be?"

He stared at her hard, trying to make her understand how sincere he was right in this moment. "I could make things work, if you'd let me. I could balance it. I-I could spend time with both of you. You don't have to break up with me to teach me fucking time-management skills, Charlotte, you're not my goddamn mother."

"And I never will be. But I wouldn't forgive myself if I was the reason something fell apart between the two of you. So, I'm taking this opportunity to give you the best chance I can." The smile finally faded away. "Listen, I still wanna be your friend. I still wanna be in your life. And I mean it when I say that when you and Logan figure out what you are to each other, if you're still interested in me, I'm gonna be right here waiting for you. You're a pretty amazing guy. You've treated me better than just about every other man I've ever been with. And if you *don't* want something with me after this...I'll always remember you fondly."

The words struck a chord with him. What did people in his hometown remember him as? That tall black kid? They'd see his name on a plaque touting him as the team's MVP two years in a row, and they'd talk regretfully about how he didn't go out for basketball, but he at least did *something* with his talent. They'd talk about how hard life was for his family, and how Christian had to go off and make something of himself to help them get back on their feet.

And, here, Charlotte was going to remember him for being kind. For being himself.

He heaved a sigh and slouched an inch or two, shoving his hands in his pockets. The realization wasn't enough of a comfort; the anger smoldered on.

Charlotte came up on her tiptoes and brushed a kiss over his jawline, and though it stoked a warmth inside him, he didn't need anything more. He didn't need to sweep her into his arms and kiss the living daylights out of her one last time. It was a simple thing.

And, for a second, he wondered if she really was onto something about the two of them, when every kiss he'd ever given Logan lit him on fire.

"Let's head back," she said. "I'm not really hungry."

"Me neither." He needed time to think about this. Did he even want to be her friend, when she thought she knew so much better than he did? Did he *know* how to just be friends with her? Friends didn't kiss or touch like he had the impulse to do.

You kiss and touch Logan now.

He wasn't ready for his worldview to be challenged like that. He didn't kiss friends, but he kissed Logan. He only fucked his girlfriends, but he was interested in fucking Logan.

Either Logan was more than a friend or Christian needed to rewrite his entire viewpoint about how he treated the friends in his life.

Or both.

The walk was silent. They didn't touch. He spent the whole time with his eyes on the ground, nursing his heart, trying to understand what was going on inside him a little better. The initial pang of being broken up with had already started to wear off as fast as it had every time before, and he had to accept that most of the sting was from his pride. It meant the only thing he had to focus on now was his pull toward something else.

Like the bottle in the drawer in his room.

Charlotte turned to face him when they were outside his dorm. "You gonna be okay?"

"Sure. I'm always okay."

She quirked a brow but didn't say anything to counter his statement—she simply squeezed his arm one more time and started to back away. "I'm serious. Friends. Hit me up if you need to talk about anything, okay? I've been where you're at right now, and you don't have to do that whole thing alone."

Even though you just made me be alone. "Be safe going to your dorm."

"Yep. Have a good night."

"Sure."

He didn't watch her go around the corner. He'd watched her disappear too many times to do it tonight.

As he climbed the stairs, taking them two at a time with a dizzying fervor building up inside him, he focused his thoughts on Logan. How would he explain this to him? How would he let him know exactly why he and Charlotte had broken up with absolutely no warning? And that it all had to do with Logan himself?

Christian stopped with his hand on the doorknob. He could taste his heart so far up his throat that it was on the back of his tongue. The knob shook with his touch.

How can I show him that he isn't a rebound?

Christian thought he heard a sound inside the door, and he stumbled back a few steps and started toward the staircase. He couldn't do this. Not right now. Charlotte could be wrong. It could be a terrible deal to make. It could be the worst decision he'd ever made, especially if it was going to alter their friendship forever.

So, he returned to the chilled air, welcoming the coolness of the night starting to fall, and walked with no expectation or destination, happy enough to let his feet take him all the way to the ocean if they wanted.

THE SECOND THE front door shut behind Christian and Charlotte, Logan was staring at the cabinet. Christian didn't keep secrets—he sucked at hiding Christmas presents longer than two days after he'd bought them. He was a giving and caring sort of guy who couldn't afford to do much for his friends, so when he had the chance to give them something, he did.

Embarrassment wasn't a huge factor either. They'd described their worst shits to each other in excruciating detail. They'd been together the first time they both puked from drinking too much. They'd recounted their sexual experiences as young teenagers over and over again without any embellishment.

Which meant there were very few secrets that could be in that drawer. And he had a feeling he knew exactly what was inside.

When he was certain they wouldn't be coming back, Logan slid off his bed and went to investigate. *Best friends don't snoop.* But he reached to open the drawer.

Just a tiny peek...

The peek wasn't enough. As soon as he saw the bottle, wrapped in a thin layer of plastic, his heart froze. He pulled the bottle out and turned it over, and sure enough, it was lube.

Newly bought too, not one he'd used with Charlotte. There was a certain charm in knowing Christian wanted this first experience they'd have together to be something fresh. Logan would be the only person on his mind when he opened this.

Shit, I'm already a little hard. He exhaled shakily and put the bottle back, shut the drawer, and leaned into the cabinet for a long moment.

He didn't need to rush Christian. There was a reason Christian hadn't gotten the lube sooner. Charlotte brought it, which probably meant fucking Logan hadn't been very high on Christian's priority list, but...

But what if it is? What if he was just nervous?

If there was anything Logan was good at, it was keeping things tidy. Making sure he had a clean environment was a way to burn off steam when he was stressed, and a way to keep the tension low on other days. Christian? Not so much. Christian's sheets hadn't been washed since they'd moved in. His desk was a mess. He had papers all over the floor that had been graded and forgotten.

Living in the middle of this was too much. And cleaning provided the perfect distraction. Logan couldn't work on homework even if he tried.

As he started stacking Christian's papers on his bed—rows by class, stacks by the months written on the top margin of the page—his thoughts began to lull. He didn't think about Charlotte giving Christian such a sincere blessing to play around with Logan that she *teased* him about bringing the lube. He didn't think about lingering touches from his best friend possibly turning into something more. He didn't think about the potential of Thanksgiving break and how Christian would relate to him at Greenbarrow—if they'd seem more than friends or if they'd be more relaxed with each other than ever.

Goddammit, you are *thinking.*

While sorting Christian's clothes, his thoughts reached a peak level of manic. Neither of them called their families much, not since arriving at FSU. And if they both went home for the break and something was different, would their parents reject it outright? Would they assume their being together was the reason they'd been so out of contact? That they were actually bad for each other? That they needed to be stopped? Would their families stand between them and force them to stay apart like when they'd ground them as kids? Could they still do that now that they were adults in college and only coming home for a week?

And what if nothing happened between him and Christian? What if he'd had his fun? Or what if he only fucked him once and decided he didn't like it? That he didn't like *him*?

The force of that last thought made him sit square on the floor, breathing too hard.

This isn't about him liking you. What do you think this is, middle school? This isn't about goddamn tingly feelings and love notes with checkboxes. This is about the two of you fucking around because it feels good, and you've never gotten to do it before. Don't make this more than it is. Don't scare him off.

Giving up on cleaning, he crawled onto his top bunk, sat on the edge, and stared at the floor far below him.

You're overthinking. You know this won't ever be more than it is right now. So, shut the fuck up and enjoy it.

Logan wasn't sure how long he sat there, staring and waiting for Christian to return. He was being illogical, waiting, especially when he and Charlotte were having a full-fledged date. But what else was he going to do? Go talk to his suitemates about wanting to fuck his best friend? That they should wear some headphones tonight just in case?

When the waiting became too unbearable, he ordered Chinese food for delivery and ate sesame chicken in the living room with the TV on, barely making any sense of what he was watching. Daiki and Noah breezed out of their bedroom at one point, talking and laughing, not giving him any notice, and that suited him fine. He didn't need their questions anyway. But emptiness in the suite was dangerous.

Before too long, it was late. Late enough that he'd wasted a whole damn night waiting for Christian to come back and *maybe* fuck him senseless. Why the hell did he think Christian would cut his date with Charlotte short to fuck him? He could fuck *her*. He *liked* her, and he didn't like Logan; he only wanted to have a little fun with him.

He tidied the living room. He brushed his teeth and washed his face. He spent one long, breathless moment staring at the door, waiting for it to swing open like in a movie...

And then he went to bed and slept like the dead.

IT WAS SO easy to keep his distance from Logan. Christian knew his sleeping patterns, when his classes were. Now that their freshman seminar was over, they didn't share any. It was simple to return to the dorm after Logan had fallen asleep and then set a vibrating alarm under his pillow so he'd wake up soundlessly. He'd grab his shit and get out of the room before Logan stirred. Christian did his homework in the library. He ate in the dining hall when he knew Logan would be in class. Everything came together perfectly—almost like it was meant to be that way.

Life, however, wasn't happy. Not really.

Christian waited for a sign every second of every day about what he needed to do, but the world seemed short on them. Nothing in his textbooks pointed to some divine providence about, say, the evolutionary advantages of men sleeping with other men. The clouds maintained their fluffy shapes rather than taking on the appearance of Logan's smile. No little forest animals came and whispered prophecy into his ear.

He didn't want to believe that every day was a wasted day, but it was getting pretty fucking hard to think otherwise.

And he *ached*. He couldn't express precisely what his body yearned for, but he hadn't been so distanced from others in a long time. He'd seen Logan every goddamn day for the past twelve years. He'd had a constant string of girlfriends to keep his bed warm. He'd had a close relationship with the members of his soccer team at home.

And now? Nothing.

His teammates weren't bad, but they weren't...good either. They wouldn't stand too close to each other or let their knees touch when they were on the bench together. During practice, if someone missed a line of shots, they'd be called *gay*. They were talented—Christian reluctantly had to admit that—but they were cocky sons of bitches who liked to pretend that breathing the same air as somebody gay would infect them with something.

What would they think if they knew their up-and-coming midfielder had swapped spit with another dude? What would they call him when he was the only one who held a strong line? What would they say when he congratulated one of their forwards on sinking a goal?

He didn't want to think about it.

Ever since he'd started putting distance between himself and Logan, it seemed the shouted slurs and foul jokes had gotten twice as bad—as though the universe could play with *that* but couldn't give him a goddamn answer.

Maybe that is *my answer. I should've known all along it was a stupid idea to think about him as anything other than my best friend.*

The thoughts weighed heavily on him during all of practice, and by the end, he was as worn thin in his mind as he was exasperated with his poor performance. He could do better. A kid on a full soccer scholarship *had* to do better. And yet, here he was, fucking up all over the pitch.

Christian gathered his things and started toward the gym to hit the showers—handling the gay jokes in the locker room would be easier than running into Logan right now.

"Hey, Daniels. Got a minute?"

Coach Atkinson. *Of course.* The man had a laser awareness for when his players wanted to be somewhere else, and he was fantastic at stopping them in their tracks. It had been a few weeks since Christian had quit hounding him at the end of every practice. His mind had been too caught up in dealing with Logan to focus on his skills, and the last thing he wanted was for Atkinson to tell him with full honesty how much he sucked.

Still, he couldn't exactly keep walking. He took a deep breath and turned around.

There was a little kick in his gut every time he was around his coach, and somehow that attraction was easier to accept than Logan—*of course*, Christian would be drawn to the first older guy who treated him like an equal. *Of course*, he wasn't fully straight. Of course, of course, of course. Everything fell into place like *Tetris* blocks, each one lining up so perfectly that the realizations fell into understanding before any anxiety could develop.

Silly schoolboy crushes aside, Atkinson wasn't too difficult to deal with. He was a good guy and a fantastic coach, and Christian could cope with a little attraction to him just like he had with his former science teacher, Mrs. Chumley. Easy as pie—and much less soul-crushing than anything he felt about Logan.

That doesn't mean anything. It's only chemistry, dude. Don't think too hard about it, okay?

Atkinson finally closed the gap between them after long seconds of Christian not approaching, a thoughtful frown on his lips. "How're you feeling today?"

Alarm bells went off in Christian. "Fine."

"You sure?"

"Yeah."

Atkinson's frowned deepened, springing wrinkles across his face. "You're playing like an amateur these days."

Later, Christian might thank him for not beating around the bush. Today, he was nothing but frustrated.

"I know there's plenty of projects and tests coming up before Thanksgiving break, but no one else seems to be struggling like you are. I wanted to check and see if something else was going on. Something you might need to talk about."

Shit, shit, shit. "Everything's fine, Coach. I'm a little stressed about school. I've just gotta adapt, right?"

Atkinson tilted his head to the side. He didn't even blink. It was as if a computer was analyzing his voice to catch wind of a lie. "Adapting to our circumstances is one thing. But sometimes, it's not always that simple."

A lecture. Fantastic.

"Sometimes, there's something going on under the surface that we might not be fully aware of. Sometimes, it's not only about adapting, but also confronting your feelings head-on—either alone or with someone we trust watching our backs for us. That's why you play on a team, right? One man can't play an entire game."

Christian scoffed.

"What's that about?"

"Nothing."

"Christian."

Having his first name spoken instead of his surname made Christian freeze. It woke something deep in his chest, coaxing the turmoil out and leaving him a little weaker than before. "Pardon my language, Coach, but the last thing I want is one of those motherfuckers watching my back off the field."

"Why's that?"

He shook his head. He didn't know how to explain his concerns. "No reason. A feeling I get, I guess."

"A feeling."

"Yes, sir."

Atkinson sighed, but he didn't speak, and when Christian glanced up, he saw him staring over his shoulder. When Christian followed his gaze, his stomach twisted in his gut.

Logan stood at the far edge of the field, books held loosely in his arms. There was no one he could be watching but Christian.

"A friend of yours?"

Christian jerked around, keeping his back to Logan, his cheeks flaming. "Don't worry about it."

Atkinson stared at him, and Christian stared back, challenging him to speak up and say what was on his mind. "Listen, if there are issues with the team, it's up to me to fix them, all right? If they're doing something upsetting—"

"Seriously, don't worry about it. I've gotta go shower, Coach."

"All right. Sure. Daniels..."

He crossed his arms. "Yeah?"

"You should probably talk to your friend first, don't you think? When he's been waiting for you?"

The heavens practically opened up, shining a spotlight on him, with little angels flying around and blowing their trumpets triumphantly. And Christian shrugged and started in the opposite direction—toward the gym. "He'll be there later."

He expected Logan to come after him—that would *really* make it a sign. But when Christian searched over his shoulder, just before walking into the building, Logan was still standing there, as deflated as a man could be.

What are you waiting on? You really think he's gonna make the first move when you've been running from him?

He didn't know what he was waiting for anymore. But the shampoo he got in his eyes while showering seemed like a pretty damn big punishment for digging his heels in the sand.

And, for once, Christian Daniels was sick of his own shit.

Chapter Eight

LOGAN

For the first time in his life, Logan regretted his deep sleeping. He'd stay up as late as he could to see if Christian would come to their room, and then he'd wake up the next day having passed out with his phone on his chest, the only sign his roommate had been there the new pile of clothes on the floor.

He could text or call him, of course. He could ask him what the fuck was going on and why he was avoiding him. He could ask what the hell Charlotte had said to him on their little date. But what would that change? And why did Logan have to be the one bridging the gap anyway?

If Christian was trying to get rid of their friendship, then that was his prerogative. Christian had to pack to move out sometime, right? He wasn't going home for Thanksgiving break with nothing from his dorm room. He couldn't be in their tiny-ass town and pretend they weren't going to run into each other.

Unless he's staying here with Charlotte. And then I might never see him again, at this rate. Bet they'd find some way to fucking move in together while I was gone.

The first few days, he kept doing his homework on Christian's bed, hoping to see him walk in like nothing had ever happened. Logan had gotten sick of himself after a while, though, and moved to his desk, where the rigid chair reminded him to sit tall with his back straight and his eyes on the page.

He considered pranks to get Christian to talk to him again. Hair dye in his shampoo, or itching powder in his boxers. Anything. But he couldn't bring himself to be so shitty, not when Christian was honest to God breaking his heart right now.

The soccer field had been the last straw. He'd been weak all day, his heart giving up the ghost, and he'd taken a different route to the dorm after class—one that took him past the field. He'd watched Christian play enough that he knew immediately he wasn't playing as well as he should. There was a second hesitation before he kicked the ball, and he let too many players get past him when he was defending. He missed every goal he shot.

So, clearly Christian was struggling with something too. It wasn't only Logan dying a little inside every day in his new isolation—weak enough that he wasn't speaking to Noah or Daiki anymore, much less the classmates he hadn't bothered to befriend. So, he thought he'd wait. He'd be there at the edge of the field, where Christian could walk to the dorm with him. He didn't need an explanation at this point. He'd take anything.

But that hadn't come to pass. Christian had taken one look at him—staring hard enough that Logan knew he'd been seen—and then he'd gone. And as Logan stood there, his thoughts frantically stirring—*come back, come back to me, you asshole*—he hadn't. And Logan had given up.

That night, he sat on his top bunk with his laptop next to him, chest aching as he clicked through the student part of FSU's website. There was a place to make a request for a new room at the end of the semester. It'd be an extra charge for him to move to another dorm, but his parents could handle the bill.

But the betrayal was too strong. Leaving without saying a word to him would be the coward's way out. Though Christian deserved the silence, Logan felt sick enough to close his laptop and put his head in his hands.

He's just a guy. You can forget him. You can get a new best friend. You're better than some man who sits here wasting his fucking life away because he did something to drive his brother away. It's not worth it. He's not worth it.

But the pep talk fell flat, because no matter what he told himself, the words were nothing more than lies.

The door swung open, and Logan whipped his head up and stared straight at Christian. The breath caught in his chest.

Christian wasn't watching him. He was standing there staring at the ground with the door open, his hands on the doorframe. Every bit of anger came rushing back through Logan.

"Well, well, well," Logan spat, and Christian stepped inside, shutting the door behind him. "The prodigal son returns. Been busy? Spending all your time with your teammates?"

Christian didn't speak. He leaned against his chest of drawers, his back to Logan.

"Or maybe you had some super fucking huge project, huh? With Charlotte? Can't spend five minutes away from her anymore, can you?"

Christian's shoulders lifted higher and higher with tension until he seemed like an imposing statue. His ribs heaved with each breath he took.

Something was going to come to a head here. He was going to turn around and rip into Logan. They'd burn the whole damn friendship, and they'd both have closure, and that was all that mattered. But Logan was weak. With every second that Christian stood there breathing hard, clinging to the chest of drawers until his knuckles turned white, Logan knew something was far worse than he imagined.

So, he gave in. He let one last little bit of tenderness rise up from his stubborn chest, even though it'd be the death of the hard man he'd been building up within. "Christian?"

Christian finally moved: he locked the door. That one click sent a shockwave through Logan, and he moved a little closer to the edge of the bed, getting ready to run if the moment called for it. Their play wrestling had done some damage to both of them before, especially in the times when tensions were high.

And then Christian pushed away from the cabinet and started toward him purposefully, his chin high. Logan had barely enough time to steel himself before Christian grabbed him behind both knees and jerked him to the very edge of the bed. He yelped when he slid into Christian's arms, caught with a grunt by strength he didn't know the other man had. The breath was knocked out of Logan when his back slammed into the edge of his bed. Pinned there, Christian seared him with a kiss.

That was the last thing he'd been expecting—but his body immediately got with the program. He wrapped his legs snugly around Christian's waist and raked his nails over his scalp, tilting his head to deepen the kiss.

The second Christian pulled back, Logan dug his hands into his shoulders and stared at him with panicked eyes. "What the hell was that for?" *The silence, the distance, the hitting me with a kiss harder than a punch...*

Christian huffed. His arms trembled in their cradle under Logan's ass. "You wanna fuck?"

Logan's eyes widened enough to hurt. "What?"

"C'mon. You and me." Christian dragged his gaze down to his mouth, and he sucked on his bottom lip, sending a pleasant spike of pain through Logan. "You're the one who brought it up first. And I've been waiting damn long enough. So let's fucking do it. Let's fuck."

Logan's cock hardened at breakneck speed—from flaccid to erect in six seconds flat—and he buried his face in Christian's neck to catch his breath. Things were happening too fast—going from dead silence for weeks to Christian dangling what Logan yearned for over his head. How the hell was he supposed to keep up with this? To keep him from yanking Logan along like a toy?

What if this is only a pit stop? What if he starts ignoring me all over again when he's done with me? What if this whole fucking thing has been about him using me as a goddamn experiment?

"You serious, man?"

"I wouldn't be joking about this. Trust me." Christian bit the shell of his ear and tugged, hard enough to make him wonder if he was bleeding, and he cried out, his fingers bruising Christian's skin as he held on for dear life. "Let me fuck the shit out of you, baby. Let's both get what we want, huh?"

Logically, Logan knew they should talk about this. Something had Christian on high alert. He was forceful and assertive in a way he'd only ever been if he wanted control—if he'd had a bad game or a shitty fight with his parents. They were about to take a huge step, and having Christian mindless with need might end with Logan hurt, physically or otherwise. They hadn't talked about fucking as something other than foreplay, and just jumping into it couldn't be a wise decision. And, when the night was over, they wouldn't be able to pretend they hadn't been together—he'd fall apart if Christian returned to the silent treatment as if he hadn't flayed Logan open with one touch of his hands.

But his body had other ideas. And Christian was right; they'd been waiting long enough for this. If Logan slowed him down, they wouldn't get there.

Having him once was better than never having him at all. Logan's heart had already been broken. Who was to say it would hurt the second time? Nothing could hurt worse than the past few weeks.

"What do you say?" Christian urged through gritted teeth.

There was only one answer. "Yeah." Logan rocked his hips forward, trying to grind his cock against Christian's hard abs. "*Fuck* yeah, fuck the shit out of me, c'mon."

Christian breathed a ragged laugh as he turned and carried Logan across the room. He planted Logan right on the edge of his chest of drawers and kissed him messily—more intent than good performance—and opened the drawer under his leg far enough to pull out the bottle of lube. "Been waiting for this," he whispered.

"Where do you wanna do it?" Logan was fine on the chest of drawers. They might as well stay there, and the couch wasn't very far away either.

Christian frowned, then pressed their foreheads together. "I'm taking you to my bed, baby. What kind of man do you think I am?"

Oh, shit. That made it ten times more intimate, somehow, knowing their first time wouldn't be messy and adventurous. Instead, he'd be buried in Christian's bed, drowning in his pheromones. And when Christian inevitably dropped him again, Logan would never forget how searing it was to be fucked hard and fast in his sheets.

That was how being with Christian would be. Soft lovemaking was reserved for someone like Charlotte. Christian was hungry for him tonight, and Logan would let him rip him open and use him—just this once.

Logan clung to him as Christian carried him back, and he couldn't help but admire Christian's strength when he let out a raw sound as he bent gently to set Logan down in his bed. He didn't want to let him go, but Christian extricated himself and pulled his own shirt over his head, tossing it on the spotless floor before tumbling down on top of him.

There was no way in hell he could get Christian naked fast enough. Logan ripped at his clothes even at the expense of missing his kisses. Christian wasn't much better. They rocked this way and that on the bed, making low grunts of effort as they got each other undressed, and for a moment, Logan wondered why neither of them were shy about this. Too many years changing in front of each other? Or were they reluctant to admit they'd had dreams of the other stripped down to nothing? Either way, he welcomed their haste. They littered the bed with clothes before they got their hands on each other and drowned in a kiss.

Logan barely got a taste of Christian's mouth before he was left cold and naked as the man kissed his way down his body in a messy mockery of how Logan had treated him that first night.

The difference was Christian apparently had no intention of stopping at Logan's cock.

Logan pushed up on his elbows so he could see better. "The hell are you doing?"

"Nothing." Christian reached for his desk drawer and pulled out a condom—and, frighteningly, a pair of scissors. "Do you trust me?"

Logan stared deep into his warm brown eyes. A question like that from a man like Christian could mean anything, especially when there were pointy things near his naked body. But there was only one answer he could give. "Yeah. Always." *Even after everything.*

Christian opened the wrapper and unrolled the condom. He made a few snips—until the latex lay flat, like a piece of saran wrap—then leaned to set the scissors on his desk. "This is a dental dam."

"Okay..." Logan blinked. "What's it for?"

"Things. When maybe you don't wanna put your tongue on something."

It obviously wasn't going on Logan's dick, then, given how they'd messed around in the living room. "So?"

Christian slung Logan's legs over his shoulders and held his gaze as he got his hands on his ass and parted his cheeks. Logan absently reached for the lube, but Christian shook his head and spoke. "Nah. I'm gonna rim you, baby."

Logan's heart hammered. "But..." His words dried up, wiped clean from his mind as he fixated on the thought of Christian spreading him open.

"We're negative from the last time we got tested, yeah, but there's a hell of a lot of nasty things that could be all over your hole. This is the way I've always done it. Feels great, I promise."

His stomach sank as he imagined Christian rimming a thousand girls, Logan at the end of a line of people who didn't mean anything. "You've done it a long time, then?"

Christian opened his mouth and then closed it, his gaze dropping from Logan's eyes. Before Logan could press him for more, Christian dipped his head.

Logan let out a sharp gasp when a peculiar sensation rocked through him. "Fuck—"

Christian hummed as he dragged his tongue over his hole. The latex over his skin barely masked the sensation. "That good?"

Logan dropped flat on the bed, hands over his face. His cheeks flushed, and he couldn't begin to imagine his expression. After everything Christian had put him through, Logan didn't want him to see how easy it was to tear down those carefully built walls, as if they hadn't existed in the first place, and see the broken man left behind.

Christian's hands squeezed his ass as he licked again and again, lighting up synapses and nerves Logan didn't know he had. Such pleasure had no business existing. He'd thought he understood everything his body was capable of, but, Jesus, he'd been wrong all along.

Christian didn't shy away from him either. As the tip of his tongue swirled over Logan's hole—like he was painting circles on a clit—Logan tried to push him away. "Dude, th-that, you don't have to do this, c'mon—"

"Want to." Christian grabbed his hand and laced their fingers and rested them on Logan's belly. "Does it feel good?"

It did, just like he'd promised but it was almost overwhelming. Like it wasn't something he was made to handle. Like his body would burst if Christian didn't stop.

"Logan?"

"It's so much." His voice trembled as he spoke, and he covered his mouth with his free hand, sucking in a shaky breath.

"Hey." Christian tugged his arm down and nestled it under their joined hands. "Lemme hear you, baby. Been wondering how you'd like this for ages now."

As Christian went back to laving his tongue over him, lighting spark after spark in his belly, Logan wrestled with the first taste of palpable jealousy. *He does this with Charlotte. He probably gives her this all the time. I bet he's doing exactly what she likes.*

What would it have been like to be Christian's first everything? If they'd figured out why they were so close and inseparable as teenagers? If the one time they'd watched porn together, Logan had minded the buzzing in his palms and reached over, pushed Christian's hand away, and jerked him off himself?

Missed opportunities didn't matter. This was what they had now—and Christian *wanted* to hear him. Maybe he thought of Logan when he was driving Charlotte wild in his bed.

So, he gave himself up to the pleasure with reckless abandon. He let the moans fly free, heedless of the others only a wall away. *Let them hear. I don't give a shit right now.*

Christian twisted his other arm awkwardly to reach for Logan's cock, clearly trying to find some simultaneous rhythm with his tongue and hand. But the imperfection was *beautiful*, and Logan didn't fight it. He tightly grasped the hand in his own and pinned his hips to the bed through sheer force of will.

He's gonna drive me crazy before he even fucks me. Logan fought a smile, but it slipped through.

"What's that for?" Christian asked as he let Logan's hand go and reached for another condom. The absence of his touch left Logan's palm cold and tingling with the need to grab him again—to have him so close he could barely breathe—but he shook his head in response. "C'mon, don't be shy. You've got a cute smile."

"Cute?" Logan wrinkled his nose, but the incorrigible grin only widened.

"You kidding me?" Christian sat up and tossed the condom on the pillow. He ripped the wrapping off the bottle of lube and dropped it over the edge of the bed. "You're the best-looking guy I know. Always felt kind of like garbage next to you."

Logan craned his neck and blinked. Going from burning physical pleasure to such surprise caused whiplash. "That's bullshit."

Christian shrugged. He focused on fitting the new condom over a finger, then covering it with lube until it was practically dripping.

"You seen yourself? You're a fucking god, man. Tall and dark and handsome, like, there's literally nobody who fits that compared to you. Could be a damn model."

Christian's lips twitched. "Listen to you. A model. Like anybody would pay me to walk down a runway."

"Just saying, it'd be a sweet-ass backup plan." He hesitated, his gaze on Christian's fingers as he rubbed them together, like he was trying to get them warm. A thought came to Logan—probably too much too soon, but he wouldn't know unless he voiced it. "Might get a little jealous, all those other people looking at you, but...I don't know, I guess I could handle it."

Christian pinned him with his gaze. Logan's heart fluttered as Christian leaned over him and pushed his legs farther apart. "And what if you couldn't? What would you do?"

Too much, too soon. Logan cleared his throat. "I, uh—"

"Would you take me home from a photo shoot and fuck my brains out?"

Logan's eyes widened.

"Maybe it'd make you feel better if you reclaimed me, huh? Isn't that what they call it?"

"I have no fucking clue," Logan murmured breathlessly. "God, Christian, would...would you let me do that?"

"Fuck me?"

"Yeah."

Christian shrugged, but his cheeks turned a vivid rose color. "Seems like it might be fun."

"Shit..."

The bottle dropped to the mattress again as Christian slid between his legs. "Hush up. You think too hard about fucking me and you're gonna come before I get my dick in you."

Logan bit his lips shut and held his breath, trying desperately to take his arousal down a few pegs. *He isn't wrong...* When a slick finger touched his hole, he gasped.

"I said hush."

Logan trembled on the sheets, clawing at them and dragging fistfuls of fabric into his palms. He exhaled sharply, trying to let all of his tension out. No good. His muscles tightened in his thighs and his ass. No matter how much he told himself he was ready for this—for Christian—his body seemed a little too nervous to play along like he wanted. Seconds ticked by as he held his breath.

Christian stared down at him. "Baby?"

Logan sucked in a deep breath. Darkness creeping in around the edge of his gaze faded away, leaving sparkles of endorphins behind. "Yeah?"

"You know how beautiful you are right now?"

He turned his head away, feeling the sudden impulse to hide his face in the pillow. "No, c'mon, that's—"

"Goddamn gorgeous." Christian's fingers kept rubbing at his puckered skin, spreading the lube in a thick, surprisingly warm layer. "Wanted you for so long."

Was that a lie to loosen him up? His ego wouldn't accept it. Instead, he took the words and buried them in his heart. "For real?"

"Yeah. Just didn't know it at the time."

"When did you know?" Logan challenged. He wanted to paint the prettiest picture possible in his head.

Christian sighed. His breath tickled the long hairs on Logan's inner thigh. "Think the first time I knew something was different about you...I must've been eleven. I didn't know any better at the time, you understand, but I was starting to notice girls, and they were things that we shouldn't be afraid of anymore, and I got to thinking about kissing—and how terrible I was gonna be." He chuckled and kissed the skin beside Logan's cock, bringing a score of tingles to life. "And I knew whatever girl I kissed first was gonna make fun of me and tell everybody not to even think about going out with Christian Daniels. So...so I thought about asking you if you wanted to practice a little."

Logan shivered. He remembered that time of their lives—when Christian was really starting to excel on the soccer field, better than the kiddy leagues where everyone pretended their kids knew what they were doing when they could barely kick a ball. There were days when they'd be walking by the creek together or laying on their backs and staring up at the clouds, and Logan would look over and Christian would be *staring* at him, like he had something on his face. He'd never really known what was wrong.

"You remember the last time I went to go see my dad?"

"Right before you turned twelve." Logan remembered asking his mom for permission to call Christian at his dad's since he'd be away all weekend. His parents had given each other a look before they said Logan should let the two of them bond a little. He'd always gotten the sense they didn't like Christian's dad, but he hadn't known why. "You went there, and he gave you a new Hot Wheels car for your early birthday present, and you got pissed because you hadn't played with them in years."

Christian's fingers finally dropped away. Silence fell heavily over them like a blanket, seconds ticking by until he took a deep breath. "There were these two old guys that lived in my dad's town. Everybody always said they were roommates, but I guess they knew better. They never got married to women. They ran their little farm together. Never came into town, never bothered nobody. And my dad, he called them..."

Ice spread through Logan's body.

"Well. He made it pretty damn clear that I was never gonna turn out like one of them. Not ever."

Just like that, the ribs cracked open in his chest, aching soul deep. Logan dug his teeth into his bottom lip and covered his eyes with his forearm and breathed out every desire he'd ever had for keeping Christian by his side for the rest of his life. *It'll never happen. Not if that son of a bitch...*

His thoughts didn't get very far, not when Christian's body pressed flush against his. Not when his lips met Logan's.

A different kiss than before, Christian cupped the back of his neck as they connected, mouths working together languidly. This was something soul-wrenching—but in the most beautiful way he'd ever known. He'd kissed a dozen girls, and his body had burned, his cock hardened, his heart pounded for them. But somehow, he hadn't experienced this closeness before, as though he was colliding with someone who perfectly complemented his body, soul, and mind.

It wasn't two puzzle pieces coming together. Logan was already whole. But something about kissing Christian so intimately—like a lover, not a one-night stand—only emphasized every bright light deep inside him, as if Christian was the spotlight shining through Logan's vivid stained glass.

Stunning flawlessness. And his body melted at the taste.

Logan turned his head, breaking the kiss so he could catch his breath and cling to Christian. Floating this high in the sky was new, but maybe he could stay aloft as long as he wasn't alone. "Want you to do it," he whispered.

"You sure? We don't have to."

"No, I'm ready. I mean it. I need you, Christian."

Christian sighed sweetly, pressing three kisses to his cheek that were more delicate than spun sugar, and nuzzled the shell of his ear. "I'm gonna take good care of you, Logan. Don't you worry."

"I'm not. I trust you."

"Okay."

When Christian pulled away to ease his latex-covered fingers between them, Logan grabbed his toned arms. "Stay close?"

"Yeah, sure." He buried his face in Logan's neck. "Don't wanna go anyway. Not if you're here."

Christian's words overwhelmed Logan. Though he was unsure of their honesty, they were exactly what he needed to hear. He clung to them like he clung to Christian, his legs spreading as wide as he could get them, welcoming him that little bit closer.

"You good and relaxed for me?" Christian's words rumbled against the thin skin of his throat, breathing sweetness straight into his blood. "I can touch your pretty cock, if you want, and see if that gets you looser."

"You've done this before." He didn't mean to sound so accusing. "With Charlotte."

"Yep."

He huffed.

"Don't you be making those jealous noises at me." There wasn't a trace of teasing or good humor in Christian's voice. "I'm not gonna tell you that I regret what I did with her or that I wish you were my first time doing this. And I'm not gonna tell you that you're better than her. Don't make me put her down to bring you up."

The words were a blow to his pride, but well deserved. "Sorry."

"It's okay. Just..." Christian's body gave a little more, as if he was deflating against him. "Listen, I'm here with you because I wanna be. Don't compare yourself to her. Don't think *I'm* comparing you to her either. You're different from her, and she was different from you, and let's leave it at that."

"Are...are you glad I'm here?"

Christian stared at him, his gaze smoldering with an intensity that licked Logan's whole body with flame. "I've never wanted you more than I do right this second. And I can't wait to fuck you just like this."

Face to face. Eyes locked. Their bodies so close they could barely breathe. Logan couldn't wait any longer. "Then you should stop running your mouth and start fingering me, huh?"

A grin broke across Christian's face. "You little shit."

"What?"

"Here I am trying to be sweet and...and *romantic*, and there you are..." Christian shook his head and chuckled. His fingers eased inside him, and Logan gasped sharply at the strange new sensation. "There you go. Feel better now?"

"Uh—" It wasn't what he thought it'd be, but he sure as hell wasn't complaining. He gulped and pushed his muscles as best as he could, opening up for him a little bit more. "Okay. Okay—"

"Gonna take my time, sweetheart, don't you worry."

The feel of Christian's hot skin under Logan's fingers was the only thing that kept him grounded. He wanted to be aware of every second of this. He wanted to replay the memory over and over again so it was *real*—so he couldn't convince himself he was making it up. He didn't want to fall under a haze. He wanted everything, discomfort and all.

Christian pulled his finger free and slathered it in more lube before he started up the process again. *It's a damn good thing he knows what he's doing.* Logan didn't know when to tell Christian he could push in a little deeper, that he was relaxed and ready for more. Every second he thought he was loose enough—that he'd taken Christian in as deep as he could—he slid in another inch farther. It was maddening.

"How long are your damn fingers?"

"Hush," Christian said again, laughing.

The stretch from his second finger nearly undid Logan. An ache deep inside his body whispered he'd be sore as fuck from a cock an inch thicker fucking the shit out of him. "Shit, shit—"

"You can take it. I know you can." Christian left precious kisses on his chest, and every time Logan's breath caught, he stilled his fingers and waited. "Not gonna hurt you."

But the ache...*God*, it was something else. Utterly satisfying—like he was stubbornly taking something his body was made for all along. As if letting himself open up under Christian's tender assault was enough to unlock capabilities he hadn't had before.

As though somehow Christian knew him better than he knew himself.

"More." Logan's voice was hoarse when he whispered. He was barely aware of the low moans and growls he'd been letting out through the entire experience. "Fuck, Christian, need *more*, c'mon."

"Yeah?" Christian's fingers pushed in a little awkwardly and pulled back again, appearing to seek something. Logan wished he had some way of seeing exactly what he was doing. "You about ready for my cock?"

"Need you so bad—*fuck*!"

"There it is..."

Logan stiffened under the new tingling inside him. He didn't have words for it—less *pleasure* and more *sensation*. There wasn't a goddamn thing he could compare it to in the universe. He gasped raggedly, his hands bruising Christian's arm as he arched. "The fuck is that?"

"I'm pretty sure that's your prostate."

The motherfucker was grinning. Logan could hear it perfectly. "What do you mean, my prostate?"

"I mean..." One more stroke had Logan's body vibrating like the growl in Christian's tone. "...I think I found something you're really gonna like, huh?"

Did he like it? He didn't know. There weren't *words*. But every time Christian fluttered his fingers inside him, Logan was flying through the air, his feet hovering above the ground, and he found he was in absolutely no hurry to come down.

"Y-you think your dick could hit that?" Logan gasped.

His words were a challenge, and they both knew it. Logan locked eyes with him, forcing himself to stare as hard as he could with eyelashes that fluttered every time he breathed, and Christian simply cocked an eyebrow.

"Why don't we find out?"

Jackpot.

Christian eased his fingers free, licking his lips, and Logan sat up on his elbows to watch as he rolled the condom on his cock. His hand moved quick and sure, smoothing it into place, and he gave himself a liberal coating of lube. Logan was half tempted to ask him to take it off, so Christian could feel Logan so much more, but the idea of his release dripping out of him made him hesitate. He didn't want anything to shorten this experience— especially not giving up the afterglow to clean himself up.

"You really want this?"

Maybe this was the wrong time for Logan to ask, when he was supposed to be confident with the level of desire he had for Christian, but...he couldn't be sure. Not when he thought about Christian's dad burning slurs into his head. Not when he was pretty sure his mom and stepfather wouldn't have done anything to undo the damage his dad might've made.

But Christian didn't look away from him for one second as he guided his cock to his entrance. "I've never wanted anything more."

He believed him. Logan believed in Christian more than he believed in God. "Then fuck me."

Christian wrapped a hand around his hipbone, holding him still, his gaze steady and strong as he began to press the head of his cock inside him.

As agonizingly slow as Christian moved—not even an inch to start—Logan closed his eyes and whined. "Oh shit, fuck…"

"It's okay," Christian whispered. "Tell me if you need me to stop. I've got all night."

"All night?" A sweat broke out across his skin at the breathtaking thought of having a whole night with Christian. "What about Charlotte? You don't have a date with her?"

Silence. "No, man. No, it's just you."

Just me tonight. Logan relaxed, trying to melt into the sheets. "C'mon. I can take it, Christian."

"Gonna take my time." Christian touched Logan's dick with slow strokes that broke goose bumps across his skin. "Wanna remember this."

"Shit…" Logan didn't cry. He never cried. And he wasn't going to fucking cry about this either. But goddamn if the thought didn't strike him.

After weeks of thinking that Christian had shrugged him off like an old jacket, that Charlotte had put her foot down and told him to pick her or Logan, that twelve years of friendship and a few months of promising changes were gone in a *second*, every little word and touch was a fresh balm on his heart. Christian pushed a little deeper inside him, and Logan rode the waves crashing through him.

"Always wanted this." Logan babbled more the farther Christian went, his shallow thrusts straddling a line between soreness and pleasure. "Didn't even know I wanted it, just, from the fucking second I started watching you really becoming a *man*, I..."

Christian thumbed over the head of his dick. "Tell me, baby, go on."

"...wanted to touch you." Logan opened his eyes and stared up at him pleadingly. "The day we watched porn together, wanted to reach over and get you off myself. Wanted to know what your cock would feel like in my mouth."

Fire raged in Christian's gaze. His hand slowed in a maddening tease. "Why didn't you?"

"You kidding me? When you would've kicked my—" He cut off with a sharp exhale as Christian pushed a little too deep with no warning, the ache lighting him up.

"Sorry, I'll—"

"No, don't stop." Logan grabbed his hips and held him firmly, marveling at the beautiful feeling rushing through him on the heels of the pain. "Shit, I like that."

"Like what?"

"When...when it hurts."

Christian chuckled. "You're a kinky little son of a bitch, huh?"

Logan's cheeks flushed. "Shut the fuck up."

"Hey, I've got you. Don't be rude when I'm taking such good care of you."

He was. Christian was obviously making a joke, but Logan couldn't help but stare up at him in wonder. The hand moved from his dick and touched his side, hesitating for a moment before Christian dragged his nails down his skin, and Logan arched under them, crying out.

"Goddamn," Christian whispered. He bucked on accident, but it was enough to shoot an ache through Logan's veins, and he threw his head back with a sharp moan.

Things began to blur. While Christian kept his hips in check, his thrusts angling deeper and deeper, Logan rode the strange pleasure from being fucked. Christian's strong hands held him in place, his nails leaving deep half-moons on the sensitive skin, until his hips finally cupped the curve of Logan's ass.

He held there like he was waiting for something, and Logan looked up at him with sweat beading over his forehead. "Don't stop now, man, fucking *do* something."

And Christian began to move.

Being fucked was a powerful, visceral experience; Christian moving to meet him in a primal rhythm was absolutely transfixing. The motion pushed the air out of him and cut off his moans, stunning Logan.

He'd had an incredible amount of sex for someone his age. He'd even have said he was good at it. But being on this side of the experience wiped his mind clean.

All he could do was ride on pure reaction. He rolled his hips in waves, meeting Christian's body with loud slaps and squeaking mattress springs. Somehow, he knew how to clench his internal muscles to shock a groan out of Christian and make him lose his rhythm. Filth poured from Logan's lips as he begged Christian to fuck him harder, bruise his hips, and ruin him from the inside out. Christian's hand wrapped around his cock, and Logan kept him close, gasping against his mouth and staring at his blurry face as those deep grinds hit an unfamiliar sweet spot inside him. It was too much—seeing him, smelling him, tasting him, and feeling every inch of his body from head to toe.

"Want you to come for me," Christian panted, sounding raw and open and completely belonging to Logan.

He had two choices: he could keep his head in the clouds, standing right at the edge of a cliff where it was safe, or he could tip over it and free-fall, hoping Christian would catch him. At the end of the day, there was no contest. There was nothing greater than Christian—not when he was the earth, the sky, and everything in between—and so Logan went with what he'd done for years.

He fell.

His own slickness soaked his skin as Christian sat up and fucked him through his orgasm, hard and fast and brutal, and Logan hovered on the verge of being overwhelmed. It was exhausting to be so thoroughly used when all his body wanted was to collapse. But to be so *needed* by Christian kept him grounded. Logan stared up at him, transfixed, his hands sliding up his strong, muscular thighs.

Christian locked eyes with him.

"You gonna come?" Logan asked.

Christian nodded. Something new and fearful was painted across his face, as if he was afraid to jump too, like he wasn't sure Logan would catch him.

Logan's eyelashes fluttered. "Want you to come so bad, Christian, c'mon."

Christian ducked his head, teeth gritted, the veins in his neck thick and swollen. And then, as Logan watched in rapture, he gasped sharply and slammed his hips against his ass, letting out an almost frantic moan. He ground against him little by little, like he didn't want this to end.

He was beautiful. Absolutely perfect.

After a few seconds of hovering there, his face moving from incandescent to embarrassed, Christian carefully pulled out and took care of the condom. It gave Logan time to muse on the open emptiness he hadn't expected, and the soreness that might be a permanent part of him from now on. It was only when he rested his hand on his stomach that he remembered the jizz spread across his skin. The tacky stickiness jolted him back to reality.

Christian was the one to determine what the hell would happen now. Was their friendship going to become awkward? They'd both said some desperate, heavy shit while they were fucking. Were those words going to disappear too?

With the condom tossed aside, Christian knelt on the bed again, and Logan immediately moved to make room for him. He might as well not have bothered; Christian grabbed his arm and pulled him back into place, then leaned down and dragged his tongue across his stomach.

"Dude!" Logan lurched, laughing. "What the fuck!"

"Stop squirming, I'm busy."

"You're literally eating my jizz, man, c'mon—"

"What?" Christian held him in place and licked another stripe. "Isn't any weirder than eating out a pussy. Hold still."

Logan shook his head. "It's gross."

"Nah." Christian met his gaze. "It's you. Nothing gross about it."

No, nothing had changed at all. Logan's nerves sang as Christian licked his stomach clean, and he shivered when Christian settled next to him and pulled him into his arms.

He fell asleep again. He didn't plan to, but he was out like a light the second he adjusted to the warmth of being held so closely.

IT WAS SURPRISINGLY less awkward than Logan expected when he woke up. It was the next day—that much was clear from how the sun was shining—and he was half-starved from not eating dinner the night before. But his soul was full. He was tucked against Christian's chest, and somehow, he'd gotten a better night sleep there than he had in the months since they'd come to FSU.

Christian was awake, too. Logan glanced up to find him watching him with a small smile, his eyelids heavy and sleepy. "Hey."

"Fuck." Logan rubbed his eyes. "What time is it?"

"Dunno. Probably about half past six."

"Shit." He'd slept like the dead. He couldn't imagine how annoying it must've been for Christian to lie there holding him after he'd already woken up. But when Logan tried to pull away, Christian's arms tightened, and his eyes burned in challenge—one Logan decided not to take. He collapsed again and snuggled close, trying not to analyze their actions too deeply. "Did...did you sleep?"

"Like a baby."

"Awkwardly? Waking up every few hours needing food?"

"Shut up." Christian ruffled his hair and chuckled when Logan frowned up at him. "Listen, Charlotte texted me a little while ago. She's getting coffee with her roommates in a little bit and invited us along."

He'd never gotten an invitation from Charlotte before. It could be awkward as shit. He and Christian still hadn't discussed the reason for him pulling away, and if Charlotte had been the cause of it, then the likelihood of Logan being civil with her was slim to none. But after so long apart, his body was eager to stay as close to Christian as possible. "Yeah, sure, why not. Should we go ahead and get ready now?"

"Probably." Christian sighed, and it took him a bit to open his arms and let Logan go. "You're like a fucking space heater, you know that?"

Logan blushed as he crawled out of bed and went to grab a fresh pair of boxers. He absently threw the discarded clothes from the night before in the hamper as he went. "Sorry."

"No, it was great, are you kidding? Barely even needed the blanket."

Things were domestic again—getting dressed close to Christian so he could study the slope of his back. It was even more intense when they shared the sink together as they brushed their teeth, and when Christian lingered in the doorframe and watched as Logan combed his hair out, meticulously working through the soft curls. He didn't complain once, though Logan was so thorough about it that the minutes ticked by like hours. Somehow, in their companionable silence, there was no awkwardness at being so closely watched.

It just made sense.

Christian chose to drive them to the coffee shop, wordlessly walking around to the driver's side door as they approached the car. They listened to the radio as they went, the mood soft. Gentle. Logan had the impulse to reach over and grab Christian's hand, but the urge spooked him, and he pulled out his phone instead.

Traffic was light so early on a Saturday morning. The sun shone beautiful rays across the ground, making the dew sparkle on the lawns they drove past. It was as if someone had masterfully painted the entire day, wanting things to be as perfect as possible.

Logan was willing to float in it as long as he could.

Once they reached the coffee shop, Logan spotted Charlotte and her two roommates through the front window, sitting at a round table near the door. He and Christian went inside together, but besides a little wave, Christian made no move to go toward them, nor did Charlotte cross the room to give him a kiss or a hug.

It's early, Logan reminded himself. *Not everybody is super gross and affectionate early in the morning.*

They ordered and got their drinks quickly, and when they wandered to the table, the three women looked up.

"Hey." A surprisingly warm greeting from Charlotte. "Logan, have you met my roommates?"

"Don't think I have." It was a little weird how she was sitting between them rather than next to an empty seat for Christian to take, but Logan tried not to read too deeply into it as he sat. "I'm Logan."

"This is Natsumi and Kavya."

"Nice to meet you both."

The two girls smiled, and then, with the introductions out of the way, Logan got to sit back and enjoy his coffee and let the conversation go on without him.

He felt a little like a detective as he watched Charlotte and Christian interacting, but there wasn't much he could focus on. Natsumi and Kavya were holding hands on top of the table, and he wasn't sure if they were dating or close friends, and that could be the reason why Charlotte and Christian weren't touching. They would've had to rest their joined hands on top of the girls'. *It'd be weird.*

He was overthinking. He was here to drink coffee and see where his temporary truce with Charlotte was at right now. It boded well that she kept smiling as she glanced between Christian and Logan, like she was trying to say something with her eyes, though he couldn't read her face enough to know what her intent was.

All of his theories went out the window when Kavya touched Charlotte's chin and turned her head and kissed her. He was eighty percent sure the pilot light in his brain went out too.

Oh.

He blinked wildly as he stared at the two girls—no, the *three* girls, because Natsumi kissed Charlotte's cheek right after—and Christian, but he had no answers. Christian was rubbing his thumb over where his name was written on his coffee cup, not giving the situation a moment's notice.

"Let me guess." Charlotte's dry tone broke the silence. "He didn't tell you."

Logan gaped at her, his mouth wide open. "Excuse me?"

"About what happened." Charlotte rested her chin on her fist, elbow propped on the table, while her other hand slid in between Natsumi and Kavya's. "No? Nothing?"

He had no idea what she was talking about, and he was pretty sure his cluelessness showed all over his face.

Charlotte rolled her eyes. "We broke up. Christian and me. And I've been dating my roommates ever since."

A pressure change rocked through him. He slumped in his chair, rapidly reconsidering everything that had happened. Christian's distance, his slow and gentle way of touching him the night before, and his invitation this morning all pointed toward something else. Logan turned his head to gape at the man in question.

Nothing. No words. Not even a glance. Just quietly tracing over his cup.

"I-I mean, that's, is everything...?" Logan barely had a grasp of language anymore.

"Everything's good! It was an amicable breakup. We're still friends." She scoffed. "You'd know all of that if he talked to you every once and a while, but...well. Whatever."

Christian's cheeks were starting to flush.

Natsumi piped up. "I'm pretty sure everybody's happy, if that's what you're worried about."

Are we? Logan wanted Christian to tell him, right here and now, but he wasn't looking at him. As though he was ashamed.

Shit, things were about to change even more than Logan suspected.

"Maybe we should go!" Kavya's voice was crystal clear, like a bell, as she hopped up. "We've got an early-bird sale we're trying to catch, and, um—"

"Yeah." Charlotte started gathering their things. "Hey. We should all get dinner sometime. I'd like to get to know you better, Logan."

"Yeah! Yeah, sure." He very quickly needed this entire encounter to end. "That'd be great. We'll be in touch."

Charlotte flicked her eyes between him and Christian with another secret smirk. He remembered the comment about Thanksgiving break he'd made ages ago—as if he and Christian were more in charge of that decision than she ever had been—and he saw the exact same expression on her face right now. "Great. Y'all have a good day."

"You too."

The three girls went outside, holding hands without any shame in the crisp early morning, and Logan turned his chair to face Christian. He wasn't going to let him get away with pretending he didn't know what was going on.

But as he waited for his best friend to comment, he got to watch how Christian nervously flicked his gaze over every few seconds, studying him for a moment before flitting away once more. "You wanna do brunch?"

He wasn't going to get a damn thing out of him unless he charged in. "Was this supposed to be a double date?"

Christian shrugged and stood up. "We can probably go get waffles before the crowd gets too big if we hurry."

Logan stayed on his heels, barely nailing the toss of his coffee cup into the trashcan. "When did you two break up? Is that why you started getting weird?"

"I had things to think about," Christian tossed over his shoulder as they went outside. "Wanted to get my head on straight."

"And you couldn't do that when I was around?"

"Logan." Christian touched his shoulder and angled him toward the car so he could trap him there with his body. He dropped his voice. "You make my head go a little funny, man. Always have. I do stupid stuff when I'm around you." He shrugged. "Thought it'd be better if I waited for a sign."

A sign. He'd spent almost a whole month heartbroken and frantic because Christian was waiting on a motherfucking sign. He gaped at him.

It made sense, of course it did, especially with everything he knew about Christian. And he had no greater fear than pushing the idea and then getting pushed back. If Logan went too hard with drilling him for answers, he might pull away all over again. But this was the first time in their twelve years of friendship, as far as he knew, that Christian had deliberately kept a secret from him, and that meant they were treading into different territory.

Christian had retreated because he didn't know what the hell he was doing, and Logan hadn't been able to help him.

He took a deep breath and relaxed against the car. He'd let the frustration go, then. He'd try his best to forget anything ever happened and let Christian take his time discovering what he needed.

Maybe all of their messing around would pay off after all.

"Waffles," Logan murmured. "You paying?"

"Fuck you." Christian ruffled his hair and moved toward the driver's side, and Logan laughed.

He could do this. He could still be his friend while Christian "got his head on straight." He'd let him have all the time he needed.

Chapter Nine

CHRISTIAN

Christian sort of liked how things returned to normal—the *new* normal.

He hadn't realized a part of his soul had been missing while he was away from Logan. The distinct emptiness in his chest made sense now. Though there was a shallow divot left behind from Charlotte's untimely breakup, most of it was filled in.

They were back to sharing space: doing homework on his bed, getting ready in the bathroom together, and getting dressed in too close proximity. But there was something new now.

Shy kisses.

They'd meet in the doorframe—one of them walking into the bathroom and one of them walking out—and every time, Logan would tilt his head slightly, and Christian would press a quick kiss to his mouth. He'd turn away before he could see the smile on Logan's face, and if Logan made a questioning sound, he'd pull him out of the way by his T-shirt to hear him laugh before he shut the door behind him.

Logan had more than once touched a fleeting kiss to Christian's neck while they were doing homework. Those times were more distracting than the little tolls to pass by him. They were already in a bed doing shit they hated and interested in a distraction, but indulging was never a possibility.

Well. *Almost* never. The three times Christian had given himself permission to hold Logan's face tenderly between his hands as he kissed the life out of him, things had accelerated. One moment, they'd be kissing, and the next, Logan would be crawling between his legs, sliding a condom down his cock, and blowing him. The lack of expertise was always more arousing than he'd suspected it would be. Knowing Logan was saving these experiences for him and him alone, and that the only way he wanted to improve was with Christian's cock in his mouth, had him going over the edge in minutes.

He'd become an old hand at getting Logan off too, either with his mouth or with his hands, always fast and messy and moving on again. No penetration. Nothing that took time or significant effort to prep. Just throwing themselves into the whirlwind and then pretending nothing had happened after.

There was always the sense that Logan was waiting for something, but whatever it was Christian didn't know. Feeling Logan's lingering gaze on him every hour of the day, no matter where they were, was enough to keep him on his toes.

He wouldn't ask, though. Not when he wasn't ready to hear the answer. Not when the mere idea terrified him.

One day after his last class in early November, Christian had just opened the door to his bedroom when his phone vibrated. It was a text from his mom asking politely if he'd call sometime about when he and Logan were coming for Thanksgiving break. But she didn't stop there.

"What's up?" Logan asked from where he was working on Christian's bed.

Christian shook his head. "Nothing. One of my cousins is getting married."

"Somebody I know?"

"Nah. Someone on my stepdad's side of the family. She's getting married sometime in January, and my mom wanted to make sure I could come." He cast a withering scowl at his armoire. "Fuck. I don't know if any of my dress shirts fit me anymore." Though his freakish growth spurt had finally ended, he'd gotten broader over the past year with the work he'd put in for soccer, and the shirt he'd worn for his high school graduation barely fit his shoulders at the time.

As he tugged off his shirt, he heard Logan shifting and glanced over his shoulder to see him rolling onto his stomach to watch him. This was new—knowing for a fact that Logan wasn't afraid to be caught checking him out— and it gave him the same thrill in his belly to be admired. He swallowed hard, wading through the fizzing inside him as he pulled out the simple button-down shirt he'd worn under his graduation robes and tugged it on.

He looked at their mirror as he buttoned it. His mom would've gotten onto him for not wearing an undershirt. She hadn't been able to afford anything expensive, and the white fabric was so thin that the rich brown of his skin, and his nipples, bled through it.

It fit. Barely. It clung to his broad shoulders and narrow waist, and his arms alone appeared twice as muscular in the tight fabric. It wouldn't do for a wedding, but he'd somehow scrounge around and find the money to buy something more fitting.

Logan was watching him in the mirror, licking his lips and tracing his eyes down his body. Though he had all the information he needed, Christian made no move to take the shirt off. Instead, he reached for a tie.

He'd always been shit at working with ties. His mom had dubbed his skills terrible and redid his knots every Sunday before church, up until he stopped going. He hadn't tried to make a tie look halfway decent in months, and his fingers were clumsy as he worked.

"Here, let me." Logan climbed out of bed, crossed the room and turned him around, and went to work charming something beautiful out of the fabric.

Christian assumed he did, anyway, since he was staring at the intense expression on Logan's face.

His arms brushed over Christian's chest as he worked, and once he was finished, his hands found his shoulders. "There." Logan smiled, admiring his work. "Perfect."

A storm brewed in Christian's chest, as feverish as the first time they'd rolled around on his bedroom floor, confusing the hell out of him. He didn't move away. He watched Logan's face shift, the smile disappearing and his eyes focusing more intently, and then he was being pulled down by the tie to kiss him.

I'll never get sick of this. The thrill that filled him every time their lips met drove him mad. He didn't know what it was about Logan, but Christian's years of rejecting his body's yearning for his best friend made every damn kiss explosive.

There was the promise of something else, too—something that would end with the both of them naked and panting in Christian's bed, playing each other's bodies like violins in this secret game—and he was willing to chase it.

Except when Logan pulled away, breathing hard, he simply smoothed down Christian's shirt, caught his eye nervously, and walked away.

He headed toward the bed—a promising direction. Christian followed right on his heels, his blood stirred red hot...and came to a clumsy stop when Logan picked up his textbooks and moved them to his desk.

Christian had been rejected before. He'd gone through it in middle school constantly, from the pristine girls who pretended they were better than him to the tomboys who didn't date any guys at all, but it rarely hit him this hard.

This was what Logan and Christian did now. They touched, they kissed, and they tumbled into bed without thought. They had a fantastic time, and then they moved onto what was next on the agenda, from homework to soccer practice to dinner to sleep. And neither of them had ever flinched away from it.

How had Logan's eyes gone from warm to anxious so quickly? And what had Christian done to cause it?

"What just happened?" Christian asked.

"Nothing." Logan shrugged as he sat in his chair and grabbed a stray pencil.

People played games all the time. This could be another one. He might be waiting for Christian to make the proper move. He crossed his arms and tried to decipher the mystery. "Nothing? Nothing happened?"

"We've got homework, man."

Of all of the possibilities, Christian hadn't considered that Logan might've been *bored* with him—maybe he was ready to stop playing around. How was that possible? Especially when Logan had initiated their kiss in the middle of the room? Surely, he hadn't changed his mind.

The only logical explanation was that he wanted Christian to make the next move.

Christian came across the room like an unsteady elephant, his steps clunky and loud. He'd lost all grace in this weird dance the second Logan changed the song. "Is this what you want?" He leaned over the back of the chair, his hands running over Logan's chest, eating up his body and tugging at the hem of his shirt. "You want me to come after you, man?"

For a moment, Logan relaxed into his touch, tilting his head in apparent invitation, and Christian tugged at his earlobe with his teeth. He'd answered correctly. He'd gotten with the program.

Except Logan then turned his head, his hands stopping Christian's before they could wander below his belt. "Is this all we do now?"

The words spread through the air, thickening it with tension, and Christian blinked. It was a slap in the face. No, he apparently hadn't done the right thing after all. He pulled away, Logan's hands squeezing him for a fleeting moment before letting him go. "What?"

Logan hunched over his homework. "Never mind."

"No, there's no *never mind* for that, brother." Christian's words were sharp, but he couldn't remember how to soften them. "What the hell did you mean when you said that?"

Logan huffed and shoved his chair back and started for the door, like he did the day all of this had started. "I didn't mean anything."

"No, don't you..." Christian grabbed his wrist and whipped him around. "Don't you run from me. If you've got something to say, then say it."

"I'm not your girlfriend." Logan jerked out of his grip. "Don't act like you can tell me to stay if I don't wanna stay."

"Well, what do you want me to do, then? You want me to read your fucking mind? Is that it?"

Logan flinched, taking a step back. "I *want* you to *forget* it!"

"Too damn bad!" Something raucous and wild stirred up inside him—a fire that wanted to burn everything down. They'd been doing fine with how things were going, and now Logan had broken their safety net. If he was going to act like it was Christian's fault for pushing the point... "Do you think there's something else going on here? Huh?"

Logan turned his head, jaw tight as if he was grinding his teeth.

"What do you want? Flowers? Candy? Want me to bring you a singing teddy bear with a big old heart on it?"

Logan stared at the floor, arms crossed over his chest, his breath audibly catching in frustration.

It didn't matter. Christian couldn't stop the words from pouring out, not when there was pure terror burning through him. "As far as I fucking know, you just wanted to *mess around*, didn't you? You asked Little Miss Kelly Anne if you could roll around with Christian Daniels in bed and play with his dick. You didn't want anything on top of that. So that's what I'm giving you."

"I didn't say that," Logan gritted out.

"No? So what'd you say, huh?"

Silence.

"What the hell did you fucking ask for?"

Logan raked his fingers through his thick curls, exposing his face in the too-bright dorm lighting, so Christian could see every inch of his reddened skin. "Listen, I-I—"

"I'm giving you what you wanted." Christian stepped closer, leaning down an inch, trying to see his expression. "Look at you. A week ago, you were begging me to fuck you. And now, you don't even know what the hell you want?"

"Goddammit." Logan's voice was weak as he knitted his fingers behind his neck, tilting his head down.

"Tell me what you want."

There was nothing but the sound of Logan breathing hard. It meant Christian was getting to him, just like every time they had a petty fight—as if this was like one of those and not something crushing Christian's soul.

As if Logan didn't care about Christian. As if he never had. As if he was mad about something trivial like Christian taking his favorite shirt and accidentally ripping it.

"Tell me!" Christian shouted, stomping his foot on the floor.

"Will you shut the fuck up?" Logan whipped his head up, glaring with daggers in his eyes. "Stop putting your fucking issues on me!"

Christian didn't know how to respond. He gaped at Logan, all the air shooting out of his chest.

"You think you know what *you* want?" Logan's voice cracked. "You think you understand what the fuck this is supposed to be? I don't fuck you *one time*, and you're out here throwing a temper tantrum? Do you know how fucked up that is?"

There were a million things he could say. *If we're not fucking, then I don't know what this is. If we're not kissing and touching, then what the fuck do I call this? Either you're my friend or my fuck buddy. Unless you're gonna tell me you want something else.*

He needed a sign. He needed Logan to tell him to his face exactly what he wanted.

Logan pressed a fist to his mouth, taking a deep breath. "I wanted to talk, man, I-I..."

Say it. Fucking say it.

"I-I just wanted to talk about what the fuck is going on, because I don't know what this is, and I'm sc..."

You're what? Just let me have it.

Logan peered up at him, his eyes gleaming. He cried so seldom that the sight of unshed tears alone almost undid Christian.

"Will you say something?" Logan asked, voice shaking.

That wasn't how this was supposed to go. Logan was supposed to tell him what he wanted. Logan was supposed to make this easy by drawing a road map they could follow so Christian could stop fucking everything up.

He opened his mouth. He closed it again. He couldn't—not if Logan wouldn't.

Logan sucked in a shaky breath and turned on his heel. Christian followed close after him, hands on the door that Logan threw open, staring after him as he grabbed his shoes.

Look at me. I promise if you look back at me right now I'll say something. I need you to give me the courage to speak up, man.

Logan opened the front door. He slammed it behind him, and Christian flinched, holding his breath.

Come back. Open the door, and I'll fix everything. Change your mind. Don't fucking leave me.

Seconds ticked by. They turned into minutes.

Like every man in his life he'd ever cared about, Logan had left. And it was entirely possible he wasn't coming back.

FOR A LONG time, Logan ran. He'd thrown his shoes on at the bottom of the stairs and sprinted outside as though he could leave the fight behind if he ran hard enough. Maybe if he put enough distance between him and Christian, he wouldn't hurt.

It didn't work. Neighborhoods blurred together until he barely knew where he was. Twice, he had to stop to lean over, hands on his knees, catching his breath and hoping the stitch in his side went away...and then the pain would catch up again, and he'd take off once more.

He had nowhere to go. No friends besides his roommates. No girlfriend to turn to. No siblings who'd have his back. He couldn't exactly call his parents and explain how the night had transpired.

"Hey, Mom, so Christian and I just broke up. Well, we didn't break up, because we were never together. We only fucked a few times. What? Yeah, no, his girlfriend was okay with it. But she's not his girlfriend anymore, and I really thought we'd finally figure our shit out and get together, but I'm pretty sure Christian might've been using me for a little bi exploration, and I..."

It made him sick, thinking about the words they'd shouted at each other.

Had he brought this on? What exactly had Christian said—that he'd *thought* Logan only wanted to play around? Had he ever come across like that?

You didn't exactly ask him out. You didn't say you wanted him to be your boyfriend.

He grabbed his chest and started the slow walk to campus. Thinking about Christian with that term—*boyfriend*—threatened to give him heart failure. An actual romantic relationship with him was something he never thought he'd have, and here he'd fucked up any chance he had.

Noah had told him months ago that both of them were stubborn to a T. He hadn't believed him. He'd thrown Christian under the bus instead. But now look at him: because he hadn't talked about what he was feeling, he might've lost everything for good.

He'd blistered his feet. They ached with every step he took as the adrenaline died down. But he deserved the agony, and he took it as penance.

He stopped in the lobby of his dorm. The desk attendant glanced up, blinking at him, but she didn't say anything and neither did he. Maybe she wouldn't care if he lived down there now. Maybe she'd blink every time she passed him on one of the couches and would keep on walking.

Eventually, though, he and Christian would have to cross paths. Unless Christian was planning on climbing down the tree outside their window to get to the dining hall, they would have to see each other, and he'd rather it happen sooner than later.

Why can't he talk to me first? Logan scrubbed his face as he took the elevator up. *Why do I have to be the one to fix shit? And why does he think fucking me or taking me out to brunch counts as fixing it?*

Christian had been the one to shout first. He'd been the first one to lay a hand on Logan. And that meant he needed to be the one to fix things. He wouldn't, of course. He'd be sitting in their bedroom with his headphones on, and Logan would have to get on his knees and plead.

Logan formed his game plan as he let himself into their suite. Noah and Daiki's door was closed, and that meant there was no one there to witness Logan's face contort in shock when he saw his empty bedroom.

Christian wasn't there. Of all of the outcomes Logan had imagined, none involved Christian leaving.

The only possible positive was that nothing was missing. Every single thing was still in place, minus a pair of shoes, and that meant he had to come back at some point. He hadn't taken off and run.

That realization gave little relief. Panic, thick and cloying, stirred in Logan's chest, and he made himself shut the bedroom door so he was alone in the darkness with nothing but the moonlight cutting through the blinds. He toed off his shoes and shakily crawled to the top bunk and buried his face in his pillow.

Everything was fucked up. Everything was ruined. There was no pretending this hadn't happened and that there wasn't more to say. Any way Logan approached it would more than likely end in tears.

At some point, he managed to roll over and force himself to take deep, even breaths, eyes on the dark ceiling. The pressure started to lift little by little. He could move again. Breathing became calmer.

But he was alone. He wasn't going to be sleeping tonight.

Eventually, the door opened and the lights snapped on, and he turned to see Christian standing in the doorway. Logan flicked his gaze over him dismissively and turned away. "It's two o'clock in the fucking morning." Logan's voice was so raw that any chance of intimidating him was gone. "Turn off the goddamn lights."

"As if you were sleeping." Christian's voice was tight as he shut the door. "You think I don't know how you sleep? When you let me hold you all night?"

Too raw. Too soon. He wasn't ready for vulnerability.

Logan took a deep breath and rolled onto his side so he could keep an eye on Christian—to track his movements in case he needed to prepare for another fight. But all Christian did was remove his shoes and look up at him again, his mouth set in a line, his eyes bloodshot. Logan frowned. "You on something, man?"

Christian huffed and came toward the bed. "You're fucking dumb." He stood at the edge, his height letting his gaze be almost even with Logan's as he lay there. "We need to talk, man, c'mon."

Panic shot through Logan. This wasn't the way the night was supposed to go. If Christian led the talk, Logan didn't know how he was supposed to follow. "No. Absolutely not." He rolled over, putting his face toward the wall. "I'm going to sleep."

"Logan."

"I'm not doing this tonight. I'm still fucking pissed at you."

"Brother, please."

He clenched his jaw and focused on those steady breaths again. "If you wanna talk so bad, you've gotta come up here. I'm not coming to you." It was a shitty thing to say, and they both knew it. There were a million reasons why Christian wouldn't come to his level.

When the bed frame shook, Logan whipped his head around. Christian was gingerly climbing up the ladder with his gaze to the ceiling.

"You're like ten feet tall." Logan sat up slowly. "How the fuck are you actually afraid of heights?"

"Shut up," Christian said shakily. He took a deep breath, then bobbed upward another few inches. His knuckles were pale where he dug them into the edge of the bed.

"Fucking incredible." With every step he took, Logan could see something new—the long, thin lines of darkened skin streaking down his cheeks, for example. Those made him catch his breath. Logan couldn't bear to think of what they might really mean. "You're kidding me. You're so scared of being up high that you started crying?"

"I didn't cry about the height." Christian finally got his knees on the bed. He grabbed the blanket like it was a life preserver. "Move over."

"Hell no." Logan plopped right back down, his chest practically against the wall. "If you wanna have this talk so bad, then you've gotta be on the outside." His last resort. His last chance to keep this from happening until he was prepared.

But Christian shocked him again. He crawled little by little until he was spooning Logan, every inch of his torso pressed flush against him.

As much as he wanted to, Logan tried desperately not to enjoy the contact. He was unused to being held like this. He'd always been the big spoon for his girlfriends after they'd had sex. To feel Christian throw an arm so carefully around his waist was almost more than his heart could take.

"We've gotta talk," Christian murmured with a gravelly voice.

Logan gulped. "I don't know if there's much to say."

"Oh, no, I think you know *exactly* what there is to say." Christian rubbed his hand over Logan's stomach deliberately, but, for once, there wasn't a trace of lust. It was comforting, somehow, with no expectations attached. "But I think you're scared of the words."

Fuck.

"I think you feel like if I lose my shit at you one more time, you don't know how you're gonna live with yourself. I don't think you believe you know *how* to live without me."

Stop. To be so easily read when he'd spent years trying to be tough was murderous.

"Just like I don't think I know how to live without you either."

Logan couldn't breathe.

"Listen…" Christian sighed against the back of his neck, face buried in his hair. "…I know you better than I know myself. Always have. When you put your mind to something, you take off after it, and I'm more than happy to follow right behind you. But the thing is, sometimes you get way far ahead of me. And sometimes it takes me a while to catch up."

Logan knew that better than anything.

"You were the one who first talked about us going to California and being big and famous. Remember? You were gonna write all my plays, and I was gonna be the star of them and make you big too. We were gonna go to college and learn how to make something of ourselves. And it wasn't gonna be easy, because we were so sure everybody around us in the industry was gonna be white as hell, but we were gonna show everybody. We were gonna fucking make our dreams come true."

Logan trembled in his arms. His eyes burned. *I'm not doing this. I'm not crying.*

"And I let you down. When our parents fought us on it, I could've stood up for that dream. But I didn't know how. I wasn't ready to be strong—not like you were. And it's my fault we're here, doing shit we hate instead of doing what we always wanted."

"No." Logan shook his head. "No, it's not—"

"It is. And I know it is." Christian kissed between his shoulder blades. "Just like I fucked this up too. You already knew what you wanted, and I was too dumb to see it." He shook his head, the tip of his nose tickling Logan's skin. "That's how I am, man. I lag behind. And you've gotta be patient while I catch up."

"I am, though. I wait for you all the time."

"I know." Christian grabbed his hand. "Because you're good, Logan. You're the best man I know."

That was higher praise than he was ready for. Logan exhaled shakily and curled into a tight ball, and Christian followed, cupping him perfectly with his body.

"You don't have to, though. You're not required to wait for me, and I know that. After the shit I've pulled recently, God knows you've got no reason to stand and watch me fumble in the dark."

"Christian." He turned his head, craning his neck to try to see him. "Don't say that."

"I fucked up. I know I did. I've fucked up over and over again while I was trying to figure this out, because, see…" Their fingers interlaced against Logan's stomach, like he needed an anchor. "…there's no guidebook to figuring this out, man. I don't have any way of knowing where I'm supposed to go. It's not the same, being with you."

"It's just me, Christian."

"But you're a guy. And I hate to say it, but that changes everything. Where we grew up, all the shit we got our heads filled with at church, my own dad pouring what he did into my head…it's not easy to shake. And I've never seen two dudes together that look like us anyway."

Logan glanced down at their joined hands, their dark skin tones perfect beside each other. But he was right. Every picture or movie he'd ever seen had nothing but two white guys next to each other. He nestled against Christian, trying to pull away from all of those conflicting thoughts.

"That's why I need time. Okay? Time to figure out exactly what I'm doing here."

It was the least Christian could ask for. There was no reason for Logan to tell him no. But things remained too veiled, and though it might be selfish, he needed a little extra reason to wait. "What exactly are you trying to figure out?"

Christian was silent.

"I don't mean that as, like, a fight or whatever, I promise, I..." He fumbled through his thoughts until he could find some way to word it. "Do you think we're just friends? Two guys who fuck sometimes? Or are we...?"

Christian gently rolled Logan over and stared down with eyes that were still wet. Logan reached to wipe the tear tracks from his cheeks, and Christian caught his hand too, pressing a kiss to the back of it. "No, man." He shook his head slowly. "No, there's never been anything about us that was *just friends*, has there?"

Their desperate closeness. The way they weren't afraid to touch. How they always found themselves rolling around on the ground to assert dominance. Watching porn together, dating the same girls one right after the other as if they were trying to taste the other man in them, staring too long, sharing the same bed until their parents were the ones to call them out...

Obviously, some people were able to handle such a close platonic friendship. But Logan had pulled back a veil, and now every single memory swam with clarity.

Of course, Logan hadn't had a bisexual crisis. Of course, it hadn't been something fervent and messy and panicked. He'd been in the thick of it since he was a kid, before he knew what it meant. It had been a part of him all along.

Christian rested his head on the pillow so they were nose to nose, holding Logan's hand in a death grip. "The thing is...like, when I kiss you and make love to you and stuff..."

Make love. His heart soared.

"...my head goes a little funny. I can't stop myself from touching you. It's like I've got a million missed chances that I'm trying to catch up with, and if I stop, I'll never get to feel it, you know?"

"Oh, I do."

"But it starts feeling like I'm using you. As if I'm doing what feels easy without doing the messy shit. Because having sex with you isn't hard. It makes sense. Figuring out what to call you the next time you and me go home..."

Logan nodded. Not only with their parents, but their old friends, and their neighbors, and every single person in Greenbarrow who knew them under one lens and wouldn't expect to see them beyond it.

Christian squeezed his eyes shut and exhaled raggedly. "So I need to stop that for a little while, I think. So I can think. So I know what exactly this is."

"Stop...everything?"

"The touching, the kissing, the sex. Like, I've gotta do the hard work before I can have the sweetness, man. Do you understand?"

He understood that his body recoiled at the thought of not being able to casually kiss Christian when he passed him in the hallway. Like a warning for the distance they'd had only a few weeks ago. "Can we still talk and see each other—"

"I'm not running this time, I promise. I'm gonna be right here. I just..." Christian chuckled sourly. "I can't keep taking the easy stuff from you and not figuring out what this is really gonna be. Not when you already know what you want."

Logan nodded, but he couldn't keep the pain from his face. "I-I'll miss it. I'll miss you."

"Hey." Christian kissed his forehead. "I'll be right here with you. We'll talk. We'll eat together. And I'll figure things out before you know it."

It'll take forever. It would be agonizing and painful. But maybe the time apart would pay off. Maybe they'd be able to make something work.

"Do you trust me?"

"I do. I'll always trust you."

"Okay, then." Christian smiled. "So, wait. I won't keep you there any longer than I have to. I promise."

Logan nodded again. They were concluding the conversation, but he was still standing on a tightrope with no way down or across. To wait there for Christian, to help him down, was the scariest challenge of trust they'd ever had. But he would do it, if that was what it took.

Christian touched their foreheads together. It was a terrible crime—how Christian could be so casually affectionate but unsure of what he wanted. "Listen, I know this is selfish as fuck after what I said, but do you wanna sleep together?"

Logan blinked. "As in...?"

"As in literally sleep together without any funny stuff. Get your mind out of the gutter."

Logan laughed. "Yeah, I guess I can do that." It would make it much harder to put an end to the touching afterward, but he couldn't bear to sleep alone after their blowout. "Your bed?"

"Please, God."

They made their way down together, Christian seeming like he was going to shit himself the entire time, and once they were on the floor, he wrapped his arms around Logan. Being held like that was simple, but...perfect. Everything he hadn't known he wanted.

"I'm sorry," Christian said.

Logan looked up at him.

"I didn't wanna let the night end without telling you straight up. I'm sorry. I'm sorry for everything that happened, and for not being honest with you about when Charlotte and me broke up, and for fucking you without telling you she wasn't involved anymore, and...I'm sorry for everything. And I'm gonna do better this time."

Logan opened his mouth, but the words wouldn't come out right. He couldn't say *it's okay*, as if what Christian had done had been appropriate. It took him a few seconds to figure out the only thing he could say back. "I forgive you."

Christian nodded. "Thank you. You don't have to do that."

"I know. But I do."

As they often had done before, they brushed their teeth together, but this time, Christian had an arm around Logan's waist, like he couldn't bear to let him go. When Logan took a piss before bed, he laughed at Christian lingering not too far outside of the cracked doorway.

Eventually, though, they were able to tangle up together in Christian's bed, flush together on their sides in nothing but their boxers. It was painful—Christian was hard against his ass, his breathing rough—but Logan steeled himself.

If he had to wait, then he would. At least until Christian thought himself into a hole he couldn't get back out of. Logan dearly hoped it wouldn't come to that.

CHRISTIAN HADN'T REALIZED exactly how much sexual tension crackled between him and Logan until the second he couldn't do anything about it.

Logan, for example, looked damn good in nothing but a long-sleeved black thermal shirt and a pair of jeans. Looked good enough to bend over a table and eat.

But he wouldn't. He was strong. Until he could look at himself in the mirror, ready to tell every asshole in the world he was dating a man, he wasn't going to toy with Logan's body—or his heart. He was better than that, regardless of what his recent track record showed.

Even if it killed him, Christian would have to make do with watching Logan smile at him across the room, knowing he couldn't carry him to his bed and worship him.

Christian had a lot to come to terms with, however, and dealing with it came at the strangest times. He'd had to leave the bedroom to protect his sanity—doing his homework at the coffee table instead of watching Logan suck on the end of a pen—and then, he'd immediately become lost in his thoughts.

He'd gotten lucky with Charlotte, though he still carried some resentment in his gut for how she'd ended things. And yet, there was no better person to introduce him to how people didn't always fit in perfect boxes. She was the first openly bisexual woman he'd met, and she was so freely *herself* that it hadn't been a difficult transition for Christian to accept his own bisexuality.

It wasn't shameful. Charlotte was so open about her interests. She'd comment on a woman being attractive as they walked together, and Christian would nod and say, "Yeah, fuck, she sure is" without worrying about any fallout. Though he didn't have the confidence to say the same thing about a man, he trusted her not to shoot him down for it.

Though he didn't *have* to fit in a box, he craved boundaries, and he searched for ones that might exist. There was the box for having a relationship with Logan and what life would look like for them together. Obviously, there were people who had closeted relationships, but Christian didn't want to live like that if he could truly and safely be himself. He wanted to brag about Logan's accomplishments. He wanted to kiss him in the middle of town. He wanted his mom to know exactly who she was asking after when she called with questions about his love life.

But that was a box they didn't have at home. People who didn't fit within perfect conservative boundaries were prayed about so they'd be healed of their *affliction*.

So maybe it was foolish to want to fit in a box regardless. Maybe he should shrug it off and be himself. But he still wanted an instruction manual to show him how to do things right: how to be a good boyfriend to another man, how to protect them both if somebody gave them shit, and how to jump through whatever hoops were necessary to get the same domestic shit everybody else had—like insurance.

He wanted boundaries. He wanted the safety of doing it *right*. One day, he'd be able to climb out of the box, hand in hand with Logan. But until then...

There was a knock at the door, dragging him from his thoughts, and he went to open it. His RA Aavai stood outside, his *dastaar* impeccably in place as always. "Hey, Christian."

"Hey, what's up?"

"Not much." He thumbed down the hallway. "I wanted to pop in and let you know that the dorm needs a count of how many guys are gonna be staying for Thanksgiving break. Nothing to worry about, but I need to know for safety reasons and how many of us RAs might need to stick around to cover the building. Will you let Logan, Daiki, and Noah know to come by my room and sign the sheet outside my door before the end of the day?"

"Yeah, man, no problem." He smiled.

"Cool." Aavai gave a little salute. "Have a good day!"

"You too!" He shut the door and headed toward his bedroom, slowing as he approached. Logan was stretching his lean arms over his head—a hint of stomach exposed under the hem of his shirt—and desire hit Christian like a truck. *Later. I'll tell him later.* It was a matter of self-preservation to hurry toward Noah and Daiki's room instead.

His mind was so muddled that he knocked once and then opened the door without waiting for a response. "Hey, guys, just wanted to—oh!"

A half-naked Daiki and Noah sprang apart on the lower bunk, eyes huge and lips swollen. Daiki moved in front of Noah, eyes now challengingly focused on Christian's face.

Christian froze in shock, his mouth hanging open as he took in the scene. After weeks of feeling like he needed to hide his explorations with Logan, he had no idea how to comprehend he'd apparently been wrong all along.

Words finally came to him as he backed into the hallway and shut the door to a crack. "I'm so sorry; I'm fucking rude... Hey, uh, Aavai stopped by to say something, and when y'all have a sec, lemme know, and I'll fill you in. It's, like, a sign-up thing, uh..."

"Can you text the info to us?" Daiki asked in an admirably strong, steady voice.

"Yeah, absolutely. Sorry again." He shut the door and stared at the wall, his head spinning with this new knowledge.

He'd seen something he wasn't supposed to have. In hindsight, he shouldn't be surprised by the two of them fucking around—they were inseparable, like Christian and Logan. But that didn't make him violating their privacy any more forgivable. He would've beaten the shit out of anybody who walked in on him kissing Logan.

He was a shitty-ass roommate. He hadn't spent much time getting to know Daiki or Noah, and Noah had been a source of jealousy from the moment he'd started taking Logan's time away from Christian. Now, with what he knew, any distance he kept from Daiki and Noah might be misunderstood and make them uncomfortable.

He didn't know how to handle this from the outside. He'd never known people, other than himself, who were closeted about a relationship before. Was it appropriate to sit them down and tell them he didn't see them any differently? That they had nothing to be scared of? That Christian wouldn't tell a single goddamn soul, even Logan?

Christian knew something about secrets now. He knew how important it was to keep them, especially when it came to safety. But he didn't want to put his foot in his mouth.

He floated toward his bedroom as if in a dream and knocked gently on the open door. "Hey. Gonna go walk and grab some coffee. You want any?"

"Not really." Logan grabbed his hoodie. "Maybe I'll walk with you, though, so—"

"No, I, uh..." Christian cleared his throat. "I wanna go alone."

Logan blinked.

"It has nothing to do with you. Don't give me those sad puppy dog eyes, man. You've got homework, and I've got some shit on my mind, okay?" Christian shook his head. "I'll get you a muffin or something if you stop looking like that."

"Like what?" The puppy dog eyes intensified.

"All right, fuck you."

As Christian left, Logan laughed behind him. The sound faded as he went into the hallway and pulled out his phone, texting the information he'd promised to all three of his roommates.

He wasn't sure this was going to be a good plan, but he'd go with it to the best of his ability.

AN HOUR LATER, after he'd enjoyed his own hot drink at the cafe, Christian returned to the suite. He wordlessly put a chocolate-chip muffin next to Logan, who had his headphones on and was typing furiously, and didn't acknowledge the nod he received before heading across the living room.

He knocked at Noah and Daiki's door, clearing his throat. "Hey, uh, I brought some hot chocolate from the cafe for you guys."

There was a long moment with no response—long enough for Christian to turn and start walking back toward his bedroom—but then the door cracked open, and he glanced over his shoulder.

Noah stood in the doorway with a familiar, nervous expression on his face. When Christian faced him, he lifted his chin challengingly, and Christian fought the urge to smile.

Noah clearly didn't need Daiki to kick ass for him. He'd do it himself, if he had to.

Christian looked over the top of his head and saw he was alone. He wordlessly held the hot chocolate out.

"Thanks." Noah took the cup carefully, staring down at it.

"I wanted to say I'm sorry for walking in on y'all again. I wasn't thinking right, and it was rude and..."

"It's fine."

"It's really not, no, but I'm not gonna do it again." It was one thing to make the promise, he knew, and another to prove it. "I hope this doesn't sound weird, but there's really nothing you've gotta be afraid of with me or Logan. Seriously. I'm not gonna say a word, and nobody's gonna know anything unless you want them to. I promise."

When Noah stared at him without speaking, the true awkwardness of the situation crept over Christian. He didn't know what the hell he was saying. He wasn't ready to tell Noah *why* he and Daiki were safe, but all he was doing right now was making Noah more uncomfortable.

His direct gaze made Christian flinch. He hated weakness in himself, but he couldn't look at him if he was going to be so strong.

"I want to tell you something," Noah said.

"Sure." Christian rubbed the back of his neck. "Shoot, man."

"Come in."

As Noah stepped aside, Christian hesitated before he entered. It was the first time he'd been in their bedroom, and he took everything in, from the colorful, overcrowded armoire filled with clothes that he recognized as Daiki's to the open and nearly empty wardrobe that must be Noah's. Card games and sheet music covered every available surface. A poster of what appeared to be a Japanese boy band was slapped on one wall. Getting a glimpse of the private lives of his roommates became twice as embarrassing when he caught sight of the unopened condom on the desk.

Noah shut the door behind Christian. "For the record, I really don't care if you know I'm gay. I've been out to my friends and family since I was in middle school. I'm pretty sure you know that if you made any trouble about it, you wouldn't be on this campus for much longer, so...yeah."

For a guy trying to act tough, Noah's voice still quavered at the end. Christian elected not to comment on it. "I wouldn't say anything. Promise. Neither would Logan. We're cool."

"That's not what I wanted to talk about." Noah crossed his arms. "I trust Logan. I think he's going to be a really good friend of mine. You intimidated the hell out of me when we first moved in, but I got over it. It's weird, but I trust you too."

"Wait, why is that *weird*?"

"I'm not done yet." Noah took a deep breath. "I'm telling you this *because* I trust you—and because my anxiety has been driving me up the wall since before we all moved in. I don't like secrets. I don't like thinking you're going to find something I didn't hide very well that tells you everything about me, and I don't like having these stupid fears that you're going to beat the shit out of me when you *do* find out, because they're not based in reality, and..."

Christian waited. He couldn't imagine what might possibly make him want to gang up on a sweet guy like Noah. He wasn't that kind of asshole, and he needed to prove it to him.

"I'm trans."

Oh. Oh, shit.

"That's it, really. That's all I wanted to say." Noah's jaw tightened. "That's...why Daiki freaked out today. He's protective. He wants me to stay safe."

Christian knew he was supposed to speak now. Noah had just opened up to him with an enormous secret, and it was on the tip of his tongue to spill one in return—his most precious one. But Logan wasn't there to agree to sharing it, and he couldn't find the words anyway. He stammered for a moment and covered his mouth, cheeks heating up. *I'm a goddamn fool. C'mon, idiot, you've got lips. Use them.* "Okay. Thanks for, uh, telling me."

That's not enough, asshole. He was about to start rambling, but Christian couldn't let this be the last damn thing he said. "I'm really glad you trust me enough to let me know. I'm not gonna tell a soul. Seriously. I've never known someone who was trans, but...well, I don't *think* I have, I..." He waved his hands in the air in front of him as he struggled to find the words.

Noah's lips quirked. "You haven't had somebody come out to you as trans."

"Yeah! Yeah, that...fuck. My bad."

"You're fine."

Words weren't going to do shit here. He could swear up and down that he'd keep Noah's confidence, but only time would show it. He set the second cup of hot chocolate on the desk and rubbed his hands together nervously. "Listen, your clothes..." As he peered at the wardrobe again, all he could see were baggy hoodies and a few pairs of pants. "This is gonna sound stupid, because I know I'm, like, ridiculously taller than you, but Daiki's a little less broad than you in the shoulder, so..."

Noah blinked up at him, wrinkling his brow.

"I guess I just mean that if you ever wanna, like, borrow any of my clothes, you totally can." He shrugged. "Also, about the, uh, the razor bumps." He gestured vaguely toward his own face, and Noah followed his finger with his gaze, his hand starting to shake around the cup. "There's this thing my stepdad got me into, but it's, like, an old-timey shaving brush, right? And when you put the shaving cream on your face with it, the bristles do some magic shit where they move the hair around so you don't get those razor bumps when you're done shaving. So, if you want, I can hook you up with the info about the company that makes what I use, and you could check it out. Might...irritate you less, I guess."

Noah closed his eyes, letting out a shaky breath, and when he opened them again, they were a little more full of moisture. "That'd be awesome."

"Yeah?"

"Yeah, totally." He rubbed his hands together nervously. "Listen, I'm...I'm sorry I didn't tell you before—"

"Stop." Christian shook his head. "Dude, that's not— No, you're fine. Please don't apologize. You belong here, okay? You're right where you're supposed to be."

Noah laughed and nodded, swiping his arm across his eyes. "Still, I'm sorry you had to walk in on me and Daiki. I mean it, I didn't give a shit if you knew, but we've been trying to keep it low-key so you guys didn't feel weird."

"You don't have to worry." *God, the things I could tell him.* "You don't have to hide anything from me or Logan. This is your home as much as it is ours. And we're not gonna be weird about anything." He paused. "Besides teasing the shit out of you guys if you're being cute."

Noah's cheeks turned a bright pink. "Thanks. Seriously. I kind of thought you hated me. I didn't know why."

"You've been a great roommate. Promise." The day might come when he would explain his past jealous urges and frustration, but not that day, not when he didn't quite know what the hell was going on with him and Logan. But it did his heart some good to see it normalized somehow—to see two guys who were different from the media standard, discovering and loving each other in new ways. "Listen, we'll hang after Thanksgiving break, okay? You going home for it?"

"Yeah. You?"

"I think so." He shrugged. "It's been a while since I talked to my parents, so I guess I owe them that."

Noah blinked up at him. "Don't get along with them well?"

"It's not that. It's..." Christian nearly let the whole story spill. There was something so unassuming and thoughtful about Noah. No wonder Logan liked spending time with him. "I've changed a lot since I got here. I don't know how they're really gonna take that."

Noah nodded. Understanding shone behind his eyes like a spotlight. "Well, whatever you decide to do, I hope it goes well."

"Thanks, man. Hey, enjoy your hot chocolate."

Noah chuckled. "Thanks again. I really appreciate it."

"No problem."

Christian returned to the bedroom and flopped on his bed—lay there staring up at the bunk above him. He glanced over at Logan, who was sitting at his desk and now carefully watching *him*. He did that a lot now; he was obviously waiting to see if Christian had gotten his head on straight yet.

Not yet, man. He flashed him a smile, and Logan gave one back before he returned to his essay. *Stick with me. We'll make it happen.* But it was clear figuring their relationship out was going to take a little more time than Christian had expected.

He could work with that. It just might not look pretty.

Chapter Ten

LOGAN

Thank God that's over... Logan pushed open his bedroom door and exhaled all of the tension that had been in his shoulders. He'd just finished presenting a project to his class—the class he had with Kelly Anne. He'd been certain she'd find reasons to humiliate him in front of the class, but he'd done well. He'd held his own, even under the weight of his professor's stern words and expression, and now he didn't have to worry about much of anything.

Only a few more days and he wouldn't have to worry about classes for a whole week. He was more ready for the break than he could say.

Christian was pacing, phone pressed to his ear, and Logan furrowed his brow as he entered, trying to get his attention. When Christian glanced over, he waved him off. Clearly there was no emergency, but his expression was severe enough to make Logan worry. "It's only a project, Mom. I promise it's fine."

Bad grade? Logan sat his backpack down and leaned against the chest of drawers. Mrs. Brown was a pretty notorious worrywart around Greenbarrow, and if Christian had done something to get on her bad side, he was going to have a hard time digging himself out of the hole.

"I've got it under control." He turned his back to Logan and mumbled, "I need to be on campus to work on it. Need primary sources from the library."

Logan stood a little taller, blinking. The way Christian was speaking, it almost sounded like...

"No, because if I check them out and bring them there, then my group members can't use the books for their part of the project. I've gotta stay here so we can share them. We're meeting, like, every day so we can exchange them. It's the only way we're gonna get work done."

Logan's heart hammered in his chest.

"Yeah. No, yeah, I know, Mom. I'm sorry. It's this one time. I'll be home for winter break. Thanksgiving's, like, nothing compared to that."

He's staying here? Over the break?

"I've gotta go. I love you too. Bye."

The second Christian hung up, Logan pounced. "You finished your last project *yesterday.*"

Christian winced as he turned around. "Yeah, I..."

Logan waited. There was no way he was jumping in. Not yet. Not when there were a million things Christian wasn't saying.

Finally, he sighed. "I needed more time to think. Where nobody was gonna see us." Christian gestured toward the door. "Both Daiki and Noah are going home for the break, okay? So it'd be you and me here, where we could be alone, and..."

What does that mean? Logan stepped forward, eyes wide. "You mean that? You know what you want now?"

"I absolutely don't." He shook his head. "I'm close, I-I think...I wanna be sure, okay?"

"We can talk about it."

"I'm not ready to talk yet." Christian started walking past him to the bathroom.

Logan touched his arm. "How are you gonna figure anything out if you can't talk about it with me when we're not either pissed off or crying or fucking, dude?"

"Logan." Christian grabbed his shoulders and held him still, his voice firm. "I. Need. Time. You said you were gonna give me that. Remember?"

He hadn't known that it would be weeks or months when he'd agreed—especially since Christian hadn't made a lick of progress yet. What was he waiting for? Did he need the skies to open up so God Himself could tell Christian to let Logan ride that dick? "Christian."

"A little longer." Christian walked away. "I promise."

As the bathroom door shut, Logan huffed and sat on the edge of his chest of drawers. It was going to be the longest week of his life. He knew it to the core of him.

Still, if Christian was staying... He pulled the phone out of his pocket, frowning as he stared at the screen.

There was only one way to make him think a little faster.

BY THE TIME Christian finished his shower, Logan was lying on his own bed, phone dangling from his hand. Even that far away, he could hear his mom talking, going through her lecture.

Christian gave him a knowing look, opening and closing his hand like a duck's bill, and Logan nodded, closing his eyes as he put the phone back to his ear.

"...just think you need to have a little more respect for your family. Your grandmother isn't going to be around forever, you know, and she and your grandfather are traveling quite a distance for Thanksgiving."

"I'll see them at Christmas, Mom."

"I think—"

Logan dropped his arm again and sighed, rubbing his eyes. When Christian touched his shin, giving it a comforting rub, he twisted on the sheets to give him what he hoped was an inviting stare. All he got in response was a quirk of Christian's lips before he moved away and started shoving papers around his desk.

So much for being inviting. Logan returned to the phone.

"...be more projects in the future. There's only one family."

"I know, but I've gotta keep my grades high so I can get those internships in a couple of years, remember?"

Silence. "I'm disappointed that you procrastinated this long on this project. If you don't come home for this break, remember this is your only chance to slack off. Your father and I are paying a lot of money to keep you in school. You could've gone somewhere local—"

Somewhere Christian wouldn't have been. "All right, Mom, I've gotta go. It's time for dinner."

"Logan Daniels, I'm not done with this conversation."

"I know you're not, but I am. Bye, Mom." And he hung up.

Christian whistled from across the room as Logan quickly put his phone on Do Not Disturb. "She's gonna have your ass, man."

"Whatever." He shoved his phone in his pocket and rolled onto his side. "Seriously, I'm done with her. She wants to hold college over my head—like she wouldn't piss her pants if I dropped out tomorrow." He rolled his eyes. "Maybe I won't be here next year. Has she ever thought about that?"

"Yeah? Where would you be?"

Somewhere there's a beach and a lot of sun and it doesn't get too cold. Somewhere I could actually write. "Who knows? The world's our oyster, right?"

Christian stared at him hard. The air stirred up, like a tornado was getting ready to whip through, like the only thing keeping Christian from Logan's arms was how high he was off the ground. Logan sat up, ready to go to him if he so much as blinked.

But he didn't. He cleared his throat and looked away, like he hadn't been practically begging Logan with his eyes to run away with him to California.

"Anyway, I'm staying for the break now." He shrugged. "In case you wanna talk about how you're feeling."

Christian nodded. "I'll keep that in mind."

The fight he'd had with his mom hadn't meant anything if Christian wasn't going to talk to him about what was on his mind. They might end up sitting in the dorm for a week watching TV and eating nothing but pizza and Chinese food.

Stubborn. We're both stubborn. Christian would go for another year thinking about this, if he had the chance, and Logan would be there stewing and getting pissy while he waited for him.

But if they never got anywhere...

He has another twenty-four hours, and then I'm making my move. And he can't stop me.

IT WAS SWEET, watching Daiki and Noah walk hand in hand out of the dorm, their bags banging against their legs. Another time, they might even go home together—

Logan wished them that pleasure. It wasn't strange to see them like that. Somehow, he felt like he'd known about them all along.

They hadn't lingered either, probably because Logan had come out of the bathroom in nothing but a towel right when they were saying goodbye to Christian.

He almost felt bad for being the reason they'd hurried off so fast. Almost. But he had a plan, and twenty-four hours had passed, and Christian was staring at him like a starving man.

Logan leaned against the doorframe, pushing his hair away from his face. Drops of water tickled his skin as they trailed down his chest and stomach. "Like what you see, man?"

Christian opened his mouth, closed it, and shook his head as he started walking past him. "I know what you're doing."

"Yeah?"

"And it's not gonna work. I asked you for time."

"You've *had* time," Logan reminded him as he trailed after him into the bedroom. "I think what you need now is to actually talk about what's on your mind so we can figure out where things stand."

"And if I'm not ready to talk?"

"Then maybe you need to do it anyway, because you're never actually gonna *be* ready. There's always gonna be something stopping you if you don't take a chance."

"You and Charlotte." Christian scoffed as he pointed at him. "The two of you always think you know better than me—about my life and my mind and my heart. Well, I'm about sick of it."

Logan crossed his arms. "Charlotte knew you for, what, two months when she did that? I've known you for twelve goddamn years. And I *know* that you're stubborn and like to dig your heels in real good. I like to do that too, but sometimes, we've both gotta stop and look at ourselves and realize we're never gonna figure everything out *by ourselves.*"

"I'm done talking about this." Christian waved him off and shut the bathroom door behind him, locking it.

Logan sighed and leaned against the chest of drawers, tugging at one of his curls. *One, two, three...*

The door flew open again, and Christian stormed out with something held right in front of Logan's eyes. "What the hell is this doing in there?"

It was their bottle of lube. He shrugged, staring at Christian with wide eyes. "I don't know, man. It's almost like if you wanna be fucked these days, you've gotta do it yourself or something."

Christian's jaw dropped. His eyes heated up as he dropped his gaze to Logan's waist, lingering for a long second—and then he dropped the lube on the floor and grabbed him and pulled him in for a fierce kiss.

Logan would have time to feel guilty for pushing him later, but right now? He needed this. He groaned and raked his nails down Christian's arms, trying to pull him closer.

Somehow the kiss wasn't enough. If he kept things moving casually—relying on the hope of a kiss accelerating things—they wouldn't get anywhere. Waiting for Christian hadn't done shit but left Logan confused and frantic. And he had other plans up his sleeve to make sure Christian was along for the ride.

Logan dropped to his knees, the towel falling loose and pooling around his legs, and mouthed at Christian's cock through his shorts.

"Fuck..."

That's it. Logan grabbed him by the ass and yanked him an inch closer, glancing up to watch Christian press a hand against the wall to keep himself upright. He was already hard. *What were you gonna do, man? Go jerk off in the bathroom when you had me right here waiting for you?* Logan moaned against the rough fabric, dragging his tongue over it in a slow tease before he started pulling Christian's shorts and boxers down together. He didn't want a condom this time, the taste of Christian's precum be damned. He couldn't take his time and miss out on anything.

"You're fucking beautiful," Christian breathed as he buried his fingers in Logan's hair.

Being with him was fucking perfect. He grabbed Christian's ass and groaned as he bobbed his head up and down his cock, desperate to breathe a little enchantment into him—to make him unable to think of anything but how perfectly they fit together.

Christian tugged at his locks, moving him into a steady pace that Logan was more than happy to keep up with, and for a few moments, everything bled together impeccably—how he moved his hips, how Logan opened his mouth a little wider, how the air was thick and crackling with tension—and then Christian swore under his breath. "Need you, man, c'mere."

Logan didn't mind the pain in his arms when Christian wrenched him up. Logan gave him another kiss, one out of millions he planned, and ground their hips. Their hard cocks moved together awkwardly, enough to make it feel *real* instead of like a perfect fantasy. "Fuck me, Christian?"

"Where's the, fuck, the lube's rolled under the—"

"Don't need it, just *fuck* me."

"I'm not fucking you dry, you little shit!" Christian ran his hands down Logan's back and dug his teeth into his neck, sucking a mark so deep it made Logan's knees wobble. The exact second Christian's fingers teased over his hole, everything came to a stop.

Christian leaned over him so fast that Logan caught himself on the chest of drawers, bent backward by their chests pushed together. Two fingers rubbed over his slick hole, and Logan held his breath as they pressed experimentally inside him, where he'd stretched himself too thoroughly during the entire shower—three fingers, then four.

"You planned this," Christian murmured in a quiet sense of wonder.

With their bodies so intimately close, Logan thought his legs might give out completely. Christian might have to fuck him on the floor. "Hoped for it," he remedied. "I need you to fuck me, man, I can't stand waiting—give me your fucking cock."

Christian squeezed his ass so hard Logan was sure he'd leave bruises peppered over his skin. Logan's cock twitched between them as he cried out. "Yeah." He whipped Logan around face-first against the bureau and shoved him a few inches higher. Logan's dick was trapped painfully against the hard surface, and he wiggled his feet in shock when he realized Christian had intentionally put him right where he couldn't touch the ground.

It's trust. Logan grabbed the far end of the chest of drawers, his entire body quivering with need. "Fuck me," he whispered again. "*Please*, Christian—"

"I've got you." He started to turn away, and whether it was for a condom or the lube Logan didn't care.

Logan threw out a hand and grabbed Christian's wrist, yanking him back. "Don't need anything, man. I'm prepped, we're negative on our testing, it's just us. *Please*."

Whatever had been holding him back flew out the window. Christian huffed and spit into his hand, rubbing it over his cock, then grabbed Logan's hip and held him firmly as he guided himself inside him.

"Fuck!" Logan arched and whined—how was it that even after stretching himself so carefully, he *still* felt the incredible thickness of Christian's cock? "Oh fuck, Christian, c'mon..."

"This what you want?" His voice was nothing but a growl. "You want me to fuck you like this? Keep you guessing? Keep you at my mercy?"

Logan tried to press back on him, desperate after his long tease in the shower, but both of Christian's hands were pinning his hips down hard enough to make his cock ache. *Perfect, it's perfect...* "Please... Hard, fast, just *take me*."

"Yeah?" Christian eased in with quick, shallow thrusts, little by little, until his hips were flush against Logan's ass. Only then did Logan feel how his lover's hands were shaking on his skin. "You need me?"

"More than anything."

Christian leaned forward, chest against his back, and nibbled on the shell of his ear. "Beg me."

Shit, that shouldn't turn me on so much. Being held in place at his mercy was bad enough, but being *commanded* to give him full submission... Logan's voice trembled as he spoke. "Christian, I need you to fuck the shit out of me 'til I can't walk straight, *please...*"

"That's good." Christian kissed his cheek, a fleeting moment of soft sweetness. "You got it."

Logan thought he was ready to handle him like that. He was so completely wrong.

Christian stood tall and drilled him with his cock, shaking him to the core. His hands kept them meeting in the middle, pushing him away only an inch every time so their bodies would slap together again half a second later. Each brutal thrust knocked the breath right out of Logan, and his knuckles went white as he clung to the edge of the bureau.

Christian owned him down to the depths of him, branding him with white-hot need and pleasure with every stroke. He made him straddle an edge—breathtaking prostate stimulation combined with the almost painful pressure on his cock, crushed between the wooden chest and Logan's body—and yet Logan wanted more. He wanted hours of this, learning his body's limitations and exactly how far Christian could push him before his control gave out.

With the burn of Christian's teeth on his neck and ear, the fingers bruising his hips, and the chest of drawers digging into his thighs, Logan was starting to think he might *never* find that edge. Maybe this was all he needed—being fucked out of his skin and only clinging to the vestige of awareness that the pain gave him.

He *liked* it. And that was terrifying.

Being pounded wasn't enough to make him come, not nearly. But being so wrapped up in Christian was like being pulled into the air above them, as if Logan was floating outside of his body, watching their aching, primal dance, with all the desperation in Christian's form and all the need in his own whining.

It wasn't until something dripped onto the wooden surface beneath him that Logan realized he'd started to cry.

Christian groaned sharply and slammed into him one, two, three more times, and then he held tight against Logan, grinding slowly as he came inside him. The second he started to pull out, Logan reached behind him and grabbed his hip, keeping them together. The tears hadn't stopped. He wasn't sure *how* to stop them; he never cried enough to figure that out.

"Logan?" Christian ran a hand up his back, as gentle as a lamb, and wrapped his fingers behind his neck.

Something about being touched there unlocked the burning in his chest. Logan sucked in a wet breath, pressing his cheek to the bureau so he could see him from the corner of his eye.

"Hey, hey, what's wrong?" Panic filled Christian's voice. "Did I go too rough? I'm so sorry, I-I thought—"

"I'm scared." Unfamiliar words, and saying them right then was like pulling his heart out and setting it in Christian's hands. This was the only way he could admit his secret—having him crushingly close, feeling their bodies so intimately connected. "I'm so fucking scared, man."

Christian stared at him for a few silent seconds, and then his face began to crumple. Tears filled his eyes. Logan awkwardly tried to reach behind him to wipe them away, but his arm refused to bend. It didn't matter. Christian slid his arms around him like two strong bands, holding him tight and shaking against him.

"I'm scared too," he confessed. "I'm sorry. But I am too."

They stayed still, time leaving them behind, and cried themselves dry. But it was okay, because they were together, and nothing was going to rip them apart.

THEY NAPPED—OF course they did—and when Christian woke, for once, Logan was the one staring down at him. Still naked and chilled in the air of their dorm, Christian pulled him closer and buried his face in his neck.

Their hands wandered, as they were wont to do. Their passionate tryst, only a couple of hours before, had opened a gate in his chest that he'd been afraid to touch, and, as he'd thought, he couldn't keep his hands off Logan anymore. He was drowning in him.

There was no intent to their touch, he realized as minutes began to tick by. Neither of them seemed able to get hard again, but their fingers still breezed down each other's chests, over their flaccid cocks, and along their inner thighs. It was a different sort of exploration than he'd gotten used to.

There was...something beautiful about it, really—that he could discover Logan's body, from the handful of stretch marks on the inside of his thighs to the way his balls fit in his palm, without the pressure to give into something erotic.

He could find intimacy with him without wearing himself raw, and that was beautiful.

Logan's hand came to a stop in the soft thatch of his pubic hair, rubbing in a wide, smooth circle. "What are you thinking about?"

Christian chewed on his bottom lip as he wrapped an arm around Logan's waist and pulled him closer. "Why didn't you want me to use a condom?"

Logan glanced away immediately.

"I'm not mad or anything; I just...I didn't realize you'd...want that." Christian envisioned copious amounts of slickness dripping out of him, making a sticky path down Logan's leg—how annoying it would be if that had really happened.

Logan took a deep breath and looked him in the eye. "I wanted to know it was real."

"Real?" Christian chuckled. "What, did you think you were dreaming the whole thing?" With how rough he'd been, he almost expected Logan to pretend their fucking hadn't happened.

"It's not that, I...man, you've been so hot and cold sometimes." Logan buried his face in Christian's shoulder, words muffled against his skin. "Thought you hated me. Thought you never wanted me. Thought I'd been wrong about everything this whole damn time. So, when you wanted to fuck me again, I guess I just wanted to really feel it."

"You wanted to have some proof that it happened?"

Logan nodded.

Christian hadn't realized hiding from Logan would have such a strong effect on him.

Logan stuck to his hip like Velcro, but he'd always given off an air of being his own man before. If Christian needed to back away from something to figure shit out—a group project, a high-level academic class, an event they'd been planning to go to—Logan would pout, but he'd eventually accept it and rally to get things done himself. He'd always known Christian was there for him.

Or maybe he hadn't. Maybe Christian had been wrong the entire time. Maybe Logan had been carrying a ticking time bomb of anxiety inside him—and Christian had ultimately been the one to press the button.

Christian wrapped both arms around him until they were crushed together. "It's real, man. All of this is real. You don't need me inside you for you to know it. You've got me. Okay? I'm here with you."

Logan nodded. For a flash, all Christian could see were the unfamiliar tears rolling down Logan's cheeks as he bent over him on the chest of drawers, and the weight of this entire relationship sank down on him.

Every second that he kept his distance from Logan, only caused him to suffer with questions and indecision and stress. Though he'd taken a step away to keep his own stress off Logan's shoulders, Logan had ultimately ended up with all of it—and more.

He'd fucked up. Every time he'd ever done this, he'd fucked up.

"I'm not going anywhere," Christian whispered against the top of his head. "You've gotta know I'm not. I couldn't leave you behind."

Logan began to shake in his arms, his fingers digging into Christian's arms.

"I don't know what the hell's happening with us, but I know that no matter what, I'm not leaving you. Even if we end up just being friends or being something more, we're gonna be close. I mean it."

"You really think we could go back? That we could...pretend none of this ever happened? That I never felt like this?"

"That *we* never felt like this." The soft correction was enough to make Logan whine—as if he was stunned Christian could ever admit he was feeling something. As if Christian could hide his pounding heart and how his body didn't feel right unless Logan was in the room with him. He needed Logan in whatever way he could get him.

And maybe Logan needed him too, in ways he couldn't imagine.

"I don't know." Christian couldn't guarantee anything anymore. But he'd fight to the death to keep his best friend with him until the day he died. Every future he imagined had Logan beside him. Whether their future involved them holding hands or not was a completely different ballgame. "I don't know what our relationship will look like. I only know you're it for me. You've got something about you I can't shake."

Logan laughed, dry and a little bitter. "Why is it we can only talk about this shit when we're postcoital?"

"'Cuz you make me feel vulnerable, man," Christian whispered. "I can't hide from you anymore."

"Is that why you wanted to stay away from me for a while?"

He squeezed his eyes shut. "I told you. I'm scared."

"But we can be scared together, can't we?"

Could we? One of them had to be tough. One of them had to have everything together, or else everything was going to fuck up. That was how things had always gone: one of them could be weak as long as the other one was strong.

Logan tipped his head back. "We can figure it out together."

The dam finally broke. "But what if we fuck it up?"

"You think we've never fucked up anything in our life?" Logan chuckled. "We've bullshitted our way through entire group presentations. We've broken hearts. We've broken *furniture.* We've had to stand in the principal's office together when he wanted us to throw each other under the bus and tell him which one of us flooded all the toilets in the men's room. Brother, we've got a trail of fucked up shit behind us." He touched Christian's cheek when he tried to turn away. "This shit is messy, okay? All of it. We haven't done it before. But maybe if we try hard and believe in ourselves, we can make something really good."

"You sound like you're telling a fairy tale. Believe in ourselves..."

"Maybe it is. But maybe they're real."

Logan had always talked crazy. But there was something charming enough about him for Christian to almost believe him every single time.

"Just think about it," Logan murmured as he snuggled close again. "I don't want you to give me something perfect. I wanna figure this out *with* you, not have you figure it out *for* me. Understand?"

"Yeah." For the first time, he understood everything, like putting on a pair of glasses and seeing that individual leaves actually existed.

Maybe Christian wasn't the tree, with Logan sprouting blossoms with his help. Maybe they were both vines—with their own leaves—that had tangled together somewhere along the way.

GIVING IN AGAIN wasn't hard. Christian knew it wouldn't be. The second he tasted Logan's lips, he knew he'd be stepping over the edge of a cliff and hoping to land in his arms again and again.

The more remarkable part was the ridiculous positions they found themselves in.

Fucking Logan over the couch, for example—not quite on it, but with Logan perched on the arm, Christian's hands digging into his plush hips. He watched how Logan gave in and leaned back, hands on the cushions, arching beautifully with every thrust.

Logan began to shake, his eyes closed and his skin flushing. "Feels incredible, don't, don't stop."

"Not gonna." Christian pushed himself, his body aching, as he fucked into him even harder. "Not gonna stop, baby, c'mon, let me make you feel good."

Logan whimpered. He put all of his weight on one hand and touched his cock with the other, and the second he made contact, he cried out. "Oh God, it's so fucking good, Christian, *please*..."

There was a whole new sense of power that came with knowing he was the only person who'd made Logan feel like this before—that they were discovering new moments together. Christian kept his eyes on him, not blinking, until Logan shouted and came all over his own chest.

"Shit—" The sight was enough to make Christian come just as fast. His release was a simpler pleasure, one that rushed over him and then left quickly, and he caught his breath, watching as Logan gradually came back to himself.

Logan slid out of his grip, his ass landing on the cushions, and a smile crossed Christian's face. It snuck up on him, like everything he felt for Logan. He let his gaze linger, drinking him in. Sighing, he removed and tied off the condom.

But before Christian could move toward the trash can, Logan sat up, grabbed him, and yanked him forward.

"Motherfucker!" Christian barely caught himself on the couch, the condom flying somewhere out of sight, and winced when the breath crushed out of Logan. "The hell are you doing?"

Logan didn't answer. He wrapped his arms around him and buried his face in his neck. And then he was out.

Of course, you fell asleep.

Christian could be an ass and wake him up, but that was the last thing he wanted to do. He liked how Logan wanted him close and how he cuddled like a sad puppy. And, as much as he'd teased Logan, he liked how he promptly fell asleep.

The only issue was there was no way in hell he'd be joining him.

Christian grabbed the remote and turned the TV on, then pushed Logan until they were lying flat on the couch. Time went by. He watched most of a sports game, holding himself perfectly still so Logan could breathe. He'd never been so patient.

By the time Logan stirred under him, the shadows from the kitchen window had wandered, and the sun was beginning to set. Christian watched him transition to wakefulness, and when Logan blinked blearily, he grinned. "About time, sleepyhead. Shit." Christian kissed his forehead, then pulled out of his arms. "Gotta piss like a racehorse."

"But Christian—"

"You're gonna give me kidney problems, man!" Christian called over his shoulder before shutting the bathroom door behind him. He took care of business quickly, already feeling the aching pull to return to Logan. He was too cute when he'd just woken up, and Christian refused to miss it.

When he came back, hands damp from the sink, Logan was lying in the same position, his pants still around his ankles, and his shirt pulled up around his collarbone. "You look like a slut," Christian teased.

"You say that like I should be *ashamed* to look well-fucked," Logan countered. He touched his chest and grimaced. "Ugh, my jizz dried."

"You're the one who fell asleep. Jesus. I was on my way to get lunch, remember?"

Logan squinted at him. "But it's late now."

"I know that. But you gave me those goddamn bedroom eyes and wanted to kiss me before I left." Christian shook his head as he pulled his shoes on. "Gotta know by now I can't resist you."

"Really?" Logan sat up.

"Shut up." Christian took one glance at him and came over to cup his face and kiss him hard. "Why're you always falling asleep right after we fuck, anyway? Can't you stay awake like a normal person?"

Logan's face was sleep soft, open and gentle. "You make me feel safe, Christian. Safer than anybody."

His heart melted in his chest. *Shit. I've got it bad.* He could repeat the words. He could say he didn't think he could live without Logan anymore, because no matter where he went, he'd see him in every shadow. But it was too much. And so, he kissed his cheek and breathed a sigh against him. "Tacos sound good for dinner, baby?"

Logan grinned. He nodded. "Sounds perfect."

"Good." Though it was like pulling teeth, he walked away just in time for his stomach to growl. "I'll be fast. Don't you go anywhere, now."

"Never."

And he *was* fast. He broke the speed limit, he went through the drive-thru to get their tacos and sodas, and he took the stairs two at a time once he reached the dorm building because the elevator was moving too slowly to the ground floor for his taste.

He walked in on Logan cuddled up on the couch in Christian's blanket, his face peeking out from where he'd swaddled himself. It was the cutest damn thing he'd ever seen.

HE'S GONNA LAUGH at you. He's gonna think it's stupid. You're a fucking idiot if you think this is gonna be cute.

The words rumbled through Christian's head as he sat on his bed, tapping his foot. He'd gone out to grab them more takeout without remembering what day it was. Thanksgiving. Every goddamn restaurant was closed.

He'd ended up in a very quiet drugstore with exactly one bored cashier, and he rooted through their tiny frozen-food section until he found something affordable and allegedly delicious. It was on the way out that he'd seen it.

He'd bought it. He came back to their room to the sound of the shower running. And now it sat on the edge of Logan's desk, waiting for him to come out of the bathroom.

Though Christian had been pacing the entire time, the second the water switched off, he threw himself on his bed and grabbed a book so he could act natural. A few minutes went by. Logan had to be dry.

The door clicked, and Christian threw the book open.

The book was upside down. He couldn't turn it without looking like a fool, so he buried his face in the pages and hoped Logan wouldn't notice.

There were quiet, wet slaps of Logan's feet, and when they came to a sudden stop, Christian peeked up.

Logan stared straight ahead, eyes wide. "What's that?" He pointed.

Christian glanced at the gift on the desk. "That...is a, uh, a teddy bear. With a heart on it."

Logan shook his head, still stunned, inching forward. He reached his hand out and squeezed the button on the bear's paw.

It began to sing.

THANKSGIVING BREAK CAME and went with no new insights, but for the first time, Logan didn't feel the need for them. The Cold War between him and Christian had broken. They'd spoken of feelings and closeness. There was no longer the feeling of being used by him.

I don't need a title. I can't ask him for one, if he's not ready. What we feel isn't any less real just because we don't call each other boyfriends.

Was this what adulthood was? Leveling up a little at a time, until he eventually reached peak adult? Would he receive a trophy for it? Engraved: Resolved a conflict using a love language not his own.

Either way, he felt brave. And that was why he sighed when he pulled out his phone while walking to Christian's first practice at the end of the break.

Ten missed calls from his mom. Ten voicemails he'd deleted instead of listening to.

If Christian could end a Cold War with him, then Logan could end one with his mom. No matter how difficult it was going to be.

As he called, he half expected her not to answer. It would be just like her to make him wait until she called back, thus keeping her parental power. But instead, she answered on the first ring.

"Hello?"

"Hey, Mom."

"Well, look who's finally getting back to me. I was worried sick about you, do you know that?"

"I had things to take care of."

"Oh, like your project? If you get any less than a hundred on that, I'm grounding you the second you get home."

It would be effortless to start a fight, like they always did—to stomp his foot and throw a tantrum and have his mom hold how much of a child he was being over his head. But not today.

"It..." He took a deep breath and tried to think of the best way to phrase his thoughts. The words came out carefully. "It's upsetting that you wouldn't let me make a decision without threatening me, Mom."

"Well, it upsets me that you wouldn't—"

"Let me finish," he said firmly. "I let you finish all the time. Can you listen to me, please?"

Silence.

"You've told me over and over again how I am an adult now because I'm going to college, but the way you've been treating me is...it's hurtful, okay? You demand I call you, and you get mad if I make my own decisions—like staying here for Thanksgiving break. It's like you want me to stay a kid. But how am I supposed to grow up and figure out my own life if you keep me a child?"

His mom huffed, but when she spoke her voice was shaky. "If you're so big for your britches, then you can go ahead and pay for your own college, and your own food, and your own clothes—"

"You want me to drop out?" Logan interrupted.

"Excuse me?"

"You made me believe my education was the most important thing, but now you're threatening to cut off your support because I want to make my own decisions here at school. I can't afford to be here on my own. You know that. That's why we compromised in the first place. But now you want me to drop out."

"I...Logan." She sighed. "No, I don't want you to drop out."

"Then why are you saying these things?"

For a long time, she was quiet, and Logan slowed to a stop under a bare oak tree. He leaned against the trunk and stared at the leaves under his feet. He wouldn't speak first. He'd fought for years to get her to think before she spoke to him, and if she was doing it now, he wasn't going to ruin it.

"I'm scared that you'll make mistakes. Okay?"

Logan closed his eyes and sighed.

"You don't know how cruel the world can be. You don't know how hard it is to get back on your own two feet when things fall apart around you. If you make a mistake and lose your opportunities..."

"I know everything about the world being mean." He breathed an unamused laugh. "Mom, do you think I've never been made fun of? I was adopted. I'm black. I was a nerdy kid for a while. Trust me, I've gotten a lot of shit."

"Watch your language."

"Okay, but see, that's what I'm talking about! I'm not a kid anymore—you *told* me that. I should be able to swear if I want without worrying you're gonna take away my phone or something. I should be able to make mistakes and learn from them. I'm not saying I want to disrespect you or Dad. I'm not saying I want to ruin my life. I just want to be able to say words, and stay on campus if I want, and..."

And date my best friend without being scared you'll never speak to me again.

"But if you listened to me, you wouldn't *have* to make mistakes. I could protect you, Logan. I could keep you safe from them."

"And then I wouldn't learn." When she stayed quiet, Logan went on. "I know if I do something wrong, it might hurt. I'll probably end up regretting some things. But I've gotta learn, just like you did. I need to know what it feels like to commit to my choices. I'm growing up. I'm supposed to be figuring things out."

"Logan..."

"I've made a lot of compromises for you. Okay? All I'm asking is for you to make some for me too."

"I'll think about it. How's that?"

It wasn't what he wanted. But it was a start. He pushed off the tree and started walking again. "Okay."

"I love you."

"I know you do, Mom." He rubbed his eyes. "I love you too. And Dad."

"You're coming home for Christmas, right?"

"Of course, I am. I wouldn't miss it."

"Okay." Quiet drifted between them. It was thick with unspoken words and tension, but they'd taken a step forward, and that was what mattered most. "I'll...I'll talk to you later."

"Okay. Bye, Mom."

Hanging up was no more freeing than usual. If anything, there was more of a weight on his chest. But as he rounded the corner, the soccer field bloomed before him, and he couldn't help but smile.

They were just finishing up practice. Everyone was collecting their water bottles and things and starting to head to the gym, and Logan sat on a bench to wait for Christian. He picked him out of the crowd easily, towering over the others. When Christian turned his head and saw him, he waved at Logan, tapped his wrist, and thumbed at the gym behind him.

Time to shower. Logan grinned and waved him off, then made a show of stretching out and getting more comfortable, and Christian's smile shone brilliantly right before he disappeared inside.

A ball rolled toward him, kicked off course, and Logan ignored it as he pulled out his phone and started going through the alerts he'd missed.

"He was fucking awful in practice, though, did you see him?"

"Who, Anthony?"

The two voices that drew closer weren't familiar, and he didn't glance up.

"Yeah, man. Didn't nail a single corner while practicing. Embarrassing. People like him are the reason we're sucking ass."

"Yeah, it's gay as shit."

Logan bristled. But before he could look up, another voice rang out. "Barker! James!"

Logan chanced a peek. A silver-haired man wearing glasses and dressed in athletic attire—their coach—was walking closer.

"What did I just hear you say?"

The two guys stared at each other. "Nothing."

"That something was...what was it, 'gay as shit'?"

Logan stiffened, shifting uncomfortably.

"It's a joke, Coach, c'mon—"

"We don't make jokes like that on this team. This is your strike. If I hear it one more time, you're off the team."

"Are you serious?"

"Completely. You get one chance to learn why using things like that as an insult is just as bad as saying a slur. Am I understood?"

"That's so stupid! That's unfair!"

"If you want, I can take you off right now. Hmm?"

"No...thank you, Coach."

"You sure?"

"Yes, sir."

"All right. Now hit the showers."

As the two guys walked off, mumbling quietly to themselves, Logan risked a glance at the coach. The man was watching him right back. He gave a smile and a nod, then turned and started walking after them.

What the hell just happened? Logan had been hit by a hurricane. But a good one. Was that possible?

He shot a text to Christian. *Your coach is a pretty cool guy.*

Stop trying to fuck my coach. Be out in a second.

Logan laughed. The sun shone just a little brighter while he waited.

Chapter Eleven

CHRISTIAN

Coffee with Noah wasn't as weird as Christian thought it would be. It wasn't as if he owed him his time; much to his surprise, he genuinely wanted to catch up with Noah after his week away.

At the very least, he had some questions, and from where they were currently standing, Noah was the best guy to answer them.

"So how was your break?" Christian smiled across the table as he sat down

Noah grinned back. "Good! Better than I thought it was going to be."

"Yeah?"

"I just..." He shrugged. "I mean, my parents know I'm gay and all, but I didn't date anybody in high school, so...me telling them about Daiki was a really big first step."

"Shit." Christian imagined a million ways that could have gone wrong. He was sure he'd repressed nightmares about this very scenario. "Was it bad?"

"No! No, not at all." Noah shook his head. "No, they took it well. They wanted to see pictures of him and asked how we got together—"

"Really?"

"Yeah." Noah stared at him. "It went well. Why do you look like that?"

Christian blinked. "Like what?"

"Like you're..." He shook his head and held up his phone, the camera on, and Christian caught a glimpse of his face. "...that."

Afraid. Stunned. Shocked. All of it came together in a split second expression. As Christian stared at the moving image of himself on the screen, he smoothed it all away into a perfect mask of calm. "Nothing."

Noah put his phone away and knitted his hands on the surface of the table. "Are we friends yet? Am I allowed to call your bullshit, or do I have to level up a few more times?"

"You're such a nerd." Christian rubbed his face. He groaned. "Goddammit. No, you can call me on it."

"Then, bullshit! Tell me the truth. I'm not going to tell anybody."

He took a long drink of his coffee, letting the rich taste and aroma ground him little by little. By the time he swallowed, the world made a little more sense. "I just can't imagine my folks ever being so chill. Like, we live in the same state and all, you and me, but things are...different here. I didn't realize how different they were gonna be."

Noah seemed to weigh his thoughts before he spoke. "Is there ever going to be a time where you'd have to tell them something like that?"

Christian pinned him with his gaze, and Noah immediately glanced away. He was obviously still a little shy around him, like he was feeling him out. Christian understood that—he was doing the same thing—and guilt pricked him for how fast he'd tried to stare him down.

He hadn't talked to anybody about this but Logan and Charlotte. They both cared about him deeply, even when he and Logan had no idea exactly what was happening, and they were invested in him figuring it out. They wanted him to succeed.

He didn't have such a guarantee with Noah. He'd just have to take a leap and see what happened.

"There's, uh…" Christian dug his nail into the side of his cup, dragging it up and down in invisible patterns. "Can I ask how you and Daiki got together?"

"God." Noah laughed as he raked a hand through his ginger curls. "A lot of dancing around each other. A lot of being touchy and teasing. There was a whole *will we or won't we* thing, like, if I'd seen it happening with two of my friends I would've called them out in a second, but…we weren't ready for that so fast, I guess. We both thought the other person was being friendly. And then, on Halloween, I think I got sick of sharing a bedroom without him knowing, and he'd stayed up the entire night helping me finish my costume for a party, and I was sleep deprived, and everything poured out."

Christian lifted his brows. "Brave, dude."

"Or stupid." He grinned. His skin turned pink under his freckled cheeks. "I didn't even get the words out. Daiki kissed me before I was done. I think I'd probably been rambling."

"And you were together the whole damn month, and me and Logan had no idea?"

Noah leveled the same hard and focused look Christian had given him, and this time, it was Christian turning his head away. "You were both a little busy."

His heart pounded in his chest. He knew they hadn't exactly been as subtle as he would've wanted, but knowing that Noah and Daiki probably knew the entire time was mortifying. *Who else knows? Has Charlotte told anybody? Does the whole damn world know?* He didn't know anyone from his graduating class who'd come to FSU with them, but Greenbarrow was a small town. Gossip flew around like nobody's business, and nothing could stop a rumor once it got started.

He cleared his throat. "You told anybody?"

Noah reached across the table and then stopped, his hand halfway in the middle. "It's none of my business."

So, they both knew each other's secrets. Christian knew he'd been cold enough to Noah in the past to give him every reason to spread rumors about him. "Thanks."

"No problem."

Christian curled his arms on top of each other and slouched, resting his chin on top of them. "It's been a lot. That's all. I still don't know what the hell's going on most times."

"Gets messy, doesn't it?"

He scoffed. "Hell, yeah."

"And have either of you ever...been with a guy before?"

"Man, I didn't even know I wanted to be with a guy before him. Maybe there were signs. Maybe there was something there the whole time. But whatever it was, I did a damn good job of repressing it. Sort of figure he did the same thing." He would've heard about Logan messing around with dudes back home, for sure. His parents would've made him stop hanging out with him too.

Noah hummed in sympathy. "So what's next? Are you together?"

"We're not *not* together." There was no less clumsy way to put it. "I keep thinking about what it might be like, if we were together. Boyfriends." Making himself say the word was hard, but the second it was out, the reality was simpler. "I know he wants that. But we've gotta go home for winter break. We've gotta be home all summer. And I know myself. Once I say he's mine, I'm not gonna be real interested in hiding it."

Noah was quiet for a long time—just enough time for Christian's mind to go through the worst-case scenarios. There were rednecks in their town. Everybody was white and conservative. Too many guns to speak of.

Best-case scenario, they'd get thrown out without any money to their name.

Logan relied on his parents to pay for college. Christian relied on his family for a roof over his head, food, any clothes that he wore. Going at it on their own, especially to a university like this, wouldn't be easy.

"Have you thought about getting a place together for the summer?" Noah asked.

"We can't afford that shit."

"What about with a job?"

"You think anything around here's gonna be hiring? They've probably been hit with a million students looking for jobs. Feel like I probably missed my opportunity a few months ago."

Noah shrugged. "People go home from college. Most students here don't live in town. They're going to be quitting their jobs for the summer. And..."

Christian met his gaze. Something was hanging in the air. He wished he was quick enough to figure it out himself—Logan was brilliant enough that he would've realized the unspoken suggestion immediately.

For once, thinking about that didn't make him jealous. It made him feel *proud.* Logan was incredible.

And he deserved any opportunity he could get. And the second Christian saddled him with a relationship, he'd lose all of them.

But could he be noble enough to break Logan's heart to save his future?

Noah finally took a deep breath. "My parents already live in town, but...listen, overall, renting an apartment's cheaper than paying to live in the dorms. It's tricky. You need to make sure you have money, month to month, to pay for it instead of paying for everything up front with a loan. But if you've got a job, that's easier."

Christian wrinkled his brow. "But I don't—"

"I'm moving into an apartment of my own for the summer," Noah finally blurted out. "My folks already know. We're figuring out everything I need to have to make it happen. But I'm going to be staying in town, and I'm going to keep my lease through the school year too to save money. And if you and Logan can both get a job before May..."

Christian's heart pounded. "Are you saying we could move in with you?"

"It'd be a two-bedroom." Noah winced. "I don't think we could afford a three-bedroom. And even if we could, I need to be saving everything I can for after college. But I've already lived with you guys. You keep things clean. You buy your own food instead of eating mine. And...and I know how terrifying it is to wonder what's going to happen when all your secrets come out."

He was dreaming. He had to be. The offer changed everything. Winter break would be nothing to get through if he had a safe place to live afterward.

It didn't matter how many jobs he'd have to work to afford his half of an apartment. He'd do it in a heartbeat if it meant being able to wake up in the same room as Logan in a town where he could hold his hand without flinching.

His eyes blurred. His tears took him by surprise, to the point that one had to drip down his cheek before he realized he was crying. "You mean it? You're not gonna take it back or nothing when May rolls around?"

Noah stared at him, eyebrows lifted, appearing stunned. His own blue eyes teared up. "Listen. I am not going to let anything happen to the two of you." He shook his head. "I'm not going to stand there and pretend I can't do anything when I have two supportive parents who've helped me transition and who were excited about my relationship with Daiki. I'm upper middle class. They can bail me out if there's an emergency. And we're...we're family, aren't we? We're both..."

Queer. Not the norm. Christian wiped a hand over his face and nodded. "Yeah." He couldn't look away. "I'm not gonna fuck this up for you. I promise. I'll work three goddamn jobs if that's what it takes."

"I trust you." Noah touched his arm. "Just talk to Logan. Don't hold yourselves back from living. You're as safe as you're going to be here. You can be happy."

There was only one thing left on his mind. "What if I break his heart?"

Noah smiled. "What if you don't?"

Christian took a deep breath. Images of Logan flashed past his mind's eye: them at their joint seventh birthday party, Christian teaching him to skip rocks, Logan grinning up at him from the ocean, and him sleeping naked in Christian's bed with his head on his chest.

He couldn't let it go without taking a risk. Not if Logan wanted it too.

"Thank you," Christian whispered as he stared across the table at Noah. "You've changed everything."

Noah beamed at him. "I didn't do anything. It's you who has to do the hard part."

"Yeah." Christian covered his eyes and groaned. "Shit. Okay. I can do this."

"You can."

"What the fuck am I gonna do?"

Noah grabbed his hand and squeezed it. "Just go tell him you love him."

I love him.

It came as clear as day, like the clouds parting overhead. Like sunshine warming his body all over. In a burst of energy, he pushed his chair away from the table. "I've gotta go."

"Yeah!" Noah laughed and held up a hand, and Christian high-fived it. "Hell yeah! Go on, go get him."

He should've thanked him again, but he was already halfway out the door.

Christian's legs pumped as he ran down the sidewalk toward campus. He practically flew, arms tucked close to his body and calves throbbing.

Shit, I haven't warmed up.

It was foolish to sprint when his body wasn't ready for it. He hadn't done a single bit of exercise over Thanksgiving break. He hadn't had practice yet. His body was as cold as a block of iron.

It didn't matter. Every second he wasn't seeing Logan was like losing a little piece of himself.

Christian whipped through the Student Living building, in one door and through the milling groups of students. "'Scuse me, 'scuse me..." Pushing past them didn't last long. They began to scatter, parting for the giant rushing toward them; for once, he didn't care. He kept his eye on the prize, flying out the other door.

He slammed to a stop.

There he was. Logan. He stood outside their dorm, chatting with Daiki as the few remaining fallen leaves scattered around their feet in the breeze. He was laughing—one of his big, beautiful, bright laughs where he'd abandoned himself completely to whatever he was feeling. His eyes sparkled. His curls rested gently on his wind-bitten cheeks.

He was perfect.

Christian approached the two of them. Though his gaze was only on Logan, he became aware of Daiki moving away, like a curtain parting on a stage. And as Logan turned his head, brow wrinkled in confusion, his smile only widened.

"Hey!" Logan held a hand out, probably for him to grasp and pull him into a hug.

Christian moved past it, pressing their bodies together and cupping his face in a warm kiss.

Logan's breath caught against his mouth. His hands tangled in Christian's coat. Christian waited for him to pull away; Logan answered by drawing him closer.

Christian's too-full heart burst open in his chest, showering the both of them with fireworks. Time slowed. Even Daiki's quick "And that's my cue to leave, lovebirds," didn't make him step back.

When they broke apart, Logan stared up at him with an open mouth. "Wh-what was that for?"

Christian grinned back. He ran his thumb down the dimple in Logan's chin, fascinated by how perfectly they fit together. "I figured it out."

"You did?" His voice was whisper thin, almost as if Christian had dreamed it.

Everything about him is a dream.

The words poured out, so fast it was a wonder they all came out the right way. "I'm tired of waiting. I'm tired of thinking I need some sign to tell me to do shit. Like, what's that about—waiting? Where did that ever get us, right?"

Logan blinked rapidly. "I—"

"Be mine," Christian whispered fervently. He buried his hands in Logan's hair and leaned down until they were nose to nose. "Fuck everybody. Fuck everything. Life doesn't make sense without you, baby. It never has. I spent seven years without you in my life. I don't ever wanna know what that feels like again."

For a moment, Logan seemed too stunned to respond. And then he breathed a wet laugh, shaking his head, finally starting to smile again. "What are you saying?"

"I'm saying I love you." He kissed his forehead, sucking in a sharp breath and feeling the tears bite his eyes again. "I'm saying you're the best thing that's ever happened to me. And I wanna know what life's gonna look like if we stop fucking around and start taking this seriously."

"This?"

"*Us.* Let me take care of you, man."

Logan laughed again. "Let's take care of *each other.* You can't even cook a pot of ramen without burning it. Don't wanna know what you'd do if you tried to take care of *everything.*"

"Fine." Christian tilted his head to the side so he could see the sheen over Logan's beautiful eyes. "Is that a yes?"

Logan bit his bottom lip. "Depends. Are you asking me to be your boyfriend?"

"Man, that's so fucking juvenile—"

"Say it!"

Christian heaved a long sigh. "Logan Brown...would you be my boyfriend?"

Logan wrapped his arms around Christian's waist and leaned back, lifting him up and spinning him in the air. "Yes!"

"Man, put me the fuck down!"

Logan practically dropped him on the ground, stumbling with him to try to catch his footing again, laughing all the while. "I love you. I love you, I love you, I love you..."

Christian dragged Logan down to the ground with him and wrapped his arms around him. The tears fell freely, and for once, he didn't care about looking weak.

He had his strength right there in his arms, and that was all that mattered.

About the Author

Suzanne is an asexual woman with a great love for writing erotic romance and enjoys spending her time confusing people with that fact. She believes there is a need for heightened diversity in fiction and strives to write enough stories so that everyone can see themselves mirrored in a protagonist. She lives with her husband and cat, and, when not writing, Suzanne enjoys reading, playing video games poorly, and refusing to interact outdoors with other human beings.

Website: www.suzanneclay.com

Email: suzanneclaywriting@gmail.com

Facebook: www.facebook.com/suzanneclaywriting

Twitter: @suzanneclay_

Tumblr: www.suzanneclay.tumblr.com

Other books by this author

Chiaroscuro Series

Painting Class

Figure Study

Life Drawing

Also Available from NineStar Press

Connect with NineStar Press

www.ninestarpress.com

www.facebook.com/ninestarpress

www.facebook.com/groups/NineStarNiche

www.twitter.com/ninestarpress

www.tumblr.com/blog/ninestarpress